SLINGS &
ARROWS

BOOKS BY TONY BLACK

The Gus Dury Series
Paying for It
Gutted
Loss
Long Time Dead
Wrecked

The DI Rob Brennan Series
Truth Lies Bleeding
Murder Mile

The Doug Michie Series
The Storm Without
The Inglorious Dead

The DI Bob Valentine Series
Artefacts of the Dead
A Taste of Ashes
Summoning the Dead
Her Cold Eyes

The Clay Moloney Series
(with Matt Neal)
Bay of Martyrs

Novels
His Father's Son
The Last Tiger
Slings & Arrows
(with Tom Maxwell)

Collections
The Sin Bin
Last Orders

Novellas
RIP Robbie Silva
The Ringer

Non-Fiction
Hard Truths

BOOKS BY TOM MAXWELL

*The Lone Rangers: An English Club's Century
in Scottish Football*
*The Fabulous Baker Boys: The Greatest Strikers
Scotland Never Had*
Set in Scotland: A Film Fan's Odyssey
First and Last: How I Made European History with Hibs
(with Jackie Plenderleith)

TONY BLACK   TOM MAXWELL

SLINGS & ARROWS

DOWN&OUT
BOOKS

Down & Out Books
3959 Van Dyke Road, Suite 265
Lutz, FL 33558
DownAndOutBooks.com

The characters and events in this book are fictitious. Any similarity to real persons, living or dead, is coincidental and not intended by the author.

Cover design by Zach McCain

ISBN: 978-1-64396-233-7
ISBN-13: 978-1-64396-233-7

Chapter 1

The whirring bottle came out of nowhere. Agnes Donnelly watched the missile hit the ground ten feet from the bus stop and explode into tiny shards on the pavement. She shrieked, stepping backwards into the shelter as four noisy teenagers appeared. The youths swaggered towards her, bursting into raucous laughter as Agnes fumbled for her balance.

'A thick ear, that's what they're needing,' she muttered at the old man stooped beside her. 'Aren't you going to say anything, Colin? Well, aren't you?'

'Like what?' His cigarette rode the ebb and flow of his words.

'*Like* "behave yourselves and get that mess cleaned up".'

The teenagers passed the bus shelter, jeering and yelling, taunting the elderly couple.

The old man removed his cigarette. 'Aye...And I'll ask them to kick my bloody head in while I'm at it, too.'

'Don't say that. I can't think about what happened to poor Willie Cameron.'

'They're bloody animals. If they'll put Willie in the Royal for kicking his bin over, what do you think they'll do to me?'

The old woman nodded and clutched her handbag closer to her chest.

'Look, let's just keep our heads down. When's our bus?'

Agnes glanced over Colin's shoulder and shrugged. The

1

youths were a safe distance from them now and had turned their attention to kicking an empty can between them as they progressed down the street. Their wayward actions caused a speeding white van to swerve and slow down as the boys wandered into the road. After a few moments, one tracksuited teen with bleached-blond hair stopped and turned to his friends. He was gesturing wildly but his words were drowned out by the sound of the revving vehicle.

'What are they up to now?' said Agnes.

'Leave it. Just leave it, would you?' Colin grabbed her arm and turned her away from the unfolding scene.

The youths had reached a house that looked more like a council refuse depot than someone's home. A battered front gate hung on its hinges, collapsing into a slabbed path overgrown with foot-long grass. At the end of the path, on either side of a pale green front door, was a pile of a dozen or so boxes of rotting magazines and newspapers.

'Wonder if Andy's in,' said the boy with the blond hair. He had reached the front of the house and was attempting to peer into windows thick with dust. His friends laughed as they gathered around him at the window. 'You going in, Lee?'

Lee grabbed a carrier bag from one of the other boys and delved inside, pulling out another bottle of beer. 'Maybe...' He thumped on the front door with the heel of his hand, yelling, 'Andy, you old minger, you coming out to play?'

The opener resulted in more sniggering. Emboldened, Lee swung his foot at one of the boxes of newspapers, sending soggy newsprint spewing into the garden. The amusement was short-lived, however, and soon the teenager returned to the door and looked through the letterbox. It was stuffed with envelopes and fast food fliers. He ripped them out, tossed them aside, and started rattling the metal flap.

'An-dy!' he called. There was no answer. Lee peered in again, 'Tell you what, it stinks in there!'

The others took turns to open the letterbox. 'It smells of

shite, so it does.'

'That's cos it probably is shite,' said Lee. 'What do you expect it to smell of? Andy's a hoarder, man.'

'I've seen them on the telly, totally manky so they are.'

'Think he might have anything?' said Lee.

'He keeps the lot, you name it. Could have anything in there.'

'You think he's in?'

'He's not answering. Maybe he got sick of us taking the piss and legged it.'

'I've not seen him for ages,' said Lee. 'C'mon, let's try round the back.'

They walked round the side of the house, stepping over smashed fence posts and empty flower pots as they went. In the back garden the scene of devastation was even worse—a filthy mattress occupying the centre of a mound of disparate household waste.

Lee walked up to the back door and gave it a kick. 'Look at this,' he said. The door swung open a few inches before hitting something on the other side. He peeked round the door and then squeezed himself inside the house, disappearing from view.

'Keep a look out,' yelled Lee to the others.

'Bollocks to that,' said one of them, 'I'm coming too. Stew can stand watchie.'

Lee stood in what he assumed was Andy's kitchen, although it was difficult to tell. In the gloom, he could make out black rubbish bags piled from the floor to the ceiling. Cereal boxes, plastic ready meal cartons, paper plates, foil trays, tin cans—if there were a sink or a cooker in the room, they were firmly hidden beneath a decade's worth of waste.

The stench was horrendous, the floor beneath his feet sticky and he could hear movement, 'Who's that?'

'It's me—Mark. Where are you?'

'Next to the Frosties boxes. There's a gap—you have to

squeeze through.'

There was a narrow opening to the side of the boxes, just wide enough to crawl into, that Lee had already pushed his way out of at the other end. He eased through another opening, crawling on hands and knees, into a narrow passageway. He could stand up now. He touched the walls—they weren't solid, but damp and spongy.

Lee took out his lighter and called back to Mark. 'In here.'

As they stood in the doorway it appeared to the boys that this must be what Andy used as a living room. Much like the rest of the house, the area was stacked with several years' worth of putrid and decaying rubbish, piled high around every wall.

'Christ,' Lee whispered. 'It's tiny.'

They continued to scan the room but there was hardly anything to see. Only the very top of the window was visible, but the panes were so thick with dust that the room's only light came from the tiny bulb on a mini cooker by the floor. The cooker was stained a dirty orange—the tomato sauce of a thousand baked bean dinners crept down the side.

Among the magazines and cardboard, Lee could make out a boxy, yellowing portable television. Barely two feet away from the screen, a slight figure wrapped in a blanket was slouched and motionless in an armchair. Lee recognised the figure immediately as Andy Cruickshank.

'He's probably pissed,' Lee whispered to Mark. 'Come on, on the count of three, we jump out and watch him shit himself.'

Mark nodded, grinning.

'One, two, *three*!'

The boys jumped into the room and roared.

The figure in the armchair didn't move.

Mark gazed at Lee and shrugged. 'Look at the state of this place, Andy,' he said loudly. 'You could've cleaned up for us.'

Lee walked over to the armchair and picked something up off the floor. He held up a half-empty bottle of Bell's whisky. He twisted off the lid and took a swig.

'No wonder he's pissed,' he spluttered, dropping the bottle.

He took a step closer to Andy, holding his lighter up to his face. Andy's gaunt-thin features were covered in thick, grey stubble—flecks of food clung to the edge of his mouth. On his head, Andy's few remaining strands of hair, thick and greasy, sat up in stray, unruly tufts.

'Wake up, you lazy bastard,' pressed Lee.

Mark intervened when there was no response, shaking Andy by the shoulder and forcing his head to loll forwards and slump at an unnatural angle to his chest.

Lee felt his pulse quicken. 'Andy, man, wake up,' he said. There was no movement. Lee reached out for the blanket and threw it aside, and at once he felt a tightness in his chest, as if the air in the confined space was rapidly running out. His head grew light on his thin neck as he stared at Andy's grey T-shirt, soaked with a dark patch of blood. As Lee looked down to the floor, he realised that this was the sticky substance he was standing in.

Lee turned and stumbled, pushing Mark aside as he lunged back to the cramped tunnel through the piles of waste. As the youths dragged themselves on hands and knees through the mess and squalor, they heard loud, angry shouts up ahead of them. The noise—which would normally be concerning—was ignored by the boys as they pushed and pressed themselves towards the escape route of the back door.

Lee burst from the gloom, his eyes taking several seconds to comprehend what was unfolding. His two friends, Dave and Stew, were squaring up to a man and woman in the garden, watched over by a crowd of jeering neighbours leaning over the fence.

A man built like a bodybuilder—flushed in the face, his movements agitated—was screaming at the teenagers. 'You little bastards just can't leave Andy alone, can you? What're you doing here?'

'What's it got to do with you?' yelled Stew.

The man turned to the woman, 'Get the police, Trish.'

The woman nodded, pulling a mobile phone from her pocket.

'The police are already on their way,' a voice from beyond the fence yelled.

As Lee and Mark ran from the house they barged into the bodybuilder from behind, catching him off balance, he fell to the ground. Stew saw the opportunity to take a kick at the fallen man, and the woman screamed. The chaotic scene was made worse when she lunged at her man's attacker and fell face-first into the dirty mattress.

'Run!' yelled Lee. 'Get out of here.'

Within seconds, the youths had disappeared round the side of the house—fleeing like a pack of rats—as the sound of police sirens cried over the rooftops.

'Are you okay, love?' said Trish, emerging from the filth of the mattress.

'Aye, but those little bastards won't be when I get my hands on them.'

Chapter 2

Home was the place you went to enjoy the comforts of your labour, wasn't it? Kenny Gillespie was undecided. As he stood before his wife, in the full glare of her pointed gaze—her arms folded brutishly, her flank butted against the jamb—he wondered if Pauline had annexed the doorway to the kitchen in an act of war.

'Well?' she said.

Gillespie stared at her for a moment before turning back to his microwave curry. 'What's up?' He started digging his fork into a piece of chicken.

'Where is it?'

Gillespie chewed for a long moment and then swallowed before answering. 'Where's what?'

'You know very well what,' said Pauline, her fat cheeks almost matching the maroon of her bobbled dressing gown.

Gillespie swallowed another mouthful. 'I'm a detective, my dear, I'm not Darren Brown.'

'It's Derren Brown.'

Gillespie shrugged. 'I'm not him either. What've you lost now?'

'I've not lost anything,' said Pauline. 'You've been bloody tidying up again and moved my book.'

Gillespie was already bored with the conversation. 'Which book do you mean?' he said. 'If it's the one about the wizards, it's in the living room, where you left it. If it's the one about the teenage girl who cops off with a werewolf, then it's in the bathroom, where you left it.'

Pauline's eyes narrowed slightly and she stomped out. Gillespie heard her go into the bathroom and then thud through to the living room. The bare walls of the hallway echoed as she slammed the door. He suspected she was still annoyed with his comment about her werewolf book, saying he preferred the movie version with Michael J. Fox.

After finishing his curry, Gillespie gave his fork a quick rinse under the tap and chucked the plastic container in the bin. He didn't bother with plates if he could avoid it, especially after a long day. He rarely had time to cook, let alone wash up, and there was more chance of Pauline missing one of her favourite TV shows than having a meal ready for him when he came home.

He was about to head upstairs for a shower when he almost tripped over a giant Amazon box in the hallway. He could only guess at what Pauline had been ordering this time. Chances were, she wouldn't remember herself. Barely a day went past without her receiving a delivery of something else she didn't need. Gillespie pondered what Pauline had bought in the past week alone: a new set of Jamie Oliver saucepans, despite the fact she never cooked, a collection of nail varnish brushes, even though she never went out, and the new *Guinness World Records*—presumably, he thought, so she could see how she measured up against the planet's biggest waste of space.

He looked at the other boxes that lined either side of the hallway. Gillespie knew she'd never be satisfied. Contrary to popular belief, there were some things that couldn't be bought online. His thoughts were interrupted by a phone ringing by the front door. He walked over to the hall table and picked up the receiver. 'Gillespie.'

'Sir?' It was Harris.

Out of the corner of his eye, Gillespie could see the living room door open slowly. Pauline emerged, taking in the scene with a sigh.

'What's the problem, Simon? I was just about to jump in the shower.'

'I wouldn't bother sir,' said Harris. 'A body's been found in Liberton.'

'Hold on a second.' Gillespie covered the receiver and swore under his breath as he shoved a pile of *Hello* magazines off the table to reveal a notepad and pen. He could sense Pauline bristle as they hit the floor. 'Sorry Simon,' said Gillespie. 'What's the address?'

Pauline watched as he took down notes for several more minutes.

'See you in half an hour,' said Gillespie. He put down the receiver and turned to Pauline. 'It'll probably be a late one. Murder in Liberton.'

Pauline scowled. 'The broadband isn't working again,' she said, holding up an iPad. 'I thought you said you were getting it sorted. How am I supposed to order that cake stand if I can't get online?'

Gillespie was incredulous. He wondered if Pauline had actually registered the word 'murder' or given any thought to what it meant—a life snuffed out. A family ripped apart.

'Why don't you use this?' snarled Gillespie, holding up the phone and slamming it down again. 'Why do we need a cake stand anyway? When was the last time you baked anything?'

Pauline was starting to get agitated, tugging at the hair above her ear. 'Well, it's your birthday next month, but I need to get some new cake tins and...'

'Jesus Christ, Pauline,' Gillespie interrupted. 'Look at this place. It's like a bloody warehouse. We don't need any more crap. Didn't you hear what I just said? Someone's been murdered. Some mother's son. How would you feel if...' He stopped himself from going any further, but it was too late. He could see Pauline's eyes welling up.

'Well I wouldn't know, would I?' She started to cry, storming back into the living room, slamming the door again. Gillespie stood for a moment in the hall and soon heard the familiar sound of the QVC shopping channel blaring out of the television.

His anger had already given way to guilt. He grabbed his coat from the peg, patted his pocket to check he had his car keys and, more importantly, his cigarettes, and opened the front door.

Gillespie sat in his Golf and lit up, something Pauline had banned him from doing in the house. He felt a sense of calm as the smoke filled his lungs.

He started the engine and put the car into first. He had barely set off when he slammed his foot on the brake as a Yodel delivery van turned into the driveway. Gillespie jabbed the horn and gesticulated that he wanted to get out. The driver, a coat-hanger-shouldered lad in his late teens, took his time backing up. Once he had reversed and Gillespie was able to squeeze his car along-side, the driver wound down his window. Gillespie did the same.

'Sorry, mate,' said the driver. 'Is this number fourteen? I've got a parcel for a Mrs P. Gillespie.'

The DCI took another draw on his cigarette and shook his head. 'You've got the wrong house.' He wound up his window and disappeared round the corner.

Driving from the west of Edinburgh to the east was never a quick process, but the detective felt it now took longer than ever. Because it was after seven, he had decided against taking the bypass from his home in Corstorphine but, as he approached the west end of Princes Street, he immediately regretted it. The traffic was backed up for half a mile down Shandwick Place, and he didn't need to be a clairvoyant to see what was causing the jam. At that very moment, he suspected, a tram would be ferrying half a dozen passengers at glacial speed over the crossroads. He'd read in the *News* that the city's new tramline, which ran for nine miles, had cost Edinburgh taxpayers nearly £900 million. How was it even possible to piss away that kind of cash? While constant police cutbacks were forcing him into double shift after double shift, the city fathers were able to spend £100 million a mile on a transport system nobody was using.

By the look of the other cars on the road, the arrival of the trams coincided with the council dishing out cab licences to anyone who asked. Every other car seemed to be for hire. Gillespie had only been in Edinburgh for five years, but he felt he knew the streets better than most of the cabbies, who now relied on sat navs to find the longest and most expensive routes through town. The city was a shambles.

As he inched towards his turn off at Lothian Road, Gillespie peered through the mist at the Scott Monument, its spire jutting into the grey sky and away from the chaos of the streets below. It had a nickname: the Gothic Rocketship. As he pondered the miserable home he'd just left and the murder scene he was about to visit, Gillespie thought he'd happily sign up for its maiden voyage out of the city.

Though he'd never commit murder, the DCI understood it and could even empathise with some people's desire to kill. Pauline looked horrified the first time he'd told her this but, he explained, he wouldn't be very good at his job if he didn't know how a killer's mind worked. The day he stopped being able to think like one of them would be the day he'd jack it all in and head to the Job Centre. What he couldn't understand, though, was a desire to hurt those who were already dead. This occurred to him as he drove past the cemetery on Liberton Brae, where several gravestones had recently been desecrated. Locals were blaming the kids but, then, locals usually did. Whoever had caused the damage, Gillespie found it unsettling to think that even the dead members of this community couldn't get a moment's peace.

It was nearly eight o'clock when he pulled up at the address given to him by Harris. Several police vehicles were already on the scene and a crowd of onlookers were jostling for position, camera phones at the ready. They were after a glimpse of blood or, even better, a dead body. One or two others were being interviewed by officers in uniform. Gillespie parked up and flashed his warrant card to a young PC, who let him through the cordon.

As he walked up to the house, he clocked what appeared to be magazines strewn across the overgrown front lawn. He winced slightly as he remembered the copies of *Hello* he'd hurled at Pauline's feet in frustration.

'Thanks for coming out at such short notice, sir.'

Detective Sergeant Simon Harris—tall, handsome and, at times, greener than Easter Road—had appeared at his shoulder.

Gillespie nodded. 'Sorry I'm late, Simon. Traffic was a nightmare. What do we have?'

'The victim is a forty-six-year-old male, sir,' said Harris, who checked his notes and added, 'Andrew Cruickshank. Cause of death appears to be stabbing.'

'Appears to be?'

'Well, there's a lot of blood loss.'

'Do we have a knife? A weapon of some sort?'

'No, sir.'

'So, it might *appear* to be no such thing, Simon.'

'Yes, sir.'

Gillespie let the sting of his last remark subside before moving on to his next enquiry. 'Pritchet taken the early bath, has he?'

'I'm not that sure...I'm presuming he's been and gone.'

Gillespie rolled on the balls of his feet and looked around for the medical man. 'Any word from the socos?'

'Putting expiry down at,' the DS took out a spiral-bound notebook, '...around twelve hours ago.'

'Any witnesses?'

'No, sir, but the next-door neighbours encountered a group of boys leaving the property shortly before the body was discovered.'

'Any luck rounding them up?'

'We think we know who they are, sir. An elderly couple saw what we believe to be the same group hurling bottles near a bus stop roughly half an hour earlier.'

Gillespie nodded his approval. 'And what do we know about Andrew Cruickshank?'

'Lived alone, sir. A virtual recluse, according to neighbours. No known enemies.'

'Okay. Let's go and see him.'

At the rear of the property a steady procession of officers in white overall-suits came and went. A group of uniforms seemed engaged in the arduous task of relocating large bundles of newsprint—lining them up in teetering pillars alongside the back wall of the house. As Gillespie watched, a young woman presented him with a small cardboard box containing blue latex shoe coverings and matching gloves.

'What the hell is going on here?' said the detective.

'Relocating the magpie's hoard, sir,' said the soco.

'It's my bloody evidence...' Gillespie pushed the small box with the gloves aside. 'Hey, you! I want this lot bagged and tagged.'

A PC turned and shrugged. 'Sir, this rubbish?'

'It's a crime scene! Now, as much as I admire your recreation of the Leaning Tower of Pisa, in triplicate, I'd sooner see this lot stored and examined for potential clues. So get to it!'

The PC turned back to face the rubbish and, appearing perplexed, unclipped his radio.

Gillespie snatched a pair of gloves from the small box. He snapped them on his wrists as he headed for the back door of the property.

'Unbelievable,' said Gillespie. 'What next?'

DS Harris stepped from behind the soco, grabbing the cardboard box, 'You might need a mask too, sir. Bit whiffy in there.'

Chapter 3

Gillespie took the mask on offer, but stuffed it in his jacket pocket.

'Aren't you going to put it on, sir?' said Harris, his voice muffled through his own face-wear.

The detective shook his head. 'I like to use all my senses. Anyway, a bit of guff never did anyone any harm.'

'*Guff*?' Harris tugged down his mask, his top lip was shining. 'Is that what they say down in the Borders, sir?'

Gillespie smiled but didn't reply. The way city folk took digs at speech from the regions was tedious. He turned to go into the shabby house, giving Harris his back. As he proceeded, something caught Gillespie's eye and he crouched over to examine a metal door handle. After a minute of silence, he spoke again: 'Did you spot this?'

Harris squinted, his eyebrows riding up and down on the blank expanse of his forehead. It was a bloodstain, not a great deal of blood, merely a smear, but more than enough to confirm the presence of something being somewhere it shouldn't be.

'McKenzie,' said Harris, calling into the house, twisting his straight shoulders at a right angle to his hips—he did not take his eye from the door handle for a second. 'Can we get a print from this bloodstain?'

A tall soco shambled up in rustling white overalls and

14

crouched in the doorway, following Harris's intent gaze. 'Hmm, we can try,' he said. 'It's a motion smear. The chances of there being anything identifiable are slim. The details, y'know the useful stuff, tend to get wiped out in the action.'

'Would you give it a try?' said Gillespie, standing up. 'The lab is matching stuff with microscopes these days, even a partial of a partial can mean a win for us.'

The soco departed and Harris rose, motioning beyond the door, then led the way inside. 'Watch your step, sir,' he said, as they entered the kitchen. 'I think the cleaner must be on holiday.'

Gillespie smirked, his usual applause for Harris's gallows humour. The amusement was short-lived, however, as Gillespie looked around at the grease-lined walls and the black, furry caterpillars that were the filth-filled dust crawling along the skirtings. He felt his stomach turn over. In his twenty years on the force he thought he'd seen it all, but the excrement-filled bathtub that was used as a toilet and the month-old suicide with rotting innards stuck to a living room carpet were the only memories that came close to the current atmosphere.

'Jesus,' he said, louder than he had intended. Harris nodded. Another soco, carrying yet another bundle of mouldy, putrefying newspapers, emerged from a gap among a pile of empty cereal boxes riddled with rat-gnawed holes.

Harris pointed through the mess. 'This way, sir,' he said, as though directing Gillespie to a room reserved in hell.

'The victim appears to have been a hoarder,' said Harris as the two men inched their way through the rubbish-strewn hallway, easing the detritus along with the toes of their shoes.

'Thank you, Simon,' said Gillespie. 'We'll make a detective of you yet.'

Harris ploughed on, either oblivious or refusing to acknowledge his superior's sarcasm. 'It was crawling room only when we arrived. I would think this "collection" goes back several years,' he said.

Gillespie spotted one of the newspapers as he squeezed

through the hallway, a Scottish redtop celebrating England's elimination from Euro '96. 'I'd say at least twenty,' said Gillespie.

The DCI was no stranger to seeing people lying dead in their own homes, but coming face to face with Andy Cruickshank, now a decaying mound of flesh slumped in a filthy old armchair, made him angry. It wasn't so much the violence of the act that got to him, more the indignity of someone left to rot in the place where they ate and slept. Andy's home might have looked like a tip and smelt even worse, but living like that was his choice. Dying like that wasn't. It wasn't a choice anyone would have made.

Gillespie held on to that last thought as he surveyed the living room. He couldn't get over how cramped it was, as though the walls, or the cardboard boxes, were closing in. Stretching out his arms wide, his fingertips made contact with the piles on both sides. How could anybody live like this? Perhaps even more perplexing, though, was how could a murder be committed in a space this small?

The detective walked over to Andy's corpse and crouched down to examine his wounds. The victim had lived in squalor and, by the looks of things, had died in agony. 'Are you sure his wounds aren't self-inflicted?' said Gillespie.

Harris gave a little smirk. 'I don't think Cruickshank is a Japanese name, sir, if you're suggesting he committed *hara-kiri*!'

'One of the first things to remember about being a smart-arse, Simon,' said Gillespie, not turning around, 'is you might not be as smart as you think...no matter what university you went to. However,' he added, standing up, 'if you're asking me if I think this man committed *seppuku*, then no, I don't. I just want to consider all the possibilities.'

'Sorry, sir,' said Harris. 'It just seems...unlikely.'

'Me having a basic grasp of Japanese is unlikely,' said Gillespie. 'That doesn't mean it's impossible. Looking at the space in here, though, I'd say there's no room to swing a cat, or a blade.'

Harris's expression changed, and he became the human

equivalent of a cartoon light bulb going on. 'Could he have been killed somewhere else?'

'And moved, you mean?'

'Yes, and later positioned like that...'

Gillespie grinned. 'After being murdered somewhere else. I think that's more likely, but let's see what we turn up by way of blood patterns before we jump to any conclusions.'

It was nearly dark by the time the two men emerged outside. Socos, clad in their white overalls, drifted ghostlike across the garden in the gloom. The excited murmur of the crowd at the front of the house had all but disappeared. Boredom, at a lack of action, had obviously set in. 'So,' said Gillespie, lighting up a cigarette and walking over to the back fence, 'assuming Cruickshank was murdered, we can eliminate robbery as a motive straight away.'

'Completely, sir?' asked Harris, joining him.

Gillespie took a draw on his cigarette and pointed back towards the house. 'It's hardly Holyrood Palace, is it? Unless there's a sudden demand for old bean cans, there's nothing Cruickshank owns—or, I'm guessing, owned—that anybody would want to steal.' Gillespie continued as Harris began to make notes. 'And it's obviously not a domestic dispute, because he lived alone.'

'Maybe a family member?' said Harris, 'A visiting relative?'

Gillespie shook his head. 'Just look at the state of the place. Any relatives Andy Cruickshank might have had gave up on him long ago.' He paused and muttered a word, 'Kids.'

Harris shook his head. 'The victim didn't have any children.'

'Not *his* kids,' said Gillespie. 'Think about how cramped it was in there. Only a kid could move about freely without disturbing anything.'

As Harris continued to take notes, a middle-aged woman strode round the side of the house, accompanied by a PC. Gillespie thought her designer trench coat and immaculately tousled hair looked out of place next to Andy Cruickshank's old washing machine. She paused outside the back door and checked a clipboard.

'Thanks for dropping by, Ms Taylor,' said Gillespie, walking over to her.

The woman looked up briefly and gave him a nod. 'Gillespie.'

'I can't remember how this works,' said the DCI. 'Are you here to declare the dead deceased, or the deceased dead? It must be a tough job, either way.'

Wendy Taylor, Edinburgh's Procurator Fiscal, sighed and shook her head. 'Keep puffing away on those cigarettes, Gillespie, and maybe I'll soon be declaring you deceased...or dead. Either would suit me.'

Gillespie gave her a grin as she followed the PC into the house.

'If you don't mind me asking, sir, what was all that about?' said Harris.

'Just one more cook spoiling my broth,' said Gillespie, stubbing out his cigarette. 'If there's a way of making the law in this country more bureaucratic, you can bet we'll find it. Besides, Lady Penelope gets on my nerves. Now, the moment she's finished in there, I want to see all that stuff cleared out and I want the body taken to the Cowgate and put on the slab. We'll see what Dr Freud makes of it.'

Harris looked flustered. 'But, sir, it'll take hours to clear the house and most of these officers are already on overtime.' He gestured towards the socos, who were busy bagging and tagging as Gillespie had requested.

'I've been on the go since five o'clock this morning,' said Gillespie. 'Let me put it this way: I want a body on that slab by first thing tomorrow. Ideally, it'll be Cruickshank's but, if you'd rather it was yours, just say the word "overtime" to me again.'

Harris said nothing. Gillespie watched as Harris went to relay his instructions to the nearest soco. He watched the man's shoulders slump. Harris walked back over and nodded to Gillespie.

'Good work,' said Gillespie. 'Now, what do the neighbours have to say?'

It took several minutes for someone to answer the door. Gillespie and Harris were about to leave when a small woman in a dressing gown emerged, a towel wrapped round her head. 'Oh, hello,' she said. 'Can I help you?'

'Sorry to disturb you, Mrs...Durham, isn't it?' said Harris, checking his notebook.

Tricia Durham nodded, a hand reaching up to balance the towel on her head.

'I'm Detective Sergeant Simon Harris. This is Detective Chief Inspector Kenny Gillespie. Do you mind if we ask you a few questions? It's about your neighbour, Mr Cruickshank.'

As they entered the brightly lit hall, they walked past a glass cabinet filled with silver trophies. Next to the cabinet was a framed picture of a bronzed man wearing nothing, as far as Gillespie could tell, but a pair of underpants. The man's teeth gleamed an unnatural shade of white as he flexed his bulging muscles.

Tricia showed Gillespie and Harris into the living room. The man from the picture, a few years older but no less physically imposing, was sitting on a white leather sofa, his feet up, watching the news on an oversized flat-screen television. It was a world away from the house they'd just come from.

'Steve, love,' said Tricia. 'These detectives would like to talk to us about Andy.'

Steve looked up and nodded. He pointed the remote and switched off the television. Tricia, the towel removed and her hair hanging in wet corkscrews, turned to the officers and said, 'Can I get you a cup of tea?'

'No thanks,' said Gillespie. Harris looked as though he was about to accept, but followed Gillespie's lead and shook his head.

'Sorry if I don't get up,' said Steve. 'Back's giving me a bit of trouble. Old injury, you know how it is.'

'Sorry to hear that,' said Gillespie, taking a seat. 'Weight-lifting?'

For a moment, Steve looked perplexed and then gave a slight smile. 'Oh, you saw the photo? That was a while ago. No, it was those bloody kids.'

'What kids were these?' said Gillespie.

'I don't know all their names,' said Steve, shrugging. 'We caught them coming out of Andy's house and the little shits...sorry...well, they jumped me.'

'One of them pushed me over,' said Tricia, who had joined Steve on the sofa. 'Covered in mud, I was. Should have seen the state of my shower.'

'Do you know who they are or what they might have been doing in Mr Cruickshank's home?' said Harris, as he pulled the spiral-bound notebook from his pocket.

Steve shook his head. 'I've seen a couple of them kicking around here before. I'm pretty sure they were involved in smashing up the cemetery a few weeks ago. You'll know all about that, I take it? One of them, Lee, I'm pretty sure he works in the Co-op. I've no idea what they were doing in Andy's house, though. Nothing good, I can tell you that. I'm sure one of them had blood on his hands when he came running out of there.'

'Blood?' said Harris.

Steve nodded. 'Well it looked like it to me. What else could it have been, ketchup?'

Gillespie sat forward, balancing his elbows on his thighs. 'This might seem a strange question, but did you see whether he wiped his hand on the door?'

Steve shook his head. 'I wouldn't know. I was too busy arguing with his friends when they came out.'

Tricia cut in, her voice wistful. 'Andy was a lovely guy, but he didn't get any visitors. That's why we went outside when we saw those boys go into his garden.'

'We were probably the only friends he had, to be honest,'

said Steve. 'Andy had his problems. He was a drinker and, well, you've seen the state of his house...' he tailed off, inflating his cheeks and exhaling slowly.

'How often did you see your neighbour?' said Gillespie.

'Only every couple of weeks,' said Tricia. 'If he was coming back from the shops or whatever, we'd stop and have a quick chat.' Her voice began to crack. 'He really was a lovely guy. I can't believe what's happened.' Steve gave her knee a squeeze as she reached for a tissue.

'We tried to help him,' said Steve.

'In what way?' said Gillespie.

'We phoned up social services. Just to see if there was anything they could do.'

'And was there?' said Harris.

'I had a long chat with a woman there,' said Tricia. 'She said they'd look into it, pay him a visit, but I don't think they ever did.'

'Do you remember who you spoke to?' asked Gillespie.

Tricia thought for a moment. 'It was a few months ago now,' she said. 'Somebody Campbell? Could it be, Maureen Campbell? That might have been it.'

Harris jotted down the name.

'Can you think of any reason why anyone might want to hurt Mr Cruickshank?' said Gillespie.

Steve and Tricia both shook their heads. 'He was a lovely guy,' said Tricia. 'A bit strange, maybe, but really lovely, in his own little way, if you know what I mean.'

'Well,' said Gillespie, looking at his watch and wondering how much longer he could take hearing the same platitudes recycled, 'it's getting late. We'll let you get back to your evening. Thanks very much for your time.'

Tricia started to get up but Gillespie stopped her, 'Oh, don't you worry, Mrs Durham, we'll see ourselves out.'

'Please get whoever did this,' said Tricia. 'Andy really was a lovely guy.'

Gillespie smiled and nodded. 'So I gather.'

Chapter 4

Gillespie was overwhelmed by a wave of fatigue as he leaned on his car and yawned, the gape of his mouth stretching his jaws to near-breaking point. From somewhere deep inside him, an old instinct forced a hand to shoot up in apology, 'Sorry, I'm just about done in,' he said.

Harris grinned. 'Does someone need their bed?'

The detective was just about to repeat his favourite line about Harris making a detective one day, but another incoming yawn meant he could manage only a nod. He opened the car door and slumped into the driver's seat.

'See you at the station at eight?' said Harris.

'Don't even think about adding bright eyed and bushy tailed.' Gillespie took a deep breath and closed the door, started the engine and was quickly out of sight. Despite his body's insistence that he was tired, Gillespie's mind was racing in sync with the car's speeding wheels.

He'd known plenty cops over the years who could switch off at the end of a shift and never give a second's thought to the horrors they might've seen, but Gillespie wasn't one of them. The lulling effect of brain-numbing television didn't work for him and he'd seen too many develop a fondness for viewing life through the bottom of a whisky bottle to go down that route. His coping mechanisms were far more complex, if no less common.

The image of Andy Cruickshank's frail, helpless body was a hard one to shake. Gillespie hadn't known the man. He'd only seen the mess he'd left behind. Now Andy, like the trash that filled his house, was being bagged up as evidence. He wondered what might've gone through the tragic hermit's head when he realised he was about to take his last breath. If he'd known his days were numbered, would he have left his house to enjoy a last day in the sunshine, or at least the Edinburgh equivalent? Then he thought about the kind of kids that were currently running amok in Andy's neighbourhood, and he figured someone like him was probably best off indoors. The detective's thoughts were rambling, but it was a familiar territory they took him to. This was the finder in him, the hunter seeking his prey; he needed to know what that bloody corpse had seen in order to serve justice on the killer.

As the traffic lights on the junction between Liberton Brae and Mayfield Road turned red, Gillespie took the opportunity to roll down his window and light a cigarette. The bitter nicotine brought the welcome taste of formality, something to distract his thoughts, but he had enough self-awareness to know that the fingers he was drumming on the steering wheel told another story.

In search of a stronger distraction, Gillespie switched on the radio, and grimaced as the unmistakable brogue of Ally Murdo— the city's self-styled 'Jock Shock Jock'—burst into life.

'...absolutely disgusting scenes outside Fairview today. What I'd like to know is, how many of these women's libbers have actually ever watched golf, let alone played it?' the DCI's grip tightened on the wheel as Murdo's voice cut through him.

'Can you imagine one of these protestors teeing off against Tiger Woods? He'd be too distracted by their pink hair and their tattoos to get his hole—so to speak. I know old Tiger has a bit of a reputation for playing the field, but even he wouldn't touch one of these munters.'

Murdo's rant continued as the lights changed to green and Gillespie turned left on to Mayfield Road. He appreciated the irony of driving past the University of Edinburgh's King's Buildings while listening to the kind of misogynistic ravings that would've made Bernard Manning blush. That was Scotland's capital all over: schizophrenic splits at every turn.

'The point is,' continued Murdo, 'the gentlemen at Fairview have been playing golf quite happily for more than two hundred years without female members. If they vote in favour of maintaining the status quo, then who is this bunch of sports bra-burning femmies to say they're in the wrong? These men pay good money to be members of Fairview, and the last thing they need is to be put off their stroke by Emmeline Pankhurst and the cast of *Rent* waving placards outside their clubhouse.'

The DJ was still in full flow by the time Gillespie reached Causewayside. He flicked on the blinkers and made to turn left through the Meadows. Under the streetlights he watched the late-night pub traffic being serenaded by a wobbly drunk with one hand on a drainpipe and the other directing the significant outflow of a full bladder.

A young couple, disgusted and amused in equal measure, laughed as they let go of each other's hands for a moment and sidestepped the yellow stream now gushing down the pavement. As he watched their hands reconnect, Gillespie's mind flashed back to an ancient date with Pauline—dinner at an Indian restaurant that had long since shut down. The thought was quickly replaced with the more recent recollection of the crappy microwave curry from a few hours earlier. It had left a bitter aftertaste, although how much was down to the meal and how much to the subsequent shouting match with his wife, he wasn't sure.

His mind wandering, Gillespie realised that, by the time he'd reached Lothian Road, Murdo was no longer shouting. He instead spoke in a threatening hiss. 'These so-called "women" are dangerous,' he said. 'Their Commie views aren't just a threat to the good men of Fairview Golf Club, they're a threat to our Western way of life. They're against tradition, all Western tradition, and they oppose it with conflict because that's what's in the little red Commie book! Mark my words, if we don't stand up to these looney leftists who want to bring us down then we'll wake up one day and find we're living in a totalitarian state. And if that's not the whole truth of the matter then you can kiss my arse and call me Comrade!'

Gillespie had heard enough. He jabbed at the button and the radio went silent. The detective had nearly reached Corstorphine but, despite his tiredness, he had no real desire to go home. He didn't know whether it was the argument with Pauline, the sight of Andy Cruickshank's body or the ranting of Ally Murdo, but the DCI was suddenly in desperate need of a pint.

In almost any other part of town, Gillespie would be able to slip into a pub unnoticed and enjoy a drink in peace. His dark suit might be mistaken for that of a banker's, or maybe someone in insurance. But in the Logie Baird he was such a 'well-kent' face that he might as well have had 'copper' chalked over his shoulders. As soon as he walked in the door, he could feel a dozen pairs of eyes turn in his direction. If this was a Western it would be the moment when the old timer at the piano would stop playing, which in turn would lead to some patrons supping up and heading for the door.

Gillespie always smirked at the recurring thought. He didn't care. He wasn't the man who shot Liberty Valance, but he'd spent too much of his life putting the bad and the ugly behind bars to be intimidated by a few old blokes with thousand-yard stares ranged on him over the dingy air of an Edinburgh boozer.

The glow of a small, bracket-mounted television in one corner of the pub caught his attention. Gillespie took a few steps closer, ignoring one man who promptly got up and left when he clocked him. A male reporter on the screen was interviewing one of the protestors who were camped outside a golf club. The sound was turned down, but the caption read 'Fury at Fairview'.

'I really don't know why they're making such a fuss,' said a voice nearby.

Gillespie kept his eyes on the screen and shook his head.

'Maybe they're annoyed because a bunch of sexist old farts has barred them just because they're women,' he said. He turned round to face the man who was paying for a drink at the bar.

The man looked hurt. 'Oh, I understand that,' he said, taking a sip of his fresh pint and then using his sleeve to wipe the froth from his moustache. 'I meant I don't understand why the guys at Fairview don't just let them join. I've got no issue with it. It's all a wee bit last century if you ask me.'

Gillespie exchanged amused glances with the woman behind the bar, who looked like she was ready to take his order. 'Sorry about that, John,' said Gillespie, patting the old man on the shoulder. 'For a moment, I must've mistaken you for an old fart.'

John smiled. 'Wouldn't be the first time, Kenny,' he said, taking another drink. 'Would it be wrong to say if any of those birds want to improve their grip I can give them a good shaft to practise with!'

The old man chuckled to himself as he meandered back to his table. Gillespie shook his head and sighed as he settled into a barstool.

'Long day?' said the woman behind the bar.

Gillespie nodded.

'Want to talk about it?'

He shook his head. 'God, no.'

'What can I get you?'

'A pint...please.'

'Anything in particular?'

The detective raised his eyebrows as if the suggestion was a tactical nuke. The woman didn't need to ask twice. She reached for a glass and placed it under the pump as Gillespie slid a crumpled fiver over the bar.

'You're full of chat this evening,' she said.

Gillespie remained silent as he quaffed the cold beer.

The woman tried again, 'Well, how's life in the detective world treating you?'

He put down the pint glass and patted his lips. 'Can't

complain, Louise. Right now, crime's probably the only expanding business in Edinburgh. It's the other stuff I find tiring.'

'I can tell by the bags under your eyes,' she said, handing him his change. 'You look like one of those pandas over at the zoo.'

Gillespie paused, the mention of the pandas altering the direction of his thoughts. 'How's my little Eilidh doing?'

Louise rolled her eyes. 'Driving me up the wall. Just when I think she's grown out of having tantrums, she goes and has another meltdown. Did it in Asda the other day, a proper sparky because they were out of Coco Pops.'

The DCI grinned. 'You can't live without Coco Pops...'

'Tastes so chocolatey they turn the milk brown, don't you know!'

Gillespie wasn't sure where to take the conversation after the foray into children's cereal so opted for another sip of beer. Louise was about to move to the other end of the bar to serve someone else when Gillespie promptly found his voice again. 'I need to see you again.'

Louise stared at him for a moment. 'You're seeing me now, aren't you?'

'You know that's not what I mean.' He shook his head, lowered his voice. 'I *want* to see you again. Soon.'

Louise gave a faint smile and then walked away. Gillespie felt a hot flush of anger and embarrassment rise in him. He felt compelled to look around him, to check no one had overheard what he had just said. Looking over his shoulder wasn't a comfortable experience for the DCI. He finished his pint in one and thumped his empty glass on the bar.

Gillespie was collecting his jacket and preparing to leave when Louise returned to pull another pint. 'Eilidh has her dance class on Tuesday night,' she said, not taking her eyes from the pump. 'One of the other mums drops her back at the house about eight-thirty. That gives us a couple of hours.'

The detective nodded and left without looking back.

* * *

It was nearly midnight by the time Gillespie pulled into his driveway, but he knew Pauline would still be up. Her night was probably just getting started. He opened the front door quietly, but needn't have bothered. He could hear the television blaring through the living room door. Every sinew in his body was begging him to skulk upstairs and collapse into bed, but guilt kept him on a tight leash.

'All right?' he said, opening the living room door and standing on the threshold. His wife, slouched on the sofa, her head resting in her hand, didn't look up. Gillespie blinked slowly and shook his head. The empty pizza box, Coke cans and chocolate wrappers made the room look uncomfortably familiar to the one he'd left earlier that night. He did his best to ignore the rubbish and sat down in an armchair.

'Good programme?' he asked. Not that he cared either way about whether she was enjoying *I'm Strictly an X-Factor Celebrity Made in Essex*, or whatever the hell it was called. All the reality shows looked the same to him, each one packed with people famous for just being famous. Infamous, in some cases. His question was greeted with yet more silence. That suited him. He turned his attention back to the television but was only able to last a few minutes before giving out a derisive snort at the rank idiocy on screen.

'Nobody's asking you to watch it,' said Pauline.

'So you've remembered how to talk? I was hoping maybe for a "How did your evening go?" or maybe even a "Fancy a cup of tea?" but it's better than nothing.'

Another long silence settled between them. 'Why do you watch this garbage anyway? It's bloody mind rot.'

Pauline shrugged. 'Nothing else on, is there? And the internet's still down. Remember that? I did mention the orange flashing light on the box before you rushed off but you didn't seem interested, not in the slightest.' She continued to drone on,

28

something about not being able to place an order, something about the irritating prospect that a product might sell out. He switched off to her voice completely.

Gillespie's cheeks burned. He wanted to yell at his wife. Her inaction was an assault on his eyes but the return home to more moaning about the internet connection struck at his heart. Had she really no concept of what he had to deal with on the other side of that front door? Was she so self-absorbed that her husband's waking hours were a mystery to her?

Gillespie had an urge to wrench the television from the wall and hurl it through the window. But he'd been running on empty for hours. His body had nothing else to give. Slowly, he stood up and shuffled over to the sofa. Without warning, he snatched the remote control from Pauline's hand, hit the off switch, and tossed it aside. She seemed ready to protest but something—perhaps it was the chilling look in her husband's eyes—told her that, this time, staying quiet would be the best option.

Gillespie began to talk in a voice so measured, so unnaturally calm, that he surprised even himself, and unnerved his wife.

'Do you know what I saw tonight?' he said. 'I saw a man, about the same age as me, lying dead in his own home. He didn't have a heart attack. He didn't trip and bang his head, and he sure as hell didn't die peacefully in his sleep. Another human being had actually gone to the trouble of taking a knife, sticking it in his guts, and watching the poor bastard bleed to death.'

He paused for a moment and let the words sink in. The little colour left in Pauline's face had drained away. 'Now, I don't expect you to want a blow-by-blow account of my day. In a lot of ways, I don't blame you. I'm even past caring that you're more interested in a bunch of bloody D-list celebrities than you are your own husband. But, after the day I've had, and you can trust me on this, my dear Pauline, I really could have done with that cup of tea.'

Chapter 5

'Christ, Kenny, what have you been up to? You look like you've gone ten rounds with Ken Buchanan.' Gillespie smiled politely as he waited for Derek McCall to finish laughing at his own joke. As always, the St Leonard's staff sergeant was squeezed into a shirt several sizes too small, which gave his jiggling belly the appearance of a giant white blancmange.

'I wouldn't know, Derek,' said the DCI. 'Ken was a wee bit before my time.'

'A bit less of your cheek, young man.' The sergeant stood up behind his desk and aimed a couple of playful jabs in the detective's direction. 'I used to box at Leith Victoria back in the day. I reckon I could've been world champion if I'd stuck at it.'

'Yeah?' said Gillespie, grinning. 'Featherweight, presumably?'

'Aye, well.' The staff sergeant stopped his shadow boxing and sat down, adding, 'I'm the champ when it comes to eating chip butties now.'

Gillespie held his waning grin a moment longer than he should have—it was just enough to incite Derek further. 'So come on, what's up with those bags under your eyes? Seriously, Kenny, you look like a...'

'Like a giant panda?'

Derek smiled. Clearly he wasn't the first person to make this observation.

Gillespie shook his head. 'A giant panda, isn't that what you had to drive before you traded it in for a desk?'

'How long have you been saving up that one?'

Gillespie's face hardened. 'I've just been having a bit of trouble sleeping. There's a lot going on.'

Derek eased back in his chair, his chin doubling over his collar as he nodded. 'If it's any consolation, there's a lot of that about right now. Some of the uniform boys have just gone on stress leave.'

'More off on stress?'

'You can only spin the barrel so many times before somebody gets a bullet. This austerity bullshit's crippling everyone except the top brass—I see there's a new Jag in the station car park.'

Gillespie's lips narrowed, like he was preparing to spit on the floor. 'Is the boss in?'

'Aye, he's in,' the sergeant said while glancing down the corridor. 'And he's in a right mood.'

'So, what else is new?'

'True, but this is worse than usual, the Fairview protestors are driving him up the wall. That's what Collins is saying, anyway.'

If there was any kind of gossip at St Leonard's Police Station, Derek would be the first to know about it. There were few men or women working there who didn't have his attention but fewer yet who actually had his confidence. Gillespie knew he was on solid ground in this regard but there was still no way he was going to start pouring out his marriage problems onto the front desk.

'Everything's a drama with Collins though,' said the DCI. 'Why would the boss be getting his panties in a bunch about Fairview? It's only a handful of protestors, from what I've seen. Have you ever heard him slavering away about the G8 riots in Princes Street? The way he tells it, you'd think he arrested half the population of Edinburgh that day, so I'm sure he can handle this.'

'Well, from what I've heard, even our Ken would have to think twice about climbing into a ring with some of these women. Some big lassies among them.'

Gillespie raised a hand to halt the tirade that he sensed was being queued up, 'Speak to you later, Derek.'

He left the sergeant testing the temperature of a mug of tea that had been sitting on the counter and made for the stairwell. As the DCI pushed open the heavy double doors a flickering fluorescent bulb greeted him—its low buzzing was the perfect soundtrack for the dingy surroundings. The carpet could have been green or brown, once, but had now been worn away almost to nothing. Over the years, Gillespie had been able to identify which stains were coffee and some that were from a less wholesome source but, short of putting in a call to Forensics, the others would forever remain a mystery. An equally indeterminate grey colour covered the walls, darkening to black in the corners and where the cracks cut into the peeling plaster.

He opened the door on the second floor and headed for the coffee machine. Coffee was, he had to admit, a generous description of the pale liquid the machine spluttered into the tiny plastic cups but, for an early morning caffeine fix, it did the job. He pulled a face as he took a sip and looked over to the opening stairwell doors. 'Morning, sir!' said Harris. Unlike Gillespie, the detective sergeant was, that strange beast, a morning person.

Gillespie nodded. 'What's that you've got?' he said, pointing to the cardboard cup in his deputy's hand.

Harris raised the cup. 'It's a skinny caramel macchiato.'

'And who's Simone?'

'Simone?'

'It's written on the side of your cup. I assumed you were just holding it for her.'

'Oh, not again,' said Harris, holding it up for a closer look. 'It's really good, though.' The two men started walking along the corridor. 'Would you like a taste, sir? I daresay it's a lot nicer than the stuff you're drinking.'

'This'll do me fine, thanks, Simon. Which room are we in?'

'We're in number four.'

Gillespie spluttered on his last swig of coffee. 'Four? I'll tell you what, why not just cram us into one of the cubicles in the gents and we'll do the investigation from there?'

'Four's like the Playhouse compared to my flat.'

'I wouldn't put it about that you have a flat, son. The way things are going I can see the day when we're all working from home.'

Gillespie led the way as they walked round the corner. He opened a door and the DS followed him into the incident room. When the overhead strip light flickered into life, the windowless space seemed even more cramped than he remembered it. Blue folders, bulging with notes, were piled on a table while the large whiteboard on the adjacent wall was covered in pictures of Andy Cruickshank.

The DCI walked over to the whiteboard and stared at the images. This was the point where the blood and gore started to lose its power. At the crime scene, Andy's corpse was close enough to touch. There was no escaping the violence, the taking of a life in such a cruel fashion. But when it was all packaged up into little plastic bags, and the incident became reduced to no more than pictures and markings on a whiteboard, then it was hard for Gillespie not to feel like he was just processing another case on Edinburgh's murder production line.

He stood staring at the crime scene photographs of Andy Cruickshank. This man had been living and breathing only a few hours earlier. He'd had a life, and all that entailed. Gillespie tried to keep that in focus at all times—for every case he investigated— because the victims deserved to retain their human dignity, no matter what else had been denied them.

He scanned the images, one after the other, trying to draw into focus a rounded impression of Andy Cruickshank and how he came to be killed in his own home, on a seemingly quiet city street. As he stared, Gillespie found himself drawn to one particular close-up of the victim's face. He compared the profile shot to another taken from a different angle and then he sought Harris for a second opinion. 'Does that look like anything to you?' said Gillespie.

Harris placed his coffee on the table and walked over. 'Where am I looking, sir?'

'Just above the right temple. Looks like it could be bruised. I didn't notice it last night.'

Harris looked doubtful. 'It could be just a smudge from the printer,' he said. 'I think the toner's getting low, to be honest.'

Gillespie ignored this last comment. 'We'll see what Dr Freud thinks. What time are we due down there?'

'In about an hour, sir.'

Gillespie picked up a piece of paper from the table and scanned the list of evidence bagged at the crime scene. 'Is this everything that we've taken from the victim's house?' said Gillespie.

'Everything, sir, including more lads' mags than might be considered healthy.'

'Was there any sign of a passbook?'

'A passbook, sir?'

Gillespie tilted his head towards his shoulder and shrugged. 'A bankbook, Simon. Andy Cruickshank doesn't strike me as the kind of man who'd have conducted his finances online, or on a phone either.'

Harris nodded. 'There was an RBS book found. I think it's listed on page three.'

'Let's get it up here,' said Gillespie as he flicked over the pages. 'It'll be interesting to see what he was living on.'

'Maybe more than you might expect, sir,' said Harris, picking up a file. 'Turnbull, the PC who was doing the door-to-doors, found out a few more things. A neighbour further down the street, an old bloke, said the victim's father made a very good living.'

'Doing what?'

'Would you believe, importing tea from Sri Lanka?'

Gillespie raised his eyebrows. 'Any particular kind of tea?'

Harris checked the file and said, 'He didn't say, but chances are it was Ceylon—it's a Sri Lankan specialty and has a lovely, rich aroma.' Noting that Gillespie's eyebrows had raised even further, Harris swiftly added, 'He also said the victim was an only child so it's fair to say that, despite the way he lived, he might have been sitting on a decent nest egg.'

Gillespie thought for a moment about how detectives might discuss his own affairs if he were the one lying in a mortuary fridge. Would they talk about his old man's gambling problem? Or the fact his marriage was a complete disaster? Yes, he thought. It wasn't just a murder victim's body that suffered the indignity of dissection—it was their entire existence.

His thoughts were interrupted by a knock on the door. A young PC entered. 'Sorry to disturb you, sir,' she said. 'But the Chief Super would like to see you.'

Gillespie sighed. 'Get some Ceylon on the boil will you, Simon? I've got a feeling I'm going to need it.'

'Come in.' Gillespie wasn't fooled by Chief Superintendent Brian Bassett's calm tone on the other side of the door. He took a deep breath and stepped into his boss's office.

'Morning, sir,' said Gillespie.

Bassett, a balding man not much older than Gillespie, was at his computer. He didn't look up and continued to type using only his index fingers. Gillespie knew exactly what his superior officer was doing, of course. He was making him wait, making him stew. Gillespie took the opportunity to examine the wall behind Bassett's desk. The various framed certificates were interspersed with photographs and newspaper cuttings. In one, he was shaking hands with the Lord Provost, sporting the kind of cheesy grin that Gillespie had never witnessed first-hand but knew had probably served Bassett well as he clambered up the ranks.

After several minutes, Bassett looked up from the monitor and something told Gillespie he wouldn't be treated to one of those grins any time soon. 'Thanks for coming up so quickly,

Kenny, I know you're busy.'

'Not a problem, sir. What can I do for you?'

Bassett picked up a pen and leaned back in his chair. 'Actually, Kenny, I was wondering if there was something I could do for you. I understand you're looking to change jobs?'

Gillespie struggled for a response. 'Sir?'

'That's correct, isn't it? Because, judging by the state of my evidence room, I think you'd enjoy a very fruitful career in refuse collection.'

Gillespie could practically see the thick sarcasm oozing from the Chief Superintendent's pale, thin lips.

'Well, I like to think I'd get the bins picked up on time, sir.'

'It's not funny, Kenny,' said Bassett, his tone turning nasty. 'I wouldn't be surprised if the city council sent the health inspectors round. But the fact you've turned the basement into a landfill isn't the problem.'

He paused for a minute to leave Gillespie to guess what the problem might be. Gillespie didn't say a word. Bassett glanced at his computer and said, 'Tell me, Kenny, how many officers did you have working overtime last night?' He didn't wait for an answer. 'Twelve,' he said. 'That's how many—twelve! Jesus Christ, Kenny, I can't afford to have a dozen officers working all night to clear out some poor bugger's cesspit of a home. I've had to post thirty men out at Fairview every day this week to keep the protestors in check. It's costing the division a fortune.'

Gillespie couldn't help himself. 'Thirty?' he said in disbelief. 'Why so many?'

'Think about the Fairview membership, Kenny,' said Bassett, his voice going up in pitch as he became more agitated. 'They're the kind of people that hold the purse strings. It won't reflect well on us if we're not seen to be out in force.'

Gillespie wanted to correct Bassett, to say that it wouldn't reflect well on him, but he said, 'Everyone in the department is well aware of the budget issues, sir. But when it comes to a crime scene, I don't like to do things, if you'll pardon the expression, sir, half-arsed.'

'I've noticed that about you, Kenny. This isn't the first time I've had to speak to you about overspending.' He gave a heavy sigh and added, 'And did anything of interest turn up? A murder weapon, for example?'

Gillespie's shoulders stiffened. 'No, sir. But we've found a bankbook, which I think might be useful.'

'I hope so, Kenny, because you're on your last warning. Pull a stunt like this again and you really will be looking for a new job.'

Bassett turned back to his computer. It was Gillespie's signal to leave. He wanted nothing more than to slam the door shut on his way out, to watch Bassett's face turn purple as he peered through the broken glass but, with great difficulty, he was able to resist the urge. As he marched down the corridor, he realised there was an upside to the confrontation. The prospect of a trip to the mortuary didn't seem so bad after all.

Chapter 6

By capital city standards Edinburgh was small, but at any given time some of its half-a-million souls would be lying dead. With any luck, thought Gillespie, they would be discovered quickly, though as he was now being reminded, this wasn't always the case.

'I blame direct debits, myself,' said the pathology technician, Keith Irwin. 'There was an old woman found in a flat in Sighthill, just after I started. Guess how long she'd been there?'

Gillespie shrugged. 'Six months?'

Keith shook his head, 'Five years! Five years, can you believe that? They only found what was left of her because the kitchen tap had a leak and it started dripping into the flat below. You know what the problem was?'

'Perished washer?' said Gillespie.

'No. The problem was she paid all her bills by direct debit. Her pension was paid into her account automatically every month and her rent, gas, council tax, you name it, was coming out regular as clockwork. So long as she was paying her bills on time, nobody gave a monkey's about the poor old dear. Do yourself a favour, Kenny, if you're planning on dying, cancel your direct debits so we'll know when to send out the search party.'

'I'll bear it in mind.'

The two men stood in silence for a moment as they heard the

clank of the approaching lift. A few seconds later the heavy doors creaked open to reveal a metal trolley. On top sat a large white bag that Gillespie knew contained the body of Andy Cruickshank.

Keith stepped into the lift and wheeled out the trolley, humming tunelessly as he went. 'We'll get him over to the PM suite. Wendy's in the viewing room if you want to join her?'

Gillespie shook his head. 'I'll stick with you guys, thanks. That woman's too cold for my liking.'

He went to join Harris in putting on a white suit and mask before stepping into the post-mortem suite where the pathologist was laying out instruments.

'Dr Freud,' nodded Gillespie.

Clements sighed. 'It wasn't funny the first time, Gillespie, so it's unlikely to be funny the thousandth time. And you know very well I'm not a doctor.'

'Neither was Dr Seuss. Why *do* people call you "Dr Freud," anyway?' Gillespie saw a touch of red creeping into the pathologist's thin features.

'*You're* the only one who calls me "Dr Freud",' he said, holding up a scalpel that glistened in the overhead light. 'I'm a pathologist, not a doctor. Just like you're supposed to be a detective, as opposed to a comedian. Now, shall we get on with this examination or should we continue to pretend we're in a playground?'

Gillespie smirked. He found winding up Clements—one of the only blood sports yet to be banned—a welcome distraction to the thought of what lay ahead.

Every time he entered the mortuary, he was reminded of the first time he saw a body on the slab—a twelve-year-old schoolgirl called Angie Bates, who'd been mown down by a drunk driver. He saw her white face again, that had never left him, and neither had her organs being yanked out and binned right under his nose.

The DCI had been trying to substitute his humanity with humour ever since. It was the only way he could cope, and it seemed to work for the mortuary staff.

He turned to Harris. 'You all right, Simon?'

'Yes, sir,' said Harris, he seemed unfazed; one less thing to worry about, then.

Keith wheeled up the trolley and started unzipping the body bag.

'Make sure you keep the sheet as evidence,' came a voice from behind them.

Gillespie turned his head towards the viewing room, which looked down on the PM suite. Despite the time of day and the setting, Wendy Taylor seemed to Gillespie like she was settling down to enjoy a night at the theatre. All the Procurator Fiscal needed to complete the illusion was a pair of opera glasses and a box of Ferrero Rocher.

'Of course, Mrs Taylor,' said Harris, his tone sailing dangerously close to sycophantic waters for Gillespie's liking.

As Keith pulled away the plastic sheet to reveal the frail, naked body of Andy Cruickshank all eyes focussed on a large, dark torso wound. But it was Andy's ribcage—clearly defined under the white skin—that grabbed Gillespie's attention.

'Christ, there's nothing on him,' he said. 'He looks like he'd be eight stone dripping wet.'

'Eight stone, two pounds, bone dry, to be precise,' said Clements, consulting his notepad. 'Let's get him on the table, Keith.'

The technician slid the body across from the trolley and Clements started work on the hole in Andy's belly.

'The wound is eight centimetres by nine centimetres gaping,' he said, before pinching the skin and taking another measurement, 'and five centimetres by one centimetre closed.'

'What's the angle of entry?' asked Gillespie.

'Upwards and steep,' said Clements, 'you're probably looking at around seventy degrees. Certainly enough to reach the heart but we'll know for sure once we open him up.'

The detective mulled over the new information, trying to

formulate in his mind a picture of Andy Cruickshank's final moments. Frail as he appeared, there was no way the hoarder would have issued an open invitation for someone to stick a knife in his body.

As though reading Gillespie's mind, Clements said, 'There's no other stab wounds but these marks suggest significant pressure has been applied to the victim's right arm.'

'And there's definitely bruising on his left temple,' said the DCI, now able to see clearly that the dark patch he'd seen on the photograph had nothing to do with a faulty printer.

'One thing at a time, Gillespie,' said Clements.

The detective didn't reply. He found the examination to be a painfully slow process, with every blemish and birthmark meticulously recorded.

'I get the impression, Dr Freud, that if a body turned up in a baked bean factory, you could tell me whether it was foul play or they'd farted themselves to death.'

Keith and Harris suppressed laughter as Clements ignored the remark and continued the examination. Gillespie looked round at Wendy Taylor, who seemed to be taking copious notes from the comfort of the viewing room. He wondered whether these were related to the post-mortem, or whether she was totting up how many times the DCI made an inappropriate comment.

'It seems you're right about the bruising,' said Clements, when he turned his attention to Andy's head.

'It's been known to happen occasionally,' said Gillespie.

'We'll take a closer look,' said Clements. 'Keith, will you do the honours?'

Gillespie watched the technician set to work, as though the sound of razor-sharp metal slicing into a human head were the most normal thing in the world. He looked at Harris, whose face remained impassive. The young man still had a lot to learn about being a detective but when it came to keeping his emotions in check, Gillespie knew there was nothing he could teach him.

'You can see how extensive the bruising is under the skin,'

said Clements, pointing to a large, dark area of tissue.

Gillespie nodded. 'So, he was hit pretty hard,' he said.

'It would seem so and, due to the skin not being broken, I would suggest it was by a blunt instrument. However, I'll have to leave it to you and young Harris here to determine what that instrument might have been.'

'Sounds fair enough to me.' After a morning of blood and gore, some more down to earth detective work suited the DCI just fine.

Gillespie inhaled deeply and wondered if he'd ever enjoyed a cigarette more. It had been six hours since he'd first watched Andy Cruickshank's body being wheeled into the post-mortem suite. If he didn't deserve a fag after all that, then he never would.

'Don't you ever think about what smoking does to your lungs, sir?' said Harris.

The DCI took another long draw and shook his head. 'Our friend in there was a non-smoker, Simon, and I've seen more impressive heart and lungs in a bag of giblets,' he said. 'Anyway, if you ever get the chance to inspect my breathing apparatus at such close quarters, I'll be past caring.'

Gillespie looked at his watch and, with reluctance, stubbed out his cigarette. 'We'd better get back inside,' he said. 'Don't want to miss the Queen's speech.'

Wendy Taylor had spent nearly an hour in the mortuary office going back over the initial findings, the main one being that Andy had died of a ruptured aorta as the result of a single stab wound. Finally, the Procurator Fiscal summed up what Gillespie knew was coming.

'There is enough evidence,' she said, 'to lead me to believe that Andrew Cruickshank was murdered.'

And Gillespie knew whose responsibility it was to find the murderer.

Chapter 7

Gillespie strained his neck and peered into the darkness. The blurred red digits of his alarm clock slowly came into focus. It was eleven forty-five. The detective had been in bed for over an hour, but sleep still seemed a long way off. He could hear Pauline snoring. Falling instantly into a coma-like state always came easily to his wife but, like a petulant child being dragged from a playground, his own mind fought stubbornly against his body's desire to rest.

He couldn't stop thinking about the day's post-mortem, of the argument with his boss, and of a woman who wasn't the one lying next to him. He'd once read that being asleep was akin to being dead. If that were the case, then right now he'd happily swap places with Andy Cruickshank. He sighed and slumped back on to his pillow. Unable to get comfortable, he sat up and punched it back into shape before lying on his side. After around ten minutes of shifting positions, he lay on his back, put his hands behind his head and stared up towards the ceiling.

It took a few moments for Gillespie to register that the din of Pauline snoring was no longer the only noise in the room. He turned his head in its direction and realised the noise was coming from his trousers, which were laid out on a chair next to the bed. He reached across and fumbled around in the pockets for his phone.

'Gillespie,' he said, answering the mobile safe in the knowledge that not even a brass band would be able to wake his wife.

'Oh, hello, Detective Chief Inspector. I'm sorry to disturb you. I know it's late.'

'Who is this?'

'This is Sergeant Bill Duncan on the night desk, sir.'

It wasn't a name Gillespie recognised. He didn't know who Sergeant Bill Duncan was and he didn't much care. All he knew was that the man on the other end of the line was now part of a global conspiracy dedicated to keeping him awake.

'What can I do for you, Bill? I know this'll come as a surprise, but even detectives need their beauty sleep.'

Bill laughed nervously but, realising Gillespie wasn't following suit, he cleared his throat and said, 'I apologise, sir, but we've had a call about a disturbance at Fairview Golf Club.'

Gillespie sat up wearily and rubbed his eyes with his free hand. 'There's been disturbances going on at Fairview for over a week, Bill. Why are CID suddenly in demand?'

'Sergeant McCall suggested I should call a DCI if anything were to come up at Fairview, sir, given the Chief Superintendent's concerns over the matter. I'm also to keep the Chief informed of anything personally.'

'Have you called him yet?'

'Not yet, sir. I thought I'd better speak to you first.'

'Why didn't you call Collins? He's the one on duty.'

'I'm afraid DCI Collins has been called away to a suspected rape in Newington.'

Gillespie paused as he mulled things over.

'Are you still there, sir?'

'Send Harris along.'

'DS Harris?'

'The very same. And do me a favour, Bill, give it half an hour before you call the Chief. We don't want the old sweetie charging out to East Lothian in his PJs for no good reason. Let's see what Simon finds out first. Goodnight.'

Gillespie hung up and put the phone on his bedside table. If Harris was serious about this business, it was time he understood what it was like to do the work of three men. He lay back down and resumed his apparently hopeless task, but after another hour of tossing and turning decided to give it up as a bad job.

Using the light from his phone as a torch, he pulled on a jumper and trudged downstairs to find a packet of cigarettes. Deeply aware that the only thing keener than Pauline's sense of entitlement was her sense of smell, he gently opened the back door and stepped outside.

He lit a cigarette and watched the exhaled smoke dissipating in the Edinburgh night. It only took a few draws to relieve his tension, and a few minutes of the cold to send him back inside. He sat down at the kitchen table and stared at his phone, scanning text messages. After a moment of thought, he started to type. 'Can't wait to see you tomorrow. Kx.'

His stomach tightened. Why was he doing this? Wasn't life complicated enough? As he waited for a response, he put the phone on the table and walked over to the fridge. He opened the door to find little more appetising than a small lump of cheese, a lettuce that was turning brown and a half-eaten pork pie. He held up a bottle of milk to inspect its use-by date and almost dropped it when the phone began to vibrate its way across the table. It wasn't a text, but another call.

'Simon?'

'Yes, sir. I hope I'm not disturbing you.'

'There's a lot of things that disturb me about you, Simon, but that's by the by. Are you at the golf club?'

'Yes, I've been here about twenty minutes. I understand you personally recommended me for this job, sir. Thank you for that.'

'Don't mention it. What's up?'

'I'm here with Mr Watson, the greenkeeper, who made the call. There's a big tournament coming up in a few weeks and he was worried protestors were trying to sabotage the course.'

'Look, Simon, if you've called me up at one in the morning

because people have been dumping rubbish on the eighteenth then I'll be sorely disappointed.'

'I'm not aware of anything like that, sir, but I thought you should know we've found a body on the ninth.'

Scribbling a note for Pauline, Gillespie threw on his suit and jumped in his car. The bypass was practically deserted and, less than half an hour later, he was pulling up to the gates of Fairview Golf Club. Several security personnel, complete with Alsatian dogs on leads, were on patrol, along with uniformed police officers.

On a layby opposite was a makeshift campsite, comprising around twenty tatty-looking tents. In his headlights, Gillespie could make out a few bleary-eyed female protestors holding up placards. Much like being a detective, the fight for sexual equality was a job where sleep was a luxury. On almost any other day, the placard that read *I don't need nuts to sink putts* would probably have raised a smile, but this wasn't any other day.

Two worlds had collided in East Lothian and now it sounded like someone had paid the price. Gillespie was waved through the gates to where Harris, along with a short man in a flat cap, was waiting for him outside the mansion-like clubhouse.

'Good evening, sir.'

'Evening, Simon. We really need to stop meeting like this. What do we have?'

'An adult female, sir. Mr Watson here was the one who found her. He's offered to take us over to the fairway in a buggy.'

Gillespie looked at the older man and shook his head. 'Thanks, but we have to keep any disturbance of the crime scene to a minimum. We'll walk.'

'Suits me,' said Watson, handing Gillespie a torch. The three men set off briskly towards the ninth fairway, torch beams slicing through the blackness.

'Can you tell me what happened, Mr Watson?' said Gillespie,

who found he was more out of breath than he expected. Maybe Pauline had a point about the fags after all.

'Aye. A couple of the security lads radioed me, said they thought they saw some women trying to flag down motorists on the main road. Bloody protestors. I live nearby so I thought I'd go and check if the buggers had done any damage. And that's when I found her.'

'Do you think she's one of the protestors?'

'Oh aye, although I have to admit I didn't get a good look at the lassie. Scared the living daylights out of me.'

They continued to walk in silence for another five minutes when Watson stopped in his tracks and pointed up ahead.

'She's just yonder, to the left of the bunker. I'll, er, wait here if that's okay.'

Gillespie and Harris slowed their pace as they approached the sand trap. The beam from the DCI's torch was first to fall on the woman, whose large, hooped earrings glinted in the light.

She lay on her back, half of her face covered by her long, blonde hair. Gillespie moved his torch over the rest of her body. Her short, white dress was stained with mud and grass, but there was no sign of blood.

'I don't think she's a protestor, sir,' said Harris, shaking his head.

'Why? Because she's not carrying a placard? She's not usual golf club clientele, that's for sure. She looks like a brass to me. What do you think?'

'Oh, yes, I'd say she's almost certainly a brass. Absolutely.'

Gillespie turned his torch on Harris. 'If you don't know what a brass is, Simon, all you need to do is say.'

'What's a brass, sir?'

'A prostitute. And the fact she's got her stilettos in her hands suggests she was a prostitute in a hurry. Now, get on the radio. I want the tent up before the dawn chorus.'

Their discussion was interrupted by a whine, which was growing louder. They looked up to see headlights approaching them at speed. A golf buggy, being driven by one of the security guards, skidded to a halt and the harassed figure of Brian Bassett, holding on to his cap with one hand and the frame of the cart with the other, sprang out of the passenger side.

'This is bad, Kenny, this is really bad,' he said, pulling off his leather gloves and striding over to the body. 'Jesus, she looks like a bloody hooker. How the hell are we going to keep this out of the papers? Get the tent up now.'

'It's on its way, sir.'

'I said *now*, Kenny. Fairview has enough problems without this. This a complete disaster.'

Gillespie wanted to tell his boss that, if the girl could talk, he was sure she would apologise for littering the pristine course with her dead body, but he knew it was pointless.

'I hope you're not too busy on that hoarder case, Kenny.'

'You could say that, sir. It's a murder investigation now. The Procurator Fiscal confirmed that today.'

'In that case, you're taking over Incident Room One. Wallace can move into number four. And you're going to get some extra help. We can't take any chances on this one. I want answers ASAP.'

By the time they got back to the clubhouse, Gillespie had no further need for the torch. The dew-covered course was bathed in the pale light of early morning. He pulled out his phone to check the time and saw that Louise had finally replied.

Chapter 8

Gillespie was only able to glance at the message from Louise when Bassett appeared beside him.

'Absolutely bloody useless, the lot of them,' said the Chief Super.

'Sir?'

'Those socos of yours. I can't believe how long it took them to put up that tent.'

'With respect, sir, they're Forensics officers—not boy scouts.'

'Nothing wrong with the scouts, Kenny.'

Gillespie nodded. 'Of course not.'

'It teaches discipline and respect. I dread to think what kind of merit badges they'd dish out to kids these days—badges for taking drugs and, what is it you call it, sexting?'

Gillespie slowly slipped his phone back into his pocket. Bassett sighed. 'If the papers get so much as a sniff of this, there'll be hell to pay, Kenny. Until we get this cleared up, everything else takes a back seat. Got it?'

'I must've missed the dead girl call shotgun.' Gillespie knew he shouldn't have said it, knew he should have done nothing more than nod and say 'yes, sir,' but that wasn't him, especially when he was watching his boss lose all sense of perspective. He braced himself for the comeback but, before Bassett could deliver it, they were interrupted by a shriek coming from outside.

'Oh, Christ. What now?' said Bassett.

Gillespie bolted out of the doors in time to see two of his officers dragging a protestor towards a police car.

'What's going on?' he shouted to the nearest officer, who was struggling to keep the woman under control.

'They'd entered the crime scene, sir.'

'*They?*'

Gillespie turned round to see three more protestors being hauled across the golf course. DS Harris was leading the way for the officers, followed all the way by the noisy chanting, interrupted only briefly by expletive-filled rants.

'How the hell did they get on the scene, Simon?'

Harris looked weary. 'Sorry, sir. They must've climbed over the wall on the far side.'

'Get them out of here, now,' said Bassett. Even in this light, it was obvious his face was darkening.

Seeing two of the officers trying to contain a particularly large protestor, Gillespie stepped in to help, only to be spat on for his trouble. He wiped his face with a handkerchief as he and Harris watched the car disappear down the driveway.

'Are you okay, sir?' said Harris.

'I'm fine. No worse than the PCs have to deal with in the Grassmarket every Saturday night. Did you and the socos find anything?'

Harris pulled out his notebook. 'We found the victim's clutch bag nearby. We've got a set of keys, a lipstick, some cash and a gym card. Her name is—was—Elena Enescu according to her gym membership, and she lives—lived—at flat 46/4, West Sullivan Street.'

'That's in Gorgie.'

'Yes, sir.'

'You look tired, Simon.'

'You could say that.'

He pulled his car keys from his pocket and gave them to Harris. 'Well, we'll both have plenty of time to sleep when we retire. Let's go and check out that flat. You can drive.'

The road back to Edinburgh was quiet, but there were enough cars around to make Gillespie wonder where each of them had to be at four in the morning.

Harris pulled up behind an Astra at the red lights of Sheriff-hall Roundabout. Gillespie gazed through the windscreen at the back of the driver's head and tried to imagine their face. He knew it was probably just someone going in to the city for an early shift, but his overactive imagination decided it was a woman fleeing an abusive husband that she'd left sleeping, without even a note.

Good for her, he thought. As they moved away and crossed the roundabout, he took out his phone and looked again at the text from Louise.

'Me neither XXX.'

His pulse quickened. He took a deep breath and exhaled as silently as he could, trying to figure out how such a short message could cause him so much excitement. He knew, though, that getting excited was a waste of energy. The discovery of the girl on the golf course meant their plans to meet up were now firmly on hold. He wound down the window, lit a cigarette and pondered how to break the news to Louise.

'The Chief Superintendent didn't seem very happy, did he?'

Gillespie wasn't one to frighten easily, but Harris, who had driven in silence since leaving Fairview, caused him to cough in surprise.

'Does he ever seem happy to you, Simon?'

Harris thought for a moment. 'I suppose not, sir, but he sounded particularly, erm, pissed off back there.'

'That's because the big sweetie hates losing. He hates losing at anything. Can you imagine Bassett playing Monopoly at Christmas? He's the banker, naturally. He's also the kind of guy who'll put four hotels on Park Lane and laugh when his five-year-old lands on it. You don't need to waste cash on the utility companies if wee Josie is providing the waterworks.'

Gillespie chuckled bitterly at the thought and took another draw on his cigarette.

'Sorry, sir, but you've lost me. What game is he supposed to be playing at the minute?'

'Right now, the boss is playing murder Top Trumps. As far as he's concerned, the girl found at the posh golf club beats the hoarder found in the hovel.'

'And does she?'

'Only if we play by Bassett's rules.'

They turned off the bypass at Lothianburn junction. By the time they arrived in Gorgie quarter of an hour later, Gillespie had replied to Louise, but it hadn't been easy.

'Got a lot on at work so going to have to postpone. Sorry X.'

He hated writing 'postpone,' as though he was telling her Man Utd v Spurs was off due to a waterlogged pitch. But it was infinitely preferable to 'sorry, babe, got to take a rain check.' If he'd written that, he'd have to put out a warrant for his own arrest. He sat in silence and sweated on her reply.

As they neared the address, a cat sprinted across the road in front of them. Harris swore and stepped hard on the brake.

'Is that good luck or bad luck? I can't remember.'

Gillespie shrugged. 'The way our week has been going, I'd say bad. But that cat was grey, so I wouldn't worry either way. I think this is us.'

He pointed to a shabby-looking building up ahead. Harris found a space next to a dumpster and the officers got out. Taking out Elena's keys, Harris opened the outer door and they made their way up the stairs. The smell of incense hit them as soon as they opened the door to the flat. Harris switched on the light to reveal a small, simply furnished apartment, all pastel colours and flat-pack furniture.

'I feel like we're at IKEA. You check the bedroom, Simon. I'll see what I can find in here.'

Harris entered the bedroom while Gillespie looked around the living room. He walked over to a bookshelf and flicked through the paperbacks but found nothing familiar.

'She's definitely from eastern Europe. Maybe the Czech Republic.'

'I'd say she's more likely to be Romanian, sir.'

'What makes you so sure?'

Harris appeared in the bedroom doorway holding up a passport, 'Romania' emblazoned across the burgundy cover.

'Just a hunch.'

'Touché.'

'I don't think there's any doubt about her being a prostitute either, sir.'

'Don't tell me she's got the paperwork for that, too.'

'No sir. Just this.'

He held up a bag and pulled out a handful of condoms. They spent another twenty minutes going through drawers but found nothing of interest. Harris followed Gillespie into the kitchen. Several photographs were stuck to the door of the fridge. In one, the girl he and Harris had last seen lying dead on the fairway was beaming at the camera in front of a café in what looked like her homeland. A man about her own age, his dark hair swept back in a ponytail, had one arm wrapped round her waist, while the other took the picture.

'You'd expect that kind of picture to be in a frame, wouldn't you sir?'

'Maybe they'd had a falling out. Or maybe it made her clients feel uncomfortable. Anyway, I don't think we're going to find a smoking gun here.'

'Maybe we should speak to the neighbours.'

'Now's not the time. I think we should both go home and try to get a few hours' sleep. We'll see what they find in the PM first. I'll see you at the station at half nine.'

Harris looked at his watch and nodded. He locked up and followed Gillespie out of the flat.

'Erm, sir?'

Gillespie turned around, 'What is it?'

'Any chance of a lift home?'

Gillespie felt remarkably fresh considering his lack of sleep. He walked into the station and greeted Derek on the front desk with, 'Good morning.'

'You're very chipper,' said the sergeant.

'I've only got the two murders to deal with, Derek. Any reason why I shouldn't be chipper?'

'Just this.'

He held up a copy of the *Edinburgh Evening News*. Gillespie felt his stomach lurch. 'MURDER AT FAIRVIEW—Body found in bunker at protest-hit golf club.'

Gillespie didn't say a word. He grabbed the newspaper and ran upstairs to the incident room. He opened the door to see someone studying the pictures of Andy Cruickshank on the wall.

'Can I help you?' he said.

The woman looked around. She looked young enough to be an intern.

'Ah, good morning, sir. I'm Detective Sergeant Gemma Dickson.

Gillespie was silent, partly in surprise, partly because she hadn't answered his question.

'I'm based in Glasgow, but I've been reassigned to help you with the Fairview case.'

'By who?'

'The Chief Superintendent.'

'The Chief? Is he in?'

'I don't think so, sir. He phoned me at three o'clock this morning to say he was putting me on this case.'

'Nice of him to let me know.'

Dickson smiled awkwardly, but Gillespie was more relieved than angry. If Bassett wasn't in, there was a chance he hadn't yet seen the news. He sat down at the table.

'Well, sorry, what did you say your name was?'

'Gemma Dickson, sir.'

'Well, Gemma Dickson, now that you're here, make yourself useful and start shifting all this stuff down the corridor to Incident Room One. You're just in time to help us move into our new digs.'

Dickson nodded and began to load files into a box as Gillespie laid out the newspaper and started to read. The story was light on details, but the only thing that mattered was the headline, which would be enough to see Bassett burst a blood vessel. Gillespie heard the door open and, jerking his gaze, saw a bleary-eyed Harris wandering in with a cup of coffee.

'Morning, sir.'

'Glad you could join us, Simon. Can I introduce you to Detective Sergeant Gemma Dickson? She's going to be working with us for a while.'

Gillespie watched Harris's mouth pinch into a tight knot as he took in the new member of the team. She held out her hand, which left Harris shuffling and twitching as he tried to figure out what to do with his coffee, before deciding finally to shift it to his left hand and shake with his right.

'Pleased to meet you. Can I, er, help you with those boxes? They look heavy.'

Gillespie intervened, 'Excuse me, Mr Darcy, but I think Detective Dickson can manage just fine. Now, come and take a look at this.'

Dickson picked up a box and walked out of the room. Harris, flustered, put his cup on the table and looked down at the newspaper. His face fell.

'Oh.'

'Oh, indeed. Although I'd be tempted to add a couple more words to that sentiment. That's why we don't let people enter a crime scene. When are we getting the post-mortem report?'

'Hopefully later on this morning, sir.'

'Let's leave the conjecture to the journalists, Simon. Go and find out exactly when we're getting it.'

'Yes, sir.'

Harris opened the door to leave and almost collided with an angry-looking man on his way in. Gillespie wasn't surprised to see him.

'Kenny.'

'DCI Wallace. Always a pleasure, never a chore.'

'Don't give me that, Kenny. Wee Gemma Dickson has just dumped a box of your crap in my incident room. Is this your doing?'

'I'm afraid it's my incident room now, Dave. We've got two murder investigations on the go. I'm sure you understand.'

Wallace stood in the doorway, his thick, grey eyebrows bunched above a red slab of forehead.

'Aye, well, we'll see what the boss thinks about this.'

'It was his idea, but by all means go and ask him. I think I'm firmly down the arse-kissing pecking order these days.'

Wallace wagged a finger, some words played on his mouth, but he thought better of releasing them. He stormed out, slamming the door behind him.

'I hope I've not caused any trouble,' said Dickson when she came back in.

'Don't worry about it, Gemma. I was in trouble way before you showed up.'

'Speaking of which, I ran into the Chief on the way back. He says he wants to see you in his office.'

'Is that all he said?'

'Not exactly, sir. But it's my first day in your team and I wasn't sure how you felt about swearing in the office.'

Bassett flung the *Evening News* down on his desk and put his hands on his hips. Gillespie wondered if his boss knew how ridiculous the pose appeared. It made him look like a Bash Street schoolmaster displaying a bag of pinched apples. Basset's voice, though, realistically conveyed his genuine doom.

'I'm waiting, Kenny.'

'We might be here a while then, sir, because I don't know any more than you do.'

Bassett thumped the desk. 'Jesus, Kenny, that's not good enough. How the hell did the *News* get on to this so quickly?'

Gillespie let some of the room's tension subside before answering. 'I can only assume one of the protestors phoned them. It's hardly surprising. We've had officers giving them a hard time all week.'

'This stops now. You're going to speak to Janet Finlay at Fettes.'

'I don't think I've had the pleasure.'

'She's the new press manager, and she knows this game inside out. You're going to speak to her about arranging a press conference for this afternoon, and you're going to play down any connection between the Fairview protest and the murder.'

'How do we know they're not connected?'

Bassett ignored the question. 'And I want you to head up the press conference, no back passing to that Harris boy.'

'Sir, we can't progress on the assumption that the murder is entirely separate from the protest just because we don't want to ruffle a few old school ties.'

Bassett had ceased to listen. 'And, your hoarder investigation most definitely goes on the back burner until further notice, understand?'

'My hoarder *murder* investigation has been trumped, sir. Got it.'

Bassett appeared to be inhabiting his own universe, directing instructions at Gillespie purely to achieve an end the detective couldn't see, and wasn't even to be consulted on. The Chief Super reeled off a list of more gripes, followed by another summary of the injustice visited upon Fairview and then he slumped in his chair and closed over the newspaper.

'This is a disaster,' said Bassett. 'You do know that, Gillespie?'

'Yes, sir.'

'Well, good. Because I'm relying on you to successfully steer this ship to port.'

'I'll man the lifeboats myself, sir.'

'What? God, no. We don't want any of that. A straight course, Gillespie, I'm warning you.'

Chapter 9

As Gillespie walked in, he spotted Harris and Dickson pinning up photographs of the two murder victims. By now the images of Andy Cruickshank were familiar reminders of the old hoarder's fate, but it was only a few days ago that DS Harris had called Gillespie out to Liberton. Broken nights' sleep, run-ins with his boss and the small matter of a dead prostitute on a golf course had played havoc with the detective's body clock.

Gillespie looked away from the board and took in the scope of the new incident room. It felt about four times bigger than the room they'd just left, which was a pointed reminder of the size of the task he now faced. Something like guilt was creeping up on Gillespie; it was the thought of having, once again, two deceased victims competing for his attention at the same time.

'Penny for your thoughts, sir?'

'You can put the penny towards your next coffee, Simon. I was just wondering where we were with the Cruickshank case.'

'Interesting you should say that, because I've just received this statement from the bank.'

He handed Gillespie a piece of paper. The detective studied it for a minute and then whistled softly. 'He knew how to splash the cash for a man who sat on a pile of old cereal boxes instead of a sofa.'

'You could say that, sir.' Harris leaned over the paperwork

and pointed to a set of figures. 'He's emptied his account of twenty-seven thousand pounds over the last year. There were regular withdrawals of just over two thousand pounds a month, almost like he was taking out a regular wage.'

'Or someone was milking an old goat.'

'It did cross my mind, sir.'

Gillespie returned the papers, pressing them into Harris's hands. 'Get back to the bank and ask for a complete breakdown of these withdrawals. I need the exact details of how they were made. If these were cheque payments, I want to know who he was being so generous to. If it was cash being withdrawn over the counter at his local branch, they might have it on CCTV.'

Gillespie left Harris nodding at the instructions and walked over to Dickson, who was perching on tiptoes to put the last photograph of Elena Enescu on the board.

'What do you think, Gemma?'

Dickson stepped back and looked at the photograph. 'Young woman, most likely a prostitute, murdered at an exclusive, men-only golf club. It would be difficult to look beyond sex as the most likely motive at this stage, but we'll have a better idea when we get the post-mortem report.'

'I meant, what do you think of our little set-up here in Edinburgh?'

'Oh, well I've not had much of a chance to familiarise myself with everything yet. To be honest, I was a bit surprised to be transferred.'

'That makes two of us. How are you with press conferences?'

'I'm not a huge fan, but I've done my fair share. We keep busy over in Glasgow.'

'That's good to hear, because I want you to handle this one.'

'What do you think Bertie will have to say about that?' said Harris, his voice pitching higher than usual, dipping dangerously close to shock.

Gillespie turned around. 'Remember when you tried to tell me about the new cushions you'd ordered for your flat? My give-a-toss levels are about the same. Now hurry up and put that call in to the bank. We've got a doctor's appointment.'

Clements was sitting in his cramped office reading a copy of the *Evening News* when Gillespie and Harris arrived at the mortuary. On the rear wall, a shelf full of thick, leather-bound tomes screamed for the attention of a feather duster. The sight made Gillespie's nose twitch, but the jars full of, he presumed human, bones on the shelf beneath took over his attention.

'I see news travels fast.' The pathologist held up the newspaper as he eyed the detectives.

'A little too fast for our liking, Dr Freud.'

Clements ignored the nickname. Gillespie was impressed he'd finally cottoned on to the fact that complaining about it wasn't going to change anything.

The pathologist leaned over his desk and picked up one of the clipboards. 'Yes, well, that young lady of yours isn't giving a great deal away, I'm afraid.'

'We'll be grateful for anything you can tell us,' said Harris.

Clements smiled, a look of practiced derision that seemed to anaesthetise the DS but bounced clear of Gillespie's stony expression.

Clements cleared his throat and turned to his notes. 'The cause of death was strangulation, almost certainly inflicted by a male, judging by the spread of finger marks around the neck. The pressure was intense, which also tends to suggest a stronger, heavier attacker, and more likely a male. There were no other signs of injury and, although we've ascertained that the victim had sex the night of the murder, there are no signs of sexual assault.'

'None at all?'

Clements shook his head. 'What's more, the Forensics team say there's no suspect DNA anywhere on the corpse.'

'Not even under her fingernails?'

The pathologist bristled. 'No. Not even under her fingernails.'

'I just find it a bit strange that she didn't put up a struggle.'

Clements leaned back in his swivel chair, crossing his legs beneath a protruding gut that worked as ballast for the screeching castors. 'As you're so fond of reminding me, Mr Gillespie, that's why you're the detective.'

Gillespie let his gaze rove the scene for a moment and then stood up to leave, pointing at the jar on the desk. 'I assume you know that's a humerus and not a coccyx in there?'

'Of course. Why?'

'Just testing a theory.'

'Maybe she had a weapon and hit him with that? It might explain why she didn't scratch him.'

Gillespie had been listening to Harris theorising for several minutes as they drove through the Grassmarket on their way to Gorgie.

'We didn't find a weapon though, did we? What happened to it?'

Harris didn't reply and instead turned his attention to the bustling street outside.

'Gosh, it's busy.'

They continued the rest of the journey in silence and managed to find a parking space in a side street opposite Elena's flat. A man in a grey hoodie and trainers was just leaving the building as they approached.

'Excuse me, sir, but do you live here?'

The man pushed his hands into his pockets and eyed Harris and Gillespie suspiciously. 'Who's asking, like?'

Harris showed the man his warrant card; it didn't improve his temperament any.

'I stay in number eight. What's the problem?'

'Do you have time to answer a few questions?'

Gillespie pulled a photograph of Elena out of his pocket and held it up. 'It's about this woman.'

'Oh, it's her, is it?'

'You know this woman?'

'Well, we're neighbours, like.' He turned back to the block of flats. 'You better come in.'

The man's flat had exactly the same layout as Elena's, but the similarities ended there. The living room floor was littered with toy cars and action figures. The man leaned over to pick up a Ninja Turtle and flung it towards the corner of the room.

'Sorry about the mess, gents. I've got the wee one staying with me this week.'

'That's quite all right, Mr?'

'Robertson. Chris, er, Christopher Robertson.'

'And you knew Elena Enescu?'

'Well, to tell you the truth, I didn't know her last name until you just told me. I just knew her to say "hi" to if we passed on the stairs, do you know what I mean?'

Harris nodded as he unfurled the pages of his spiral-bound notepad.

'I just can't believe she's dead, though. What happened to her?'

'We're still trying to establish the full details, Mr Robertson.'

'Aye, I understand. She just seemed like such a nice lassie, really friendly, you know? I can't imagine anyone wanting to hurt her.'

Gillespie paced over to Mr Robertson. 'Do you know what Ms Enescu did for a living?'

The man frowned. 'Like I say, I didn't really know her. She hadn't lived here that long. But I would quite often see her coming in when I was heading out for a night shift. I know she must've loved the clubs, because she was always coming in late and dressed a bit, you know.'

'No, I don't know. Why don't you tell me.'

After some gestures to indicate a short skirt, he indicated a low-cut top, 'She was a striking-looking lassie. If you've got it, show it off, I say.'

'Did you ever see Ms Enescu enter this building with a man?'

'No. Any time I saw her she was on her own. Actually, I tell a lie, one time she had another girl with her.'

'So you weren't aware that she was a prostitute?'

The man's mouth gaped for a moment and then he shook his head vigorously. 'No, no. I'd never have thought anything like that. Not for a second. She didn't seem the type.' He inhaled deeply and leaned backwards onto the wall, 'I just thought she loved the nightlife. I'd never have put her down as a prostitute, not in a million years.'

The pattern continued for the next hour and a half, as the detectives knocked on doors and questioned seven other neighbours in Elena's building as well as the one next door. They stood by the car as Gillespie lit a cigarette.

'Well, from everything we've heard, she was certainly one of the friendliest hookers you could ever have hoped to meet,' said the detective.

'They all seem so surprised to hear she was a prostitute.'

'I guess it's like people who still watch *Big Brother*. It's not something they'd ever admit to in public. So, we know she wasn't working from home, and she'd never been spotted by a patrol, so chances are she wasn't walking the streets.'

'Which means?'

Gillespie stubbed out his cigarette and opened the car door. 'Which means we'll need to let our fingers do the walking.'

'Excuse me?'

'Probably before your time, son. I mean, we need to start checking the good old Yellow Pages for local saunas. Someone was clearly employing Elena.'

'Ah, indeed. It might not reveal why she was found strangled on that fairway but we have to start somewhere.'

'There are any number of reasons why she might have been out there, Simon, but one thing I do know about sauna bosses is that they tend to get a bit annoyed by employees who breach their terms.'

Chapter 10

Gillespie stepped out of the car and looked beyond the turreted, baronial clubhouse towards the carefully manicured greens of Fairview. In broad daylight it was hard to believe this was where—just a few short hours ago—Elena Enescu was forced to the ground and had the life choked out of her. The action didn't fit the tourist-brochure setting, didn't seem right.

Murder happened in grimy back alleys with overflowing dumpsters, Fairview was too peaceful a place for that, too well-heeled a location for violent death. The club's sweeping Scots spires and castellated gables had long since traded in their bloody heritage and become upper-crust clichés. The only conflict that arose came from a disgruntled player who'd shanked his drive and landed in the rough. The more familiar sounds now were the gentle click of golf balls, polite ripples of applause and well-spoken banter from the club's clientele.

But that was the thing about murder. Those who were prepared to carry it out had no respect for human life, let alone the ornate splendour of their surroundings. Looking around, Gillespie suspected very little had changed since Fairview had first opened its clubhouse doors a century and a half ago—except, of course, for the police cars parked outside and the officers swarming over the lawn.

No doubt that was just how the club's members wanted it to

be. That was why, when the majority of the world was moving with the times, the group of old men that comprised its board were sticking fervently to their policy of refusing to allow women to join them. That was the way things had always been, so that was the way they'd always be. But at least one woman had been on the premises the previous evening and Gillespie wanted answers. Elena Enescu might not have belonged to Fairview, but she belonged to the human race and someone had decided to terminate her membership.

Harris got out of the car, flicking through his notebook.

'Who's up first, Simon?'

'Henry Montrose, sir. The club president. I thought we should start at the top, but he...' Harris tailed off.

'What?'

'Apparently he sounded a bit crabby on the phone, like he was going out of his way to come and speak to us.'

'That sounds about right. I've seen him interviewed on TV a couple of times. He's a busy man, Simon. He doesn't want interruptions from a couple of plebs trying to solve a murder.'

'Doesn't that kind of attitude annoy you?'

'Of course.'

'So what do you do if someone like him tries to, erm, play hardball?'

'Don't worry about that, Simon. I think he'll find my balls are harder than most.'

The detectives were led in to an oak-panelled office, the ornately-framed portraits of a dozen former Fairview presidents glaring at them from the opposite wall. Gillespie felt he was being judged by the club's founding fathers—what right did he have to question the integrity of their members?

He almost wanted to be proved wrong, for his preconceptions about the type of men that ran Fairview to be misplaced. But, within a minute of meeting Henry Montrose in person, he knew his preconceptions were bang on. The blue blazer said a lot, the white hair scraped back on his head said the rest. As the president sat down he let out a loud, irritable sigh.

'This won't take long, will it? I've got an important meeting in Glasgow this afternoon.'

'We'll try not to take up too much of your time, Mr Montrose,' said Harris.

Gillespie almost cut off the DS mid-sentence. 'How long it takes will depend on what you're able to tell us. You'll understand, of course, that this is a very serious matter.'

'Well of course I understand that. A girl has been found dead on my golf course. I'm well aware of the implications—I was just asking a question.'

'I appreciate that, Mr Montrose, but we'd be grateful if you could leave the questions to us for now.'

Montrose shook his head, leaned back in his chair and wafted a hand towards the detective. 'Fire away.'

'What do you know about Elena Enescu?'

'Very little, I'm afraid, other than the fact she's dead.'

Gillespie crossed his legs, his way of saying he wasn't going anywhere in a hurry. 'Do you have any idea what she might have been doing at Fairview last night?'

'I'm afraid I don't know that either.'

'And where were you last night?'

Montrose pursed his lips before answering. 'If you must know, my wife and I were entertaining a client at the Usher Hall.'

'What was on at the Usher Hall?'

'The RSNO were performing Beethoven's 6th.'

Gillespie nodded. '*The Pastoral.*'

Montrose raised his eyebrows. 'A fellow enthusiast?'

'Not especially. I just like to know what's going on in my city. It sounds like your clients take up quite a bit of your time.'

'They do, but if you aren't prepared to invest in your clients, they won't be prepared to invest in you.'

'I suppose it's slightly different in my line of work. Most of my clients would prefer a hands-off approach.'

Harris spoke up. 'What is it you do, Mr Montrose?'

'I'm an accountant.'

'And you like to keep busy?'

'My son handles most of the day-to-day running of the practice now, but I like to keep an eye on things. Plus I've got a small matter of a golf club to run.'

'Then these protests are probably something you could do without?'

'They've been an inconvenience, I'm not going to deny it. It's sad that some people refuse to respect the democratic process.'

Gillespie tried not to sound cynical. 'The democratic process?'

'Yes, Detective. At the last AGM, each and every one of our members was given a vote on whether we should break with tradition and admit women. The overwhelming majority of them agreed to keep our policy as it is.'

'But does part of you wish they'd voted otherwise? I can't imagine all this negative media attention has been good for the club.'

'Frankly, I don't care whether people disagree with us or not. It's our club and we'll run it the way we see fit. What does bother me is the thought of these protestors trespassing and causing damage, but I think we can rely on Brian and his team to keep them in line.'

'Brian? Do you mean Chief Superintendent Bassett?'

Montrose laughed. 'Sorry, yes, Chief Superintendent Bassett or "boss," as I suppose you have to call him.'

'I call him a few things. How long have you known the Chief Superintendent?'

'We go back some years. Sometimes I think he should have brought a bucket and spade, given the amount of time he spent in the sand out here. Do you play golf yourself, Mr Gillespie?'

'No, but I played a few rounds over in Ayrshire when I was younger.'

'Oh really? Where was that? Dundonald? Turnberry?'

'Butlins. I used to go there on holiday with my mum and dad. Brilliant course. I'd have got a hole in one if it hadn't been for that bloody windmill.'

Gillespie watched Montrose do his best to feign a smile before hitting him with another question.

'Do you think Elena's murder will damage the club's reputation, Mr Montrose?'

The president's brow furrowed. 'I don't quite see where you're coming from. You'll know better than anyone that murders can happen anywhere, often when people are in the wrong place at the wrong time. I recall one taking place on the Royal Mile a few years ago but it doesn't seem to have deterred the tourists. Yes, we've had the misfortune of a murder taking place on our premises, but I fail to see why people would think less of our club as a result.'

'You're right. I'm sure they won't.' For an opener, the interview had gone about as well as Gillespie had expected. He rose and extended a hand. 'Thank you for your time.'

'Is that all?'

'For now, anyway.'

Outside the office, Harris waited for the door to close before exhaling loudly.

'How was that for you, Simon?'

'I think frosty would be an understatement. That was absolutely Baltic.'

'Well, don't expect a thaw any time soon. The captain's up next, isn't he?'

Harris gave a grim smile and nodded, but both detectives were pleasantly surprised when Alexander Dean breezed into the office. He looked a good twenty years younger than the Fairview president, and it looked like the club captain would take a different approach.

'Sorry I'm a bit late, gents,' he said, shaking their hands. 'I was stuck at Sheriffhall for ages. God knows what the hold-up was. I might have got here on time, but I didn't want to get caught speeding. Just imagine the headlines.'

Harris smiled. 'We're grateful for your time, Mr Dean. This

is Detective Chief Inspector Kenny Gillespie, I'm Detective Sergeant Simon Harris. You obviously know what this is about.'

Dean took a seat and nodded vigorously. 'Yes, of course. It's horrific, absolutely horrific. I'm still struggling to take it in, to be honest. I couldn't believe it when I got the call.'

'Who was it that called you?'

'It was Bernie. Bernie Watson, the head greenkeeper. I think you've met him?'

'And where were you when he called you?' said Gillespie.

'In bed. It was, what, about two in the morning? Where else would I be?'

'As we explained to Mr Montrose, it's our job to ask questions.'

'Of course. Sorry, I've just not had a lot of sleep, as you can probably imagine.'

'I can indeed. Did you know Elena Enescu?'

Dean shook his head. 'No.'

'Do you know why she might have been at Fairview last night?'

'No. You've probably gathered we don't have women members.'

'It's been mentioned.'

'So you'll understand why I'm as confused as you are when I find out that some bloody girl has been found dead out there?'

He pointed agitatedly out of the window behind the two detectives. Gillespie and Harris sat in silence, waiting for Dean to regain his composure.

'Look, can I be frank?'

'By all means.'

'This is one of the most exclusive golf clubs in the country. We don't just let anyone in here. It costs fifty thousand pounds to join Fairview, and we've got a fifteen-year waiting list. Whoever that girl was, I can assure you she's got no connection whatsoever to Fairview. Our members are doctors, dentists, architects, accountants and lawyers. *Top* lawyers. I hope you understand.'

'I understand. Thanks for your time.'

* * *

'That, Simon, is a lesson in how to play defensively.'

They were driving back through the East Lothian countryside towards Edinburgh. Gillespie sitting at the wheel, shaking his head bitterly as they went over the list of six golf club interviewees, all of whom had proved less than helpful.

'We'd better find out how Gemma got on with the presser. Give her a call, will you?'

Harris took out his phone and dialled the number as Gillespie reached for a cigarette. It was frustrating to hear only one side of the conversation, and Harris's repeated use of the words 'oh, I see' didn't fill him with confidence. The DS said goodbye and hung up.

'Well?'

'Well, Gemma said things started okay. The reporters were just asking about the girl but then they kept asking her whether she was one of the protestors. She said we didn't know at the moment but they wouldn't leave it alone. Things got a bit heated and she er, decided to cut it short.'

'Jesus Christ.'

'The Chief won't be happy. Should we tell him?'

'Don't bother. He'll find out when he sees tomorrow's papers.'

It was only after he'd dropped off Harris at his Newington flat that Gillespie realised he hadn't eaten since early that morning. He could almost hear his stomach over the sound of the car. There was a burger joint nearby. It was hardly haute cuisine but the thought of processed meat and a bagful of cardboard-like fries made his mouth water. He placed his order at the drive-through and listened to the radio as he waited. Forth 1 was reporting hold ups along the bypass because of an accident. He wondered for a moment whether he should attend, but then he was handed a paper bag and the smell became too intoxicating to ignore.

Gillespie parked up and dug into the burger. It took him less than two minutes to scarf it down. He felt bloated and a little grubby but his head cleared. The day's worries seemed to have floated off and been replaced by different matters. He wanted to see Louise. He turned the key in the ignition and set off for her home.

She might have been in her pyjamas, but Eilidh was wide awake and, judging by the impressive distance she was putting between herself and the mattress with every jump on the bed, Louise's little girl wasn't going to sleep any time soon.

Sitting in his car across the street, Gillespie watched her mum come back into the bedroom. She folded her arms and wore a look of tired resignation. Gillespie thought about what his own mum would have done if she'd caught him jumping on the bed. Maybe not quite take the skin off his arse, but she'd give it a go. Thank god it was his dad who had caught him smoking behind the hay shed that day. He was as strong as they come—a farm labourer and an amateur rugby player for Melrose—but he only ever lost his temper with stubborn machinery or runaway sheep. Never with Kenny. Instead of shouting at him, he took him along for a ride in the tractor and told him why smoking was just a thing that stupid grown-ups do.

Gillespie looked at the overflowing ashtray of his Golf and smiled. He wondered what kind of relationship he would have had with a daughter of his own? Or a son? Even coming home exhausted, would he make the time to read them stories the way his dad made the time to read to him? Would he take them swimming or to play football at the weekends? Would they hug him after a hard day at the station? Or, just imagine it, laugh at his jokes?

He muttered under his breath. 'Christ, Kenny, get a grip.' Even the thought of it was painful. He and Pauline had decided to let that ship sail and there was nothing he could do about it.

Gillespie looked up to see the light going off in Eilidh's room—the closing ceremony to the bedtime Olympics. He took a deep breath and got out of the car. He and Louise had some serious making up to do.

Chapter 11

The look of surprise on Louise's face must have lasted all of two seconds before it contorted into one of anger. She glowered at Gillespie through a gap in the door, which she refused to open wider than a few inches.

'What do you want?'

The detective was relieved in a way. At least she was still speaking to him.

'Can I come in?'

'What for?'

Gillespie paused. He didn't think he'd need to explain himself.

'I thought we could have a chat.'

'You didn't seem so keen to chat the other night, when you dingied me by text.'

'Sorry. I couldn't speak. Someone was in the car with me.'

Louise looked sceptical.

'Look, can I come in or not?' He shuffled his feet. 'I'd rather not do this on the doorstep.'

Louise left the door open and disappeared inside. Gillespie slinked in behind her, watching her tensed shoulders as she strutted ahead. When she reached the living room, Louise popped her head back into the hallway and hissed. 'Keep it down, will you? The wee one's trying to sleep.'

Gillespie couldn't have been any gentler if he'd been handling the crown jewels. Louise was spoiling for a fight. He decided not to push it and stepped, sheepishly, into the living room.

Louise was sitting cross-legged on the couch, her arms were folded in what looked like a defensive posture. The room was small and, with a hyperactive six-year-old as a housemate, was obviously quite a task to keep tidy. Anyone with bare feet would have to navigate the pieces of Lego scattered across the floor. He picked up a little Power Ranger and placed it on the mantelpiece.

'So, how are things?'

'Fine.'

'How's Eilidh?'

'Huh. Same as usual. She's got the attention span of a gnat— a really bored gnat. She's just unsettled. She won't play with anything for more than thirty seconds. I watched her doing that Peppa Pig jigsaw for quarter of an hour the other day and I thought I'd entered the Twilight Zone.'

'I loved jigsaws when I was a kid. I spent days doing this one of a cockerel, but I couldn't get any of the pieces to join together. Then my mum told me to stop messing about and put the cornflakes back in the box.'

Louise put her head in her hands. 'Oh my god. I think my granddad told me that joke when I was Eilidh's age.'

'The old ones are the best.'

Louise finally allowed herself a smile. 'I bet you say that to all the girls.'

'The cheek!' Louise was thawing a little—talking about her daughter always helped.

'Look, I'm sorry for being in a mood. I was just gutted when you said you couldn't come round. I missed you.'

Gillespie sat down on the couch. 'I missed you, too. But you know I wouldn't have cancelled if I didn't have to.'

'I know. I just think you push yourself too hard. You need to learn to relax sometimes.'

She rested her head against his shoulder. Her soft hair brushed against his cheek. He couldn't remember the last time he'd enjoyed this kind of closeness with Pauline. At this moment, he didn't want to think about his wife at all. Louise wasn't wearing perfume, but he found even the smell of her shampoo intoxicating. His stomach swarmed with butterflies. He felt like a teenager on a first date, wondering how to make the next move. He didn't have to. Louise was already kissing his neck. It was gentle at first, but quickly became more intense as she began to suck and bite at his earlobe.

All thoughts of Andy Cruickshank, of Elena Enescu, of Pauline, evaporated. He grabbed Louise by the shoulders and pulled her on to his lap. He kissed her hard for what seemed like several minutes before she pushed him away. She sat up and looked at him for a moment, before leaning forwards and pulling his jacket off his shoulders. He took it off and threw it on the floor. She lay on top of him and they continued to kiss. Just as things were getting interesting, Gillespie became conscious of his phone ringing in his jacket pocket. Instinctively, he reached out his hand to answer it.

'Just leave it,' Louise whispered, kissing his ear.

'It might be important.'

'And it might not. Do you really care enough to find out?'

Gillespie decided the answer was no. He turned his attention back to Louise and the ringing stopped, before starting again a minute later. Louise sat up, looking less than impressed, her eyes narrowing to slits.

'Gillespie.'

'Evening, sir. It's Sergeant Duncan.'

'Bill, I should've guessed. What is it?'

'There's been an RTA on the bypass, sir. I've been asked to see if you're able to attend.'

'An RTA sounds like one for Traffic, Bill.' He looked at Louise; she was getting up, tucking in her top and turning away from him.

'Yes, sir, but they'd like a detective on the scene.'

Gillespie flared, 'Then call someone else. Get the Keystone Cops for all I care.'

He hung up and turned back to Louise.

'I'm really sorry. There's been an accident on the bypass. I've got to go.'

She looked confused. 'What do you mean, you've got to go? You just told him to sod off, didn't you?'

'I did, but they'll phone back in a minute. They always do.'

He reached out for his jacket and gave her a resigned smile. Louise was furious. She struggled to speak through gritted teeth. 'Why does it always have to be you?'

Gillespie shrugged. 'Believe me, I've spent years asking myself the same thing.'

'And?'

He didn't have time to think of an answer. His phone rang again.

'Hi, Bill. I know, I know. I understand. I'm on my way.'

Louise rose, indicated the door.

He put the phone away and apologised again on his way out, 'I'm sorry…'

Louise cut off his apology as she slammed the door behind him. He thought he could still see her eyes, burning through the door, two pin-sharp laser beams directed right at him.

Why *was* it always him? Gillespie asked himself the question again as he crawled in his car along the city bypass towards the scene of the accident. He guessed in some ways that it was a compliment, that his experience and expertise were valued. He then thought of a more likely reason—that he had the word 'mug' tattooed across his forehead.

Eventually, the blue flashing lights of the fire engine, squad cars and ambulance came into sharp focus near the Straiton Junction. He parked up and walked along the verge to the nearest soco.

'Thanks for coming, Detective.'

'What's the situation?'

'Male driver of a BMW 7 Series appears to have hit the central reservation at speed and then flipped over. He's in a bad way. They're still cutting him out.'

Gillespie glared at the wreck. 'There's not much left, are they using a tin-opener?'

'He's still with us, apparently. But only just.'

'And were there any other vehicles involved?'

'If there were, they didn't hang around.'

Gillespie thanked the soco and walked over to where three firefighters were trying to extract the driver from the mangled wreckage. He continued to watch as they removed the roof and the paramedics gently lifted him clear.

Gillespie stepped forward and put his hand on the stretcher, signalling them to stop. He looked for a minute at the man's face. His eyes were closed. A deep cut on his head had matted his grey hair and left a large, red stain on his white shirt.

Gillespie leaned in and sniffed around his mouth.

One of the paramedics wasn't impressed. 'When you're quite finished, we need to get him to hospital.'

Gillespie stepped back and watched as the man was loaded into the ambulance and it sped off, siren wailing, in the direction of the Royal Infirmary.

'Paul.' Gillespie signalled to a nearby officer.

'Sir?'

'I want every part of this car looked over. If there's so much as a nut out of place, I want a note of it.'

'What are we looking for?'

'There were no other vehicles involved and I couldn't smell alcohol on the driver's breath—I want to know if there are any signs of sabotage.'

'Sabotage?'

'Yes, Paul, sabotage. It's French for do as you're told.'

'You might want this.' Gillespie turned round to see Dickson handing him a piece of paper. 'It's the driver's name and address. Gerald Thompson. Lives in Stockbridge.'

'Somehow he didn't strike me as the Niddrie type. What are you doing here anyway, Gemma? Don't tell me you got a call, too?'

'Actually, I was just leaving Asda. I heard there'd been an accident on the radio so I came over to see if I could help.'

Gillespie laughed. 'I used to be all about the job too, love.'

'Used to be? What happened?'

'Life happened. Do you have time for a coffee?'

Gillespie and Dickson sat alone in the supermarket café. Gillespie sipped at his coffee and pulled a face. So that's what £2.50 tasted like.

'I remember when I was eighteen, I put my Mini through a hedge near Duns. I was out cold for about half an hour. I fractured my ankle and I had to hobble to a pay phone to call for help. I don't remember anyone sending for CID. Somehow there's a difference when there's a sixty-grand Beamer involved.'

'I know what you mean. Top brass don't attach the same value to boy racers, do they?'

'No. But as far as I'm concerned, a life is a life, and a body's a body. Anyway, I wasn't a boy racer. I genuinely thought I was going to be the next Jim Clark.'

'Jim Clark?'

'That's right. Double Formula One world champion? Chirnside's finest, don't you know.'

'I think you'll find Jim Clark was originally from Kilmany.'

Gillespie frowned. 'I didn't have you down as a Fifer, Gemma.'

'I grew up in Dunfermline, but I've been in Glasgow a few years now.'

'And now here we are in the Straiton branch of Asda. Funny the different roads we take and still end up in the same place.'

Dickson took a sip of her coffee. Gillespie knew she wanted

him to get to the point, not listen to his second-rate philoso-phising.

'What happened at the press conference?' he said.

Dickson paused mid-sip and put her cup down slowly. 'Sorry about that.'

'Don't be sorry, I just want to know why you cut it short.'

'The journalists just kept asking me the same questions, over and over again, only louder each time. My answer wasn't going to change, so I didn't see the point in carrying on. Was I wrong?'

'Well, I can't promise the Chief will be happy.'

Dickson rubbed her forehead.

'I think I'll buy some wine while I'm here. I might have to drown my sorrows tomorrow.'

'I wouldn't worry about it. It was my call to leave it in your lap so I'll be the one to wear it.'

'I'm sorry.'

'Stop saying sorry. We'll sort it out and tomorrow's another day.' Gillespie looked at his watch. 'Speaking of which, it's time to head for home.'

'At least we still can, unlike himself.'

'There is that.'

'What do you think happened here?'

'Well, it didn't look medical, and cars like that don't just drive off the road by themselves. I'm calling shenanigans, but maybe that's just my way.'

Dickson smiled. 'Maybe that's the best way to be, sir.'

Chapter 12

The droning voice of a vapid TV presenter woke Gillespie from uneasy sleep. It was wafting from downstairs. The detective rubbed his eyes and focussed on the indent Pauline had left in the mattress. It wasn't often she was up before him. He dimly remembered the early days when they first moved in together. It was a time when they would happily lie in bed; what Pauline would call snuggling, then. They'd talk about pointless things like what colour to paint the bathroom and they'd talk about the things that really mattered—like what they'd call imagined children that might one day come into their lives. Gillespie turned away from his past and rolled off the bed, his mind turning to happier thoughts, like Louise.

He thought of the all-too-brief moment of intimacy they had shared the previous evening. He reached across to the bedside table for his mobile. He hoped that she'd had time to calm down, maybe even send him a message. He had eight voicemails, all from the station. Every one of them could wait. He got up and showered, before dressing and heading downstairs.

A wall of heat and the sickly smell of freshly-made waffles greeted him as he entered the kitchen. Pauline sat at the table, cramming a waffle into her mouth. Her hair was disheveled and a large patch of what he assumed was maple syrup was smeared down her dressing gown. He opened the back door to let out some of the smoke. His wife grumbled through a mouthful of waffle.

'Shut the door, it's freezing.'

Gillespie pretended not to hear over the sound of the television on the counter, which he now realised was displaying the irritating features of Piers Morgan. Watching the impossibly smug presenter was obviously more important to Pauline than keeping warm, because she made no attempt to close the door. Gillespie made himself a coffee and sat down.

'Why's he spitting the dummy out this time? Did someone forget to put sugar in his tea?'

Pauline ignored the comment. Gillespie smirked, but the sight of a man paid stellar sums purely to be objectionable was enough to put him off his drink. He snatched the remote from the table and hit the off switch.

His wife screeched. 'Why do you have to keep doing that?'

'You've got all day to watch crap on TV. Sitting in silence for ten minutes won't do you any harm. I've barely seen you in days and you've not even so much as asked me how I'm doing.'

'Why can't you just leave me in peace?'

'Leave *you* in peace? That's a joke, considering you're the one who constantly has the volume turned up to eleven. This isn't *Spinal Tap*, you know.'

'What the hell are you talking about?'

Gillespie wasn't surprised Pauline didn't get the reference. The only things on her watch-list these days were the shopping channel and reality shows aimed at the dumbest of normies.

'Why don't you try watching kids' TV for a change? The bloody *Teletubbies* talk more sense than that guy.'

'How would you know?'

'If I watched as much as you I suppose I'd be an expert as well. The difference is I actually get off my arse and leave the house.'

'What's it matter to you if I leave the house or not? You're never here anyway.'

Gillespie stood up and chucked the rest of his coffee down

the sink. 'That's right, I'm never here. That's because I'm out there every day, knocking my pan in, while all you can do is sit there and stuff your bloody face.'

He watched Pauline's eyes reddening. 'Do you remember why we decided not to have kids, Pauline?'

'Please, don't do this.'

'It was so you could concentrate on your career. Remember that?'

Pauline looked away, her eyes locked on the middle distance. She nodded. Gillespie saw her tears coming; she dabbed her cheek with the sleeve of her dressing gown. He hated himself, but he was past the point where it mattered.

'We made that decision together, Kenny.'

'Yeah, but what happened? How long did you last as a lecturer before you were signed off with stress? Christ, I wish I could pull that trick. "Sorry, Chief, that murder case will have to wait, I'm going home to put my feet up for a few months". Now look at us. You've got no job, we've got no family, we've got no marriage— we've got *nothing*.'

Pauline screamed. She picked up the plate and threw it at him. He watched it smash against the fridge. Then she was on him, pushing him backwards and trying to claw at his face. He held up his hands and deflected the blows until she sank back, exhausted. The exertion had been unexpected, and too much for her.

Pauline sobbed, 'Why don't you just have the guts to come out and say it, Kenny? You hate me. You probably always hated me.'

Gillespie thought about picking up the pieces of the broken crockery, but left it as it was.

He walked past his wife, pausing in the doorway. 'Not always.'

Derek McCall sat behind the station's front desk and pretended to look busy as the DCI approached. Despite the ritual teasing he dished out to Gillespie, one glance at the detective's face told the desk sergeant to keep his mouth shut.

'Morning, Derek.'

'Oh, hello, Kenny. I didn't notice you come in.'

'I knew there was a reason they put you on the front desk. How's things?'

'All fine, thanks.'

Gillespie leaned on the desk, 'Then why are you acting jumpy?'

'I don't know what you mean.'

'I'm a detective, Derek. I can tell when people are hiding something. You wouldn't last two minutes under interrogation. Let me take a wild guess, we've been shafted by the local rag again?'

Derek looked sheepish. He scratched the side of his nose for a second or two, then reached under the counter and brought out a copy of the *Evening News*.

'I was going to pull your leg about it but didn't think you were in the mood.'

Gillespie stared at the headline: 'COPS IN CHAOS'.

It was accompanied by a picture of Gemma Dickson at the press conference. The photographer knew exactly what he was doing, snapping her at the moment her mouth was wide open, hands up as she called a halt to proceedings.

'Catching flies,' read the words preceding the caption. Gillespie shook his head, scanning the rest of the article, which ranted about the police being in disarray and refusing to answer questions on the golf course murder.

'It could be worse,' said Gillespie, in a tone that was clearly trying to disguise his fury.

'It is worse. Bertie Bassett's seen it.'

'Oh, no…He's seen it already?'

'I'm afraid so, and it wasn't pretty. I thought he was going to blow up. I was seriously anticipating the foyer to be showered in liquorice allsorts.'

'Well at least that would get you out from behind that

desk—can you handle a dustpan?'

'You may mock, Kenny. But I'm not the one he wants to see in his office.'

'He said that?'

'Told me to pass it on as soon as you appeared.'

'Christ's sake.'

'Want me to look out a flak jacket for you?'

'Maybe you should, Derek. Just to be on the safe side.'

Chapter 13

Gillespie was in no hurry to get to Bassett's office. His mind was filling with conflicting grievances, about work and home, and their accompanying emotions. Normally, it was his way to bury all emotions as deeply as possible. He liked reason and logic, things he could put to use. If emotion had a purpose, for the detective, it was as a warning sign: when the red light showed he knew to be on guard.

There was a bollocking coming his way, he reasoned that much from the chat with Derek, but an earful from the boss was probably preferable to the silent treatment he was getting at home. One thing to avoid was mixing up the two conflicts. The ammunition he'd stored up battling Pauline would be no use on Bassett; a clear head was needed for that engagement. Gillespie made for the vending machine and selected his usual foul-tasting excuse for a coffee. As the grey liquid sprayed loudly into the white plastic cup he tried to focus on the here and now, but he couldn't.

For two hours after he'd got in and for another hour that morning, Pauline had avoided saying a word to him. Not that he could blame her. He couldn't remember the last time they'd had a civilised conversation, so why bother trying? He saw that he could continue to walk around her, to slink in and slink out through the front door, but he was only avoiding the inevitable confrontation.

Pauline might ignore her actions, the way she had given up on life and living, but she couldn't ignore the consequences of her actions. He'd once read stories about couples who led completely separate lives, while continuing to live under the same roof, and been utterly baffled by them. How did it happen? How did the years tick by in such misery? He didn't know the answer, but what he did know was that it happened. Regardless of how or why, he knew it happened.

Gillespie headed down the corridor, sipping the bitter coffee, one wince at a time. When he reached his destination he binned the dregs in the plastic cup and knocked on Bassett's door. His mind was clearing, shifting focus. There was only so much attention he could give to his marriage before he lost all interest. Jousting with the big sweetie had more of an attraction, it was like a blood sport, not exactly enjoyable but invigorating, of sorts.

Bassett's greeting didn't disappoint. He began to unleash his fury—and a healthy dose of spittle—in Gillespie's direction the second he entered the room.

'You threw that poor girl to the bloody lions yesterday, Kenny. What the hell were you thinking?'

The Chief Superintendent was pacing back and forwards in front of his desk, jabbing his finger at the detective every few seconds. Gillespie stood by the door, hands folded behind his back. 'I had full confidence in Sergeant Dickson, sir. I still do.'

'I told you to take care of that press conference, not palm it off on the newbie.'

'With respect, sir, it was you who assigned Sergeant Dickson to my team. I'm sure you wouldn't have assigned someone you didn't think was up to the job.' Start as you mean to go on was the strategy; Gillespie had no intention of playing the beta yes man—he'd never seen it work for anyone else.

Bassett's eyes narrowed. The white collar pressing on his neck seemed to make the red flesh look even darker. 'I brought her in to help you out, Kenny.'

'And she has been helping me, starting with taking the press conference. I thought she handled it pretty well.'

Bassett reached for his copy of the *Evening News*, which was fast becoming a favourite tool for beating Gillespie over the head with. Metaphorically, at least for now.

'You call this handling it pretty well?'

'Journalists can be a hard bunch to please, you know that as well as I do. They knew we didn't have anything else to add, so what was the point in Gemma prolonging it? To be honest, I'm not sure I'd have done things that differently.'

'The fact of the matter is you should've been the one answering those questions.'

'In my defence, I'm handling three cases at the minute.' He was pressing his luck and he knew it, but previous experience told him that an enraged Bassett was easier to handle. With any luck the boss would get so wrapped up in his own rage that he'd soon be scrabbling for words.

'Are you going out of your way to annoy me, Kenny?'

'No, sir.'

'Then why are you ignoring my orders? I told you to put your hoarder case on the back burner.'

'Well, I don't think the Fiscal would approve of that, sir, given that she's already declared the death of Andy Cruickshank as a murder.'

Bassett hissed loudly through gritted teeth, but Gillespie, spying an opening, continued.

'I know he might've looked like a bloody jakey, but he happened to be sitting on pots of cash. Substantial pots of cash which have subsequently disappeared.'

Bassett raised his eyebrows. 'Substantial?'

'Yes. Believe it or not, his family were tea importers who made an absolute mint selling to the Edinburgh delis. Andy was an only child so he copped the lot. Tens of thousands by the last count.'

'I see.'

'I thought that might infuse your interest, sir, no pun intended.

Large amounts have been withdrawn from the victim's account. If we can find out who's been taking the money, then I think we'll find the killer.'

Bassett shook his head, easing himself into his chair. He tapped his fingers delicately on the rim of the desk and then gripped the arms of the chair. There seemed to be something resembling thought going on behind his drooping eyes. 'Well, I suppose there's no harm in pursuing your lines of enquiry in the Cruickshank case, but I shouldn't need to tell you that Fairview takes precedence. And the next time I ask you to take a press conference, it'd better be your mug I see in front of those cameras. If you even think of taking any more short-cuts, you'll be taking a serious short-cut—straight to the dole office!'

Gillespie nodded. He knew that this line must have sounded good in Bassett's head, that the Chief saw himself as Edinburgh's answer to Popeye Doyle, but he came over as what he was: A pompous desk jockey who loved the sound of his own voice. The detective didn't say anything, but took the barb as his signal to leave. He nodded and turned towards the door.

'Three cases?' said Bassett.

Gillespie could practically hear the sound of the penny dropping. 'That's right.'

'What was the third one?'

'An RTA on the bypass last night. The old boy's in a pretty bad way, but I'm trying to offload that one to Traffic.'

'Hmm, that might not be so easy.'

'Why?'

'They're a bit stretched at the minute. It's probably best you keep hold of that one too.'

Gillespie felt an urge to take that short-cut to the dole office, by punching his boss's lights out. 'We're all a bit stretched, sir. And I am a murder squad detective.'

Bassett sneered. Gillespie knew he was enjoying this.

He barked back, 'But, maybe it's a murder, Kenny.'

'And maybe it's a bloody blowout.'

'Well, if it turns out to be a blowout, then I'll take it off your hands. In the meantime, keep up the good work, Detective.'

Chapter 14

Gillespie stepped out of Bassett's office balling his fists. Had his job really just got even more difficult? He found it hard to believe, but it certainly had. He felt his hands starting to ache and released the grip on his fists—it probably wasn't a good look to be marching down the corridor with, anyway. As he moved he found himself retreading the boss's threat about the dole queue. It was a tempting consideration, if he brushed aside all his desires to do some good in a world that seemed to be growing darker by the day.

Perhaps he could just keep walking, pick up his coat and head to the car park. But, what would be his next move? What the hell would he do for a living? He'd need what the employment agencies called 'transferable skills'. He could cuff suspects and interrogate scrotes but he couldn't imagine these skills being useful in a regular office job—not unless someone found a body in HR. It was all a fantasy, all escapism. He had a mortgage and a wife. A regular life that was hanging like the proverbial millstone round his neck.

He slouched into the incident room and immediately spied Dickson looking through a collection of photographs. She looked up and gave him a rueful smile.

'Pictures from last night's RTA. It's growing into quite a collection. I think we're going to need another board.'

Gillespie glanced at the boards bearing the multiple images of Andy Cruickshank and Elena Enescu. 'I don't think the big sweetie will stretch to giving us another board, but I'm sure DCI Wallace has one we can borrow.'

Dickson gave a nervous laugh, unsure whether her boss was joking. 'Don't worry, it can wait.'

He looked at his watch. 'We've got a lot to do. Can you get the rabble together?'

Dickson nodded and scurried out of the room. Within five minutes, Gillespie's entire team of twenty had filed into the incident room and gathered round the boards, creating the familiar buzz of whispered exchanges and shuffling feet. The DCI knew he had a good bunch, but they could do with a kick up the backside now and then. He had started to feel the heat from Bassett and he wasn't getting answers as quickly as he wanted. If he'd been a football manager, right now he'd be thinking about hurling a cup of tea against the wall.

'Morning, everyone,' he said, the sound of his voice—something like a low growl—startled even himself.

'Morning, sir.'

'As you're all aware, we're currently working on two murder cases—Andrew Cruickshank and Elena Enescu. I know this hasn't been easy the way we're resourced, but we're going to need to up our game if we want to see results. And, whisper it among yourselves, but I've a sneaking suspicion that there may well be a third case coming our way very soon.'

The room filled with the sound of disconsolate murmuring and muttering. Detective Constable Peter Hopcroft, known to the team as Peter the Welsh, folded his arms across his chest. 'What do you mean, on the way?'

'All in good time, Peter. I've just been to see the boss and he's told me, in no uncertain terms, that the Enescu case has to be our priority. I'm not one to take issue with any of our esteemed leader's orders, as you know, but I've told him that the Cruickshank case should be given equal attention.'

'Did he agree?'

'Not exactly, but I don't want us taking our foot off the gas on that one either. I don't think I need to tell you that this is going to create a lot of extra work for everyone.'

There was another collective groan around the room, a hissing sound like air being squeezed from a deflating party balloon. Gillespie wanted to reach for the nearest teacup to restore order. 'You can cut that out, for starters. If you'd wanted short hours and massive pensions, you should've run for government. I hear UKIP are looking for Nigel's replacement, again.'

The laughter broke the tension.

'Right, now I want to make some serious headway into the Enescu case today. There are plenty of things we don't know, so let's start with what we do. We know she was Romanian, we know she was working as a prostitute in Edinburgh, and we know she was murdered at Fairview Golf Club. What we don't know is the answer to three very important questions: who, how and why? From what we've ascertained so far, she wasn't a street walker, so she must've been employed somewhere, most likely one of the saunas populating our fair city. We also don't know what she was doing at the golf club on the night she was murdered.'

Peter Morris piped up again. 'Maybe it was a kinky golf John. I hear that Tiger fella likes playing a round.'

The sniggering resumed. Gillespie felt like a teacher in a classroom.

'If you've got gum, Peter, I hope you brought enough for everybody.'

'Sorry, sir. Maybe it was just a short-cut that went wrong.'

'Went wrong is certainly one way of putting it.'

DC Dan Holland offered a serious suggestion: 'Maybe it was an opportunistic rape by a stranger.'

Gillespie shook his head. 'A passerby on the course at night? I don't think so. And, there was no sign of a struggle, so there's a strong possibility she knew her attacker.'

'Well, maybe it was just a regular John, then. Maybe she had a few clients at the golf club,' said Holland.

Gillespie turned to Harris, hoping he'd have something to contribute. 'Simon?'

Harris thought for a moment. 'Perhaps it was a lover.'

'There's no suggestion she had a lover,' said Gillespie.

'There was the photograph in her flat of her with a man.'

'That was an old picture and taken abroad. She clearly lived alone. We've got nothing that rules out an unknown connection, but who? We need answers, and quickly, so I want you all to get out there and keep asking questions until we find some. If there's any neighbours you've not spoken to yet, I want their statements by this afternoon. I also want you to pay a visit to the saunas. She had to be working in one of them. Speak to the girls there. Find out what they know, and who they know.'

'Oh, they're going to love that.'

'You're right, Peter. They won't be very keen to talk to cops, not even your good self, but they'll want to find out who killed one of their own. If that's the only in you have, then go for it.'

Gillespie dismissed the team. The grumbling undertones had diminished now, replaced with a more focussed vibe. If he had been successful in instilling some of the urgency he felt then that was something. What he didn't want to pass on was the deep-seated feeling that the case was slipping further into uncertainty; if he didn't find something to get things moving soon, then Elena Enescu was likely to end up as just another grim statistic. Gillespie didn't want to admit that to himself, but every investigation relied on getting a break, and he wasn't feeling lucky.

The detective called over Harris and Dickson.

'While they're out speaking to the neighbours and checking out the saunas, we're going to keep on the golf club mob. They're far too cosy for my liking.'

'What are you thinking, sir?' said Harris.

'At the moment, every member of the Fairview Mafia is singing from the same hymn sheet.'

'So what do we do?'

Gillespie took out a packet of cigarettes and forced on a weak smile. 'We take the hymn sheet away. We interview them separately, in their own homes. Go and get their addresses. They'll not be in the mood to sing hallelujah when we're finished with them.'

Chapter 15

Gillespie manoeuvred his dirty, seven-year-old Golf among the spickly-polished Range Rovers and Mercedes of Ann Street, wondering if his exhaust was going to set off an emissions alarm. As he parked up, he was still a little distracted by the grandeur on display and managed to ding a front wheel on the kerb. For a second or two, his first thought was guilt for possibly scraping the pavement and then he snapped back to sense. The detective stepped out of the car and looked down at his wheel-trim; it was far too grimy to reveal any damage, but it was still there, and he felt relieved about that.

Harris joined him on the roadside, emitting a reedy whistle that was obviously the forerunner of sniping commentary.

'How the other half live, eh sir?'

'Not exactly the other half, Simon. More like a tiny fraction.' He was still looking at the wheel-trim. 'Thought I was going to be sued for that, think I got away with it.'

'Not many VWs around here, sticks out a bit.'

'Of course it does. Volkswagen means people's car.'

'I suppose we're a bit far from the plebs.'

'Simon, we are the plebs. Know your place, son.'

Gillespie lit a cigarette. He took a draw and shook his head, shifting his gaze up and down the street. The Georgian architecture of the New Town was designed to be imposing, to intimidate, and it had done its job.

'There was something in *The Scotsman* the other week about how much the Queen Mother loved Ann Street,' said Harris. 'Apparently, she used to tell her chauffeur to swing down this way any time she was in town.'

'Hitler had a thing for neoclassical architecture as well. Maybe that rumour about the royal family being closet Nazis is true.'

Gillespie lifted his cigarette in greeting as a woman with a couple of Westies shuffled past. She gave a hurried nod that was unconvincing as either greeting or friendliness and then eyed Gillespie's car suspiciously.

'She's for sale if you're interested? Three grand and I'll even empty the ashtray.'

The woman smiled nervously and quickened her pace.

'She'll be back.'

'The way she looked that'll probably be with a tow truck.'

Gillespie conceded the DS was probably right. 'Come on, let's get this over with. I feel like part of a dog and pony show out here, all eyes are on us.'

Harris pointed at one of the houses and led off across the cobbled street. When they reached the polished flagstones and filigreed railings on the other side, it sounded like Harris had been running some calculations in his head.

'How much do you think that one would go for?' he said.

'Well, put it this way, if you save all your wages for the next thirty years, you might be able to scrape together a deposit. And that's only assuming you kick your fancy coffee habit. Keep that up and you'll struggle to buy me lunch.'

Harris nodded thoughtfully. 'Maybe I won't have to wait thirty years if I make Chief Super.'

Gillespie took a long draw on his cigarette. 'The day you make Chief Superintendent, Simon, is the day I give up the fags.'

'You don't think I've got the brains, sir?'

'I know you've got the brains, Simon, but looking at our dear leader, I don't think brains are a requirement for the top job.'

Harris snorted at Gillespie's joke, but his boot-licking instincts quickly kicked in and he covered his mouth. Gillespie smiled and looked around for somewhere to stub out his cigarette. He gave up and, bending slightly, flicked it down a drain.

'Hopefully the neighbourhood watch don't come after me. What number is El Presidente in?'

Harris pointed down the street. 'That's Mr Montrose's house, sir; the one with the silver Merc in the drive.'

'Naturally.'

The pink gravel crunched beneath their feet as they walked past the outsized vehicle and a row of geometrically clipped shrubs and trees. Gillespie wondered if Henry Montrose called on the Fairview groundsman to cut his own grass into such precise shadow striping. He wouldn't put it past him.

Harris marvelled at an ageing lump of metal on the doorstep. 'What a fabulous boot scraper.'

'Probably necessary, in case Mr Montrose steps on any members of the working class on his way home.'

Gillespie thought about making another joke but decided against it, worried his cynicism was starting to sound too much like jealousy. Who knows? Maybe he did envy Henry Montrose with his New Town mansion and Mercedes Benz, when all he had to show for two decades of dedicated police work was a miserable home life, a mistress who had taken the huff and a battered VW that stank of stale tobacco. But everything was relative. To some of the pond life he'd arrested over the years, he probably sounded like Little Lord Fauntleroy.

He clearly hadn't picked a good time to call on the president of Fairview Golf Club. Henry Montrose, a thick, hardback book in his hands and half-rimmed spectacles hanging from a chain around his neck, answered the door.

'Can I help you?'

It had only been a day since they'd interviewed Montrose in the equally plush surroundings of East Lothian, but that was apparently long enough for the president to forget who they were. Gillespie didn't buy it for a second, but he was happy to play the game. He stood in silence, waiting for the gerbil inside Montrose's head to start running on its wheel.

Harris blinked first. 'Mr Montrose? Detective Sergeant Simon Harris and Detective Chief Inspector Kenny Gillespie. We spoke to you out at Fairview yesterday?'

'Ah yes, of course.' His tone changed. 'Good morning, gentlemen. I was under the impression that you had everything you needed from me.'

Gillespie answered genially. 'I'm afraid murder cases are rarely that simple, Mr Montrose. There are a couple more things we'd like to ask you.'

The president flustered. 'Couldn't you have asked me yesterday?'

'It's not an exact science. It's a big case. We're learning new things all the time, and new information invariably leads to more questions. However, if you don't have time to speak to us now, we could always make an arrangement for you to attend at the station this afternoon.'

Montrose forced his mouth into an insincere smile. 'Of course I have time, Mr Gillespie. I just thought I'd clarify what you needed. Please come in.'

The detectives were about to follow when Montrose paused in the doorway. 'Would you mind giving your shoes a quick scrape before you come in?'

Gillespie cast his gaze over the high-ceilinged living room. The glass cabinets and stuffed mammals reminded him more of the National Museum than someone's home—it seemed a sterile living environment. There was silence but for the loud tick of a grandfather clock, the noise echoing discreetly in the hallway. Gillespie and Harris sat on a sagging and well-creased Chesterfield sofa, while Montrose sat opposite them on an equally well-used armchair. He folded his arms, then crossed his legs to reveal a pair of bright yellow Argyle socks that wouldn't have looked out of place on the links.

'Well, here we go again.'

Gillespie didn't waste time, starting as he meant to go on. 'Do you think a member of Fairview Golf Club had anything to do with the death of Elena Enescu, Mr Montrose?'

For a split second, Montrose looked taken aback, but the shutters quickly came down.

'No, I don't. Of course I don't.'

'No one?'

'Absolutely not. We're a very respectable club, I'll have you know.'

'Do bodies turn up at all the respectable clubs, then?'

He bridled. 'These are exceptional circumstances, as I'm sure you know.'

'Well, I don't recall any other incidents of this nature, so I'll assume you're right.'

'Detective, we do not, as a rule, select members from the criminal classes. None of the board are murderers. I hardly think I need to press that point to you.'

Gillespie eased back in the sofa, the leather creaking loudly. 'Very few advertise the fact, in my experience.'

'Oh, this is getting tedious. Can we move on, please?'

'Very well. Can you tell me if you know of any members of the club who might have financial difficulties?'

'What kind of financial difficulties?'

'The kind that might, for example, come about through being blackmailed. Perhaps by a prostitute, or someone who knew about an association with a prostitute.'

Montrose stood up and strode over to the fireplace. He picked up a small ornament from the mantelpiece—a china pheasant. Gillespie thought for a moment that he was going to smash it on to the hearth in frustration, but Montrose breathed deeply and put it back down. 'No, I don't. To be frank, I find that question utterly absurd.'

'What is it you find absurd? The bit about the financial difficulties or the bit about the blackmail?'

Montrose snapped. 'Both.'

He quickly held up his hand in apology, but Gillespie was unfazed.

'I'm sorry, Mr Gillespie, but I can honestly say that I can think of no member of my golf club who is in any kind of financial difficulty.'

He sat back down. 'I only wish I could say the same about the club itself.'

Harris looked surprised, leaning forward on the creaky sofa. 'You mean Fairview is struggling for money?'

Montrose nodded. 'I know I might have appeared bullish about the impact all this negative publicity has had on our club, and that I couldn't care less what the public has to say.'

'The thought had occurred to me,' said Gillespie.

'Well in some respects, it's true. I don't believe members of the public have a right to tell us how we should run our club, but I'm not completely naïve about the way the world works these days. The protests, the court cases—it's crippling us. What's more, QCs don't come cheap—even if we do get, what is it you call it, "mate's rates"?'

'So what are you planning to do?'

'What am *I* planning to do? I'm going to step down as president. The board is split on how to deal with our cash flow problem and I no longer have the stomach for this kind of squabbling.'

Gillespie almost felt a twinge of sympathy for the old man, but the feeling soon passed. It was hard to feel anything for a man who had clearly been granted access to the greased slide of prosperity his entire life.

'What do you mean by split?'

'One of our members has offered to buy the club, but some are more keen on the idea than others.'

'Who made the offer?'

'A chap called Henderson. David Henderson.'

* * *

The interview over, the two detectives got talking on the way back to the car.

'I must admit, I wasn't expecting to hear that they were having money problems, were you, sir?' said Harris.

Gillespie shook his head distractedly. 'No, not at all.'

'The fact the club's broke probably isn't something they wanted to advertise.'

'I'd say it's the last thing they'd want out in the open. Those that are used to projecting wealth don't like it when the cash flow dries up. Does strange things to people.'

Harris looked concerned. 'Are you okay, sir?'

'I'm fine.'

'You look miles away.'

'I'm just thinking...I've heard the name David Henderson before, bloody sure of it.'

Chapter 16

Detective Constable Billy McNab looked up from his computer and furrowed his brow in confusion.

'Sorry, sir?'

Gillespie took a deep breath. 'It wasn't a trick question, Billy. I just asked you if you'd seen Sergeant Dickson. Gemma Dickson?'

'Oh, Gemma. Of course. Sorry, sir, I wasn't with it. No, I haven't seen her.'

'Thank you, Billy. You've been very helpful. I'll let you get back to work.'

McNab smiled and turned back to his monitor. Gillespie joined Harris at the whiteboard. He nodded subtly in McNab's direction.

'I just can't seem to get the staff these days. Did I do something wrong in a past life, Simon?'

'Sorry, sir?'

'Forget it. I wonder what's keeping Gemma. She was only meant to be doing a couple of interviews, not researching for *This Is Your Life*.'

'What's that, boss?'

'Eamonn Andrews.'

Harris shrugged. 'Eamonn who?'

'Never mind. Obviously a reference to something long before your time. Don't worry, I'm getting used to being a dinosaur.

Perhaps Gemma thinks I bite.'

'I get the impression she likes to be thorough.'

Gillespie looked at his watch. 'Well, I'll be thoroughly pissed off if she takes much longer.'

He was about to pick up the phone when Dickson, her cheeks glowing, burst through the door.

'Speak of the devil. I was about to send out a search party.'

'Sorry about that, sir. I've been back for a while but I was upstairs. I had to run something through the system but I couldn't get logged on.'

'What was the problem?'

Dickson looked embarrassed. 'Colin in IT explained it. Turns out I'm supposed to spell "St Leonard's" without an apostrophe, but that's not the way I was taught.'

The two men exchanged amused glances.

'We'll open a "missing punctuation" file as soon as we get these pesky murders out the way,' said Gillespie. 'What did you find out from your interviews?'

'The captain, Dean, was exactly what I expected. He seemed to like talking about himself and his golf club, so I just sat there and let him. It didn't take him long to admit that the female membership block has hit them in the wallet. None of it's his fault, of course. It's the protestors, the media for hyping them up, and us for not doing enough to stop them.'

'Trust me, I'd love to gulag the media, but unfortunately I'm not Uncle Joe.' Gillespie was rocking, heel to toe, on his feet, while angrily rattling the change in his pockets. 'Honestly, everyone needs someone to blame these days. Nobody ever holds their hands up.'

'Look on the bright side, sir. We'd all be out of a job if that were the case,' said Harris.

'Oh, I don't know. I could gleefully command a firing squad or two for the Reds; they're not that different to my current employers when you think about it. You, on the other hand, Simon, would definitely be breaking rocks.'

Harris simpered, 'I don't think I'd last very long.'

'You'd get to the end of the first week, if you started on a Thursday, that is.'

Dickson giggled, then raised a hand towards her mouth to shield her outburst from Harris. Gillespie seized the opportunity to play favourites—divide and rule kept the team on their toes. 'I knew there was a reason we hadn't sent you back to Glasgow, Gemma, that's good work and ties nicely with what we found. The president told us the Fairview kitty's empty. He also said the board is split on whether to sell the club to one of the members.'

'That would be David Henderson,' she said.

'That's him. I was just telling Simon I think I recognise the name.'

Dickson held up a file. 'I wouldn't be surprised. That's the name I was running through the system. He's got multiple convictions.'

'*Really?*'

She put the file on the table and added: 'But I suppose the only thing that matters to the Fairview membership committee is the fact he's got a penis.'

Harris spluttered on a glass of water. Gillespie shook his head as the DS cleared his throat and opened the file. He began to read, his eyebrows gradually moving higher as he made his way through the list.

'Definitely not one of your friendly sorts. There's several counts of affray, and then another for assault and battery. Then he did six months in Saughton in the mid-nineties for GBH. He and a friend set about a man in Dalkeith High Street on a night out, apparently at random.'

Dickson folded her arms and nodded. 'Probably just looked at them funny.'

'The poor sod's lucky to look at anyone full-stop, these days. The attack blinded him in one eye. This is serious stuff, not at all what you'd expect of a Fairview regular.'

Gillespie was growing frustrated; he felt like he'd been

messed around by those that had something to hide. 'Anything else?'

'Let's see. Yes, Henderson was re-arrested about three months after he was released. This time for dealing cocaine. That was his most recent conviction. But there's a note here at the bottom. Apparently he started a tanning business with a partner back in 2003. He now operates five saunas in Edinburgh. That explains how he came into enough money to join Fairview and, if he runs that many saunas, that'll be how *you* know his name, sir.'

'Don't give Gemma the wrong idea, Simon. You're right, though, that's how I know him. Strange that captain Dean didn't list "knocking shop proprietors" on his list of noble Fairview professions. I think I met Henderson just after I moved to Edinburgh. Big guy—had a thing for sovereign rings then. Didn't strike me as the golfing type though.'

'Things might be a bit different in Glasgow, but a sauna's just a brothel by any other name, isn't it? He's hardly legit.'

Harris looked confused. 'But paying for sex isn't illegal if it's in a sauna.'

'It's still a bit of grey area. Prostitution is the hardest thing in the world to police because there'll always be people desperate enough to sell sex and others who are desperate enough to pay for it. We used to be in a position where every council in Scotland was allowed to tackle it in their own way. The Edinburgh way was to let them slap a sauna sticker on the window and let nature take its course. But things changed when all the forces merged a few years ago. A lot of the saunas were shut down. Personally, I didn't see the point. Like I said, it's the hardest thing in the world to police. Sometimes it's just easier to look the other way.'

Gillespie could tell Dickson was unconvinced. Harris chuckled. 'Prostitution. It's the oldest profession, isn't it?'

'Hardly,' said Dickson.

'What do you mean?'

'Well, if it's the oldest profession, where did the first customer get the cash to pay for it?'

'Don't confuse him, Gemma. I can hear the cogs whirring from here.'

Harris reddened. 'Whether it's legal or not, I can see why the Fairview board are swithering. It's one thing to give Henderson a membership, it's another to hand him the keys.'

Gillespie nodded thoughtfully. 'I don't know, sounds like he could be the perfect candidate to run a golf club. He's got plenty experience dealing with fannies.'

'With all due respect, sir, that's not very PC.'

'That's the great thing about being a dinosaur and not a millennial: I don't have to be PC. I have some cracking views on the myth of equality that I've gleaned from my experience of living this long in the real world, if you really want to go there, Gemma.'

Dickson sucked in her lower lip, looking like she wished she hadn't said anything. She turned to Harris for support and the pair shared nervous smiles, both utterly unwilling to challenge Gillespie's assessment of their generation.

'I take your point, though,' said the DCI. 'If the board sell the club to a guy like Henderson then it's not going to go down well with the protestors.'

'You can say that again, sir. It'll be like a red rag to a bull,' said Dickson.

'Well it's important we don't lose sight of what this is all about. Where are we with the lab report on the girl?'

'I spoke to them an hour ago. They were still writing it up.'

'That means they've had another hour to finish it. Give them another chase, Gemma. We need to get moving on this.'

As Dickson gathered up her papers and made to leave the room, the phone rang. Harris answered, 'I see. Really? Yes, of course, we'll be down shortly.'

Gillespie could have sworn the colour drained from the sergeant's face. As he replaced the receiver on its cradle, Harris's mouth was gaping open.

'Who was that?'

'Someone's ears must have been burning. That was Derek from downstairs. He says Elena Enescu's partner has just turned up at the front desk, and he wants to speak to someone. Right now.'

Chapter 17

Gillespie felt his mouth dry over. Delivering bad news wasn't the problem—it was "fries with that?" to him by now—but the unexpected arrival of Elena Enescu's partner complicating his caseload. And he had enough to contend with already, without having to tiptoe around the grieving. It was his experience that those connected to murder victims couldn't be summarily dismissed. It was a procedure that had to be handled carefully; it couldn't be rushed. Circumstances needed to be went over, usually again and again, until something approaching understanding was reached. That was always the problem: the human mind usually didn't want to comprehend that a loved one had been taken brutally. Escape from the immediate pain was wanted—something the police could never give them. Sympathy was all Gillespie could guarantee—justice was a mere hope—for those grieving a lost murder victim. He knew it was never enough.

Harris broke the detective's train of thought. 'Forensics have promised they'll have the report with you before lunch.'

'Thanks, Simon. Can you get typing up the notes from our interviews? And Gemma, come downstairs with me. There's something I could use your help with.'

As they walked down the corridor, Dickson spoke in hushed tones.

'Was there a reason you didn't ask Simon to do this, sir?'

'To be honest, yes, a very good reason.'

Gillespie saw Dickson's eyes widen, eager for a slice of St Leonard's gossip. Gillespie stopped at the door to the stairwell and looked at her.

'Don't ever tell Simon this, but the boy's becoming a very good detective.'

'Except?'

'Except he doesn't have what I need on this particular occasion.'

'Which is?'

Gillespie smiled. 'What used to be referred to as "a woman's touch".'

Dickson's face darkened. She seemed to be taken aback, resentful. 'A woman's touch? Are you serious? I've been working as a detective in one of the most dangerous cities in Europe for five years and you just think I'm Doris bloody Day?'

'It's a matter of horses for courses. Now, I'm very sure your feminist professors at uni told you there was nothing you couldn't do that a man could, and vice-versa, but outside the classroom you'll quickly discover that the law of nature rules.'

'They'd have told me to call you a sexist pig, sir.'

Gillespie grinned widely. 'You can call me what you like. That's another thing you'll learn on the job: silly little shutdown terms like that only work on those that don't see them for what they are.' He turned to walk away, 'So, I think the term you're actually looking for is *realist*. You'll thank me when I have to ask Simon to utilise his thirty per cent greater body strength to tackle the next aggressive drunk we encounter.'

'But, sir. I just hope I've got your respect as a detective.'

'If you didn't have my respect, Gemma, you'd have been on the first train back to Glasgow. Look, this is a delicate situation and I feel you're better suited to it. Simple as that.'

Dickson inhaled deeply, seemingly unsure if she'd just received a compliment or an insult. She nodded towards the DCI and they began to trudge downstairs.

'Being a detective is like any job, Gemma, you're always going to find yourself questioning the person calling the shots.'

'*Que, sera*, sir.'

The ponytail had gone, in favour of shaved back and sides, but there was no mistaking the man Gillespie had seen in Elena's photograph. He was sitting in the reception area, his gaze fixed in the distance as he nervously rubbed his hands together, like he was washing them in an invisible sink.

'Says his name's Nicolae Grozan. He's in a wee bit of a state, but I suppose that's understandable,' said the desk sergeant.

'What do you mean, Derek?'

'He's tranced out, look at him. Some of them box it away, don't believe it, until they hear it from the horse's mouth but not him. He's tearing himself apart, I'd say.'

'Well, we've got the bloody paper to blame for that. I'm sure we'd have delivered the news with bows on, eh Gemma?'

'Pink ones, sir.'

Gillespie felt an involuntary grin creep onto his face and brushed it away. The detectives turned from the desk and walked over to the visitor.

'Mr Grozan?'

The man looked up at them with a pair of deep-set eyes, the shadows around which betrayed emotion and perhaps tiredness, sleeplessness looking to be one of his problems. He trembled slightly as he nodded.

'I'm Detective Chief Inspector Kenny Gillespie. This is Detective Sergeant Gemma Dickson.'

'Yes…' His accent was heavy.

'Would you like to come with me, Mr Grozan?' Inwardly, Gillespie cringed. He sounded like a beat cop making his first arrest. He led the way down the corridor to a comfort suite, a place he'd always thought of as a bit of a misnomer. There was little comfort to be found in a blue plastic sofa and a stack of magazines that, even if they weren't several years old, would leave you struggling to find any articles of interest.

Nicolae perched himself on the edge of the sofa, while the detectives sat down on the chairs opposite. Gillespie was about to open his mouth when the Romanian, in soft tones, began to speak.

'I got here on the first plane I could get from Bucharest,' he said.

'Bucharest?'

He nodded again. 'I found out from the television. Can you believe that? I was watching the news and then, suddenly, I see a story about a Romanian girl being found dead in Edinburgh. I felt my blood run cold. I prayed and I prayed that the dead girl wasn't Elena. *Oh please, God, let her be safe*, I said. But I guess my prayers were not answered.'

Grozan attempted a weak smile but quickly covered his eyes and began to sob. Dickson handed him a tissue. He thanked her and wiped his eyes.

'We're very sorry for your loss, Mr Grozan. How long had Elena been in Edinburgh?' said Gillespie.

'Let me think, it must be nearly a whole year now.'

'What was she doing here?'

'She was a cleaner. You can make a lot more in Scotland than in Romania. We were saving up to build a home and to start a family.'

'You had everything planned?'

'Yes, right down to the names of our children and even what type of flowers we'd have in the garden. She would stay over here for three years and then she'd come back to Romania.'

'Do you know where she worked?'

'Yes, at a hotel. The big one next to the train station.'

'The Balmoral.'

'Yes, that's it. The Balmoral. Very beautiful. The last time I wrote to her, I said that, one day, we would stay in that hotel as guests.'

'You said that was the last time you wrote to her. When was that, approximately?'

'Two, maybe three weeks ago.'

'Did you get a reply?'

'Yes, of course. She said she was very busy and was looking forward to seeing me again.'

'So, you'd made an arrangement to meet up?'

'Yes, but only a loose one. I said I would try to get over here to visit in October, if I could get the time off work. I just wish I'd got here sooner.'

His eyes welled up again and he broke down. Dickson let a couple of minutes pass before taking over the questioning.

'What is it you do, Mr Grozan?'

'I work for a building firm, but I don't make as much money as Elena does. I mean, I don't make as much money as Elena did.'

'I'm afraid that Elena may not have been working where she said she did.'

'What do you mean?' Grozan double-blinked. 'She wasn't working as a cleaner at the Balmoral?'

Gillespie took over once more, softening his voice as much as he could. 'I'm sorry to break it to you like this, Mr Grozan, but she wasn't working as a cleaner.' He grabbed a shallow breath. 'She was working as a prostitute.'

Grozan stared at Gillespie for what seemed like minutes, but was probably no longer than a few seconds. His colour changed, like a light had dimmed inside him. 'A prostitute?'

Gillespie nodded.

'That's impossible. There must be some mistake. My Elena would not do that.'

'There is no mistake.'

'I've seen Billy Connolly on television. I know you Scottish are famous for your sense of humour, but this joke I don't understand.'

'That's because it's not a joke, Mr Grozan. It's not something I would joke about.'

He ignored the sideways glance from Dickson who, despite knowing him less than a week, appeared to understand there were very few subjects her boss wouldn't joke about.

Gillespie could see Grozan begin to shake, a volcano ready to erupt. Instinctively, he stood up, just as the visitor sent the stack of magazines flying across the room. He screamed something in Romanian. Neither detective spoke the language, but they didn't need a translator to know Grozan was hurt, and angry.

'I can see this has come as a shock to you.'

He glared at Gillespie, tears streaming from his bloodshot eyes. 'How would you feel, if someone accused your woman of being a prostitute?'

Gillespie didn't answer. He turned to Dickson, who was holding out the box of tissues, and he lowered her arm with his fingertips. As the DCI nodded Dickson towards the door, Grozan fell onto his knees and started pounding on the floor with his fists.

'Leave him,' whispered Gillespie.

Chapter 18

The relentlessness of Grozan's tears reminded Gillespie of Pauline. The difference was that, despite the tragic circumstances, the detective was at least able to have a semi-normal conversation with the young Romanian. This was something he hadn't been able to do with his wife for years. She now had only two settings: screaming hysterically or ignoring him altogether. There was no middle ground.

Just thinking of his wife made Gillespie want to see Louise more than ever. He was desperate to make things up with the only person in the world who made him forget he was trying to do an impossible job and live with an even more impossible woman. But there was one thing that burned stronger than his desire—his guilt. Knowing it would make little or no difference to Pauline whether he was late or not, a misplaced sense of being a good husband caused him to call home. He smirked at the sight of that four-letter word when it appeared on the dashboard. Home—not exactly where his heart was any more. He was on the verge of hanging up when she eventually answered.

'Yes?'

'Hey, I was just wondering how you were doing?'

'What do you mean?'

Through the car's tinny speakers, he could almost feel the hot spittle of her hatred.

'I mean, how are you doing?'

'Fine, but why are you phoning? Corrie's just starting.'

'Sorry, I should've realised I'd be interrupting something important. Anyway, I just wanted to let you know I'll be home late. There's something I need to look into.'

'Well, don't expect any dinner waiting for you.'

The idea was laughable, and as his response queued, she hung up. He stared contemplatively at the dash for a moment, then switched on the radio. If he thought the action would improve his mood, Ally Murdo made sure he was mistaken.

Edinburgh's 'Jock Shock Jock' didn't seem to have moved on from the last rant Gillespie had tuned into. The Fairview protestors were still firmly in the DJ's crosshairs, and the murder at the club had done nothing to dampen his enthusiasm for calling them 'blue-haired munters' at every opportunity.

The DJ was in the middle of suggesting all golf clubs should follow Fairview's lead by banning women when Gillespie pulled up at the pub. He found himself strangely fixated on the ranting, wondering if Murdo would mention the murder.

'The worst mistake we ever made was giving them the vote— it just encourages them to believe anyone actually cares what they think. Who cares if this rabble of social justice warriors and late-in-life lesbians wants to chain themselves to the gates of Fairview and screech like banshees? I say let them, and let the media show them in all their glorious petulance, like children left out of the gang hut!'

Gillespie paused. He was quite sure he'd take the greatest of delight in putting Murdo in this place—he loathed loudmouths— but there was something about an angry man in full rant that he found gripping. Where was he going with this?

'It's not about these men in tweed having the odd game of golf without the girls, y'know. No, it's not about that. It's about much more than that. It's a political agenda. When these feminazis say let us into your golf club, or let girls into the boy scouts, what they're really saying is get in line, mister! Get on your side of the fence. It's not about man versus woman, it's about everyone—man or woman—for themselves. Because if we're so occupied fighting each other we'll never look at who is above the rot, ruling over us.'

Murdo took a breath. He stilled his voice and a little of the ire left. 'I genuinely feel sorry for these women, these protestors, because they're political pawns in all of this and they don't even know it. And now a poor woman has been murdered, which saddens me deeply. My sincere condolences go out to the family and my only hope is that our boys, and girls, in blue apprehend the culprit in a quick fashion.'

The detective had heard enough, the merest mention of the word politics was enough for him to want to stick his fingers in his ears. Like most people he met, he just didn't care because the alarm still went off every morning and the mortgage didn't pay itself. He cut off the radio and took the key from the ignition. On the way into the pub, Louise looked up from pulling a pint. She clocked him and gave what Gillespie thought was the faintest of smiles before turning her attention back to the bar. Ignoring the usual glares from the regulars, he made his way over to her.

Louise closed the till and turned to face him. 'Evening, Detective. What can I get you?'

'So you're still speaking to me?'

'I find it's easier to serve customers this way.'

Gillespie grinned. 'Pint of the usual, please.'

Louise picked up a glass and placed it under the tap. She hissed, 'Wouldn't you know it?'

'What's up?'

'We're all out. I'll need to change the barrel.'

Louise turned round and muttered something to her boss. He nodded and said: 'Make it snappy.'

Gillespie got the message when Louise winked and gave her a ten-second head start before following out the door. He found her round the side of the pub, standing next to a dumpster, arms folded. She looked cold, close to trembling.

'Sorry, bit slow on the uptake,' said Gillespie.

'I thought the wink would do it, or did you think I greet all my customers like that?'

'Maybe you should try morse code, or semaphore, next time.'

Louise's laughter wasn't long or loud, but it was enough to make all seem well again in the world of Kenny Gillespie. He wanted to grab hold of her, to kiss her and feel his troubles melt away in her arms. But the feeling didn't last long.

Her smile faded. 'Rob turned up at the house the other day.'

Gillespie froze, a reality he had been ignoring was slapped across his face. 'Rob?'

'Yes, Rob.'

'You mean, as in your husband, Rob?'

'No, as in Rob Roy the bloody sheep rustler! Of course I mean my husband.'

'Shit.'

Louise nodded, her expression turning gloomy.

Gillespie didn't know what else to say. The news had been coming, or was at least a possibility, for some time, but he had shoved it so far to the back of his mind that to see it forced in front of him now was a shock. He lit a cigarette.

'What the hell does he want? Has he got tired of causing trouble in Aberdeen?'

Louise leaned against the side of the dumpster and sighed. 'He wanted to see me, but he wanted to see Eilidh more. You can't really blame him.'

'So what did you do?'

'We talked.'

'And?'

'And what? We just talked.'

'Inside?'

'No, Kenny, not inside. I didn't want him in the house. He stayed on the step. But Eilidh came to the door and saw him, then he pulled the world's cutest teddy bear out of his bag. She's not stopped talking about him since.'

Gillespie sneered. 'That figures.'

'Look, I know he's made mistakes, but he's still her dad.'

'Yeah, and does Eilidh know what kind of man daddy is?'

'He says he's off the drink.'

'A leopard never changes its spots.'

'Since when were you one for clichés?'

He took a draw on the cigarette. 'Since I became one. Do you believe him?'

Louise looked at the ground, wondering how to reply. 'I don't know, but what can I do? He's desperate to see Eilidh and she's desperate to see him.'

'And what about you?'

'What about me?'

'Do you want to see him?'

'I moved to a new city and had to start a new life just to get away from him. What the hell do you think?'

Gillespie felt a hot flush of shame. Louise was confiding in him and all he could do was act like a jealous teenager.

'Look, I'm sorry. I'm worried about you. The guy's trouble. You know that.'

Louise nodded. 'Been there, got the bruises.'

'Then why are you even thinking about letting him back into your life?'

'Because things get complicated when kids are involved. You wouldn't understand.'

Gillespie didn't say anything; he had no comeback card to play. He wondered how Pauline would take a comment like that. He could see the flouncing hysterics playing in his mind. He let the moment pass.

'So where is he now?'

'He says he's staying in a B&B for a couple of weeks. He says he hopes we can iron a few things out.'

Gillespie dropped his cigarette and stamped it out. He pressed so hard he could feel the pavement through the sole of his shoe. 'I just hope you know what you're doing. I don't want to have to send the boys round.'

'Look, the only cop I want in my house is you. I'll be okay, honestly. But I like it when you're all protective. Makes me feel wanted.'

'It's your husband being wanted I'm worried about.'

'You just can't help yourself, can you? I was just trying to be nice and all I get is a yet another sarky comment.'

Even in the fading summer light, Gillespie could see her eyes start to glisten. His heart sank. He wasn't sure if he could deal with any more tears today. And what made these ones even worse than Grozan's were that they were his fault, and his fault alone. Why couldn't he just learn to keep his mouth shut? He took a step forward and patted her awkwardly on the shoulder. He wanted to give her a hug, but he knew this wasn't the right time or the right place.

'Look, I'm sorry. You're right, I know I say stupid things. I don't mean anything by it. You know how I feel about you.'

She looked up at him, wiping her eyes. 'Do I?'

'As soon as I've got these cases wrapped up, I'll try to take some leave and we'll get away somewhere.'

She sniffed. 'Like where?'

'Anywhere.'

'What about Pauline?'

'I doubt she'd even notice I had gone.'

'I'd like that, but...what's that?'

Gillespie cursed himself for not switching off his phone. Its piercing ring was getting louder.

'Christ. *Yes?*'

'Sorry to bother you, sir. This is Sergeant Duncan.'

'I don't believe it. Do you have a hidden camera somewhere, Bill?'

He gave Louise a smile. She didn't return it. Instead, she looked at her watch.

'Never mind. What is it this time?'

'I'm afraid Mr Thompson, the gentlemen involved in the

RTA on the bypass, has died.'

Gillespie knew instantly what this meant. Instead of two murder investigations on his hands, he might well now have a third. It also meant that he could forget making any plans with Louise.

'Are you still there, sir?'

'Yes, I'm still here. Are the family still at the hospital?'

'They are. We've got a couple of PCs with them at the moment, but they've requested someone from CID.'

'Tell them I'll be there in half an hour.'

Louise shook her head. 'I don't know how much longer I can carry on like this, Kenny.'

'Me neither. I'll be in touch soon, I promise.'

She shrugged and went inside. He watched her disappear and wondered when, or if, he would see her again.

Chapter 19

The old woman in the pink and white dressing gown took a long, final draw on her cigarette before dropping it on the ground and crushing the remains of the glowing ash beneath a well-worn slipper. She coughed loudly, her shoulders shaking, and then shuffled up to Gillespie, smiling. 'The doctor keeps telling me to give them up, but I'm too set in my ways.'

Gillespie forced out a half-hearted grin. 'I know the feeling.'

They were standing outside the Royal Infirmary, Gillespie finding himself among half a dozen pyjama-and-anorak-clad smokers who had sneaked from their wards for a quick fix. He couldn't help but admire their devotion, being buffeted by the damp winds in such inappropriate attire. His own call for nicotine was more diversion than ingrained craving. He needed to get Louise out of his mind and focus on the job at hand.

There was no place for personal life in an investigation; it messed everything up, the two competing factions cancelled each other out every time. The number of divorced, alcoholic, or plain screwed-up detectives on the force was testament to the fact there was just no balance to be found. No matter how hard he tried, Gillespie couldn't get it right. He'd so thoroughly blitzed his own marriage that it was a miracle to him that his wife could still tolerate him long enough to launch her attacks. Just this morning he had felt revulsion for even being in the same room as Pauline—and he knew she felt the same. He wondered where it was going, but not with any great effort—his real focus was on Louise, and the return of her ex.

'That wind's picking up,' said the old woman. She was trying to start another cigarette, her lighter sparking but failing to ignite.

'Here, let me.' Gillespie took the lighter and cupped his hands around the flame.

'Thanks, son.'

The subtle kindness, being called 'son' again—a rare occurrence and getting rarer—melted Gillespie's mood and brought him out of himself.

'You should get yourself out of the cold,' he said.

The old dear gave an agreeable nod. 'So what are you here for?'

'Oh, I'm just visiting someone.'

'Well, I'm sure they'll be pleased to see you.'

'I wouldn't bet on it.' He stubbed his cigarette and headed towards the sliding double doors.

Gillespie found Harris sitting in the reception area on an uncomfortable-looking row of blue plastic chairs. The bright and pitiless lighting shined on the faces of everyone in the room and Harris was squinting, furrowing his brow as he leafed through a folder.

'Looks like an interesting read.'

The sergeant looked up, startled. 'Sir, I didn't see you come in.'

'Sorry, Simon, I'd have got here sooner but I was trying to find a space. Can you believe how much it costs to park here? I'm going to have to sell a kidney to get out again.'

Looking from side to side, Harris leaned closer and began to whisper, 'Could we find somewhere quiet to discuss this before we head upstairs?'

'I assume you mean the contents of the folder rather than the actual price of one of my kidneys. Let's go over there.'

They made their way over to a remote corner of the overly-lit reception area and sat down.

'What do you have, then?'

'Your instincts were bang-on, sir. Gerald Thompson's collision was no accident. It was definitely sabotage.'

'Which means we're definitely dealing with another murder. Which means I'm definitely due for a nervous breakdown. What have you found out?'

Harris opened the folder and shuffled pages until he found what he was looking for. 'Nothing very sophisticated, by the looks of things. Two bolts from the front wheel on the driver's side were removed.'

A crime-scene photograph showed an intact wheel. Red marker-pen had circled the exact points where the bolts were missing.

'And there's no way these bolts could have come loose on their own?'

'Not a chance. It was a brand-new Beemer, not some old banger. This was definitely done deliberately—someone was trying to take him out.'

'Or at least give him a scare.'

'You don't think they'd know the consequences of doing something like that?'

'Maybe they were very stupid. I'm keeping my options open right now.'

Harris closed the folder and started to drum his fingers on the cover. 'The victim's a banker, I know what you're thinking.'

Gillespie looked at him. 'That I can probably narrow the suspects down to a few hundred thousand in the city.'

'Something like that, but who would go to this extreme?'

'Well, someone who wanted to do away with him. And someone who knew he liked to put the boot down. If our banker had been your Driving Miss Daisy type, then he'd probably still be here.'

Gillespie clocked the sheepish look on Harris's face, 'What's up?'

'Gemma already thought of that, sir. She looked up his record and found he had several speeding offences. He even made the *Evening News* last year because he kept his licence despite being caught doing over one hundred on the A1. His lawyer argued that he could lose his job if he wasn't able to drive.'

'Our Gemma's some girl.'

'Oh, she certainly is.'

Gillespie cocked an eyebrow as he observed Harris's gushing appraisal. 'Just you behave yourself, Simon.'

'I just mean she's very good.'

'I'm sure she is, but just you behave yourself.'

'I mean a very good detective.'

'Simon, some of the guys at the station have a poker school, so if that's your idea of bluffing then perhaps you should come along and help me fill up my pension pot. But yes, we're lucky to have Sergeant Dickson.' Gillespie made for the wards. 'Come on, they're waiting for us.'

'Here comes the cavalry.'

Gillespie looked the young PC up and down. He was going to ask if he was being facetious, but he thought he'd do a Ronald Reagan and put the comment down to youth and inexperience. He looked about twelve and, in all likelihood, wouldn't know what facetious meant.

'I've been called worse, Constable, but I'll settle for "sir" from now on. Which members of the family are here?'

'The mother and the daughter, sir.'

'How are they coping?'

The PC puffed out his cheeks. 'The mother's pretty cut up, as you can imagine. But the girl, well, she's just a bit...'

'What?'

'Well, sir, her dad's dead but—and pardon my French—she doesn't seem to give two shits.'

Gillespie peered over the officer's shoulder and through the round window on the door. He could see a woman hunched over in a chair, her face hidden in her hands. The girl, probably about twenty, stood next to her. One hand was lazily patting her mother on the back, while the other was in the middle of typing something on her phone.

'What do you mean?'

'Like she's not bothered, sir. Like she's lost a shopping list, not her dad.'

Gillespie returned to the window. He wondered if the girl was posting news of her dad's death on Facebook, or Twitter, or wherever the hell kids posted stuff these days. He thought about the day he lost his own dad. He couldn't face speaking to anyone for almost a week, let alone share his sorrow with the entire world. There was a generational gulf that seemed to be growing wider every year, and he didn't understand it.

'Grief's a funny animal, son, affects people in different ways. You'll have to get used to it.'

'Yes, sir.'

The women looked up when they came in. Harris closed the door gently.

'Mrs Thompson? And Jane, isn't it? I'm Detective Chief Inspector Kenny Gillespie, this is Detective Sergeant Simon Harris. We're both very sorry for your loss.'

The widow, smartly dressed in a grey skirt and white blouse, looked at him through blood-rimmed eyes. Her voice was barely audible, 'Thank you, detective.'

The young girl, wearing all black but for a splash of purple on her T-shirt, stared at him for a second, before turning her attention back to her phone. Gillespie felt like a youth club coach. He wanted to rip the pink chunk of plastic from her hands and tell her she'd get it back at the end of the day. But he reminded himself of his own words to the officer outside.

'I understand this is a very difficult time, but I'm afraid I do have to inform you that we are treating your husband's death as suspicious. I'll be conducting a murder investigation,

Mrs Thompson.'

The woman's mouth gaped. She seemed to be trying for words but none came. The girl looked up but remained impassive.

Harris spoke, 'It's okay, Mrs Thompson, take your time.'

She paused for a minute to gain composure. 'Murder? But this was a car crash? How can it be a murder? Who would want to? To?'

She broke down again. Gillespie let the sobs subside. He looked at Jane, who was staring at her mother with a look he would only be able to describe as contempt.

'We have evidence to suggest that Mr Thompson's car was deliberately tampered with, causing him to crash.'

There was another look on the girl's face. Not contempt this time. Gillespie could barely believe it, but he was certain that, just for an instant, a smirk passed across her lips. The mother was oblivious, and was once again overcome with emotion.

'I know this is very hard to hear, Mrs Thompson, but it's important we move quickly. Now, can you think of anyone who might have had some kind of grievance with your husband?'

She shook her head, the tears flowing down her face.

'Please try to think carefully, Mrs Thompson,' said Harris. 'Can you think of a time when he might have been threatened? Did he ever mention being in a confrontation at work, or maybe when he was out with friends?'

'Definitely not. He wasn't the type of person to get into fights. And he wasn't some hoodlum who goes looking for trouble. He was a professional. Who on earth would want to kill him?'

'That's what we'd all like to find out, Mrs Thompson. It's been a rough few years in the financial sector. Emotions have been running high.'

The widow stared at him and spoke softly, deliberately. 'My husband, Mr Gillespie, was a gentleman.'

The girl snorted. Even after all the strange looks and the odd behaviour, Gillespie and Harris were taken aback.

'My dad, Mr Gillespie, was a bastard.'

'Jane!'

'Oh come on, Mum, stop kidding yourself and tell it like it is. You know you're not supposed to lie to cops. He was a bastard to everyone, except maybe that little tart of his.'

Mrs Thompson clapped her hands over her ears. She begged her daughter to stop, but Jane was only getting started.

'Why are you trying to protect him? He was a bastard to you and he was an even bigger bastard to me.'

For the first time since he'd known him, Gillespie saw a complete look of shock on Harris's face. He appeared dumbstruck, without any reference for what he was witnessing. Things were getting out of control.

'Look, Jane, we know you're upset. It's a lot to take in. I think perhaps we should leave you both to calm down. We can come and see you tomorrow.'

Jane was defiant. 'I'm totally calm, *Kenny*. You want to know who had a beef with my dad? How would you like a list?'

Chapter 20

'What's that you've got there, Simon?' Gillespie studied the flickering computer screen, his morning eyes thinning to beady points.

Harris looked up from his terminal, taking in the DCI. 'Oh, morning, sir. I'm just finishing this presentation.'

'Presentation? On what?'

'On the paper trail that shows how Andy Cruickshank's money consistently found its way into Steve and Tricia Durham's bank account.' Harris sounded proud, as if showing his mum a picture he'd drawn at school.

'And what's that?' Gillespie pointed to a large piece of text on the title screen.

'It's Copperplate Gothic Bold. I was just trying to make it look nice.'

'I appreciate the gesture, Simon, but if you've got time to piss around on PowerPoint then I'm obviously not giving you enough to do. I'm interested in facts, not fonts. I'm going to get a coffee. I want this ready to go in five minutes.' He was aware how contradictory his order sounded, and the gruff tone didn't help, but with three cases on the go, Gillespie knew his demeanour was only going to get worse. He justified the outburst to himself as easing the team towards the storm he was forecasting.

The coffee machine spluttered into life as he went over the events of the previous evening. He thought of the girl at the hospital who had reacted with such ambivalence, even pleasure, after learning that someone was responsible for her father's death. In all the years he'd spent breaking the hardest news of all to family members—that their loved one had been murdered—he'd never seen a reaction quite like that.

Regardless of what Thompson may or may not have been like as a person, it was Gillespie's job to find out who had killed him. He just hoped he could cope with the pressure of leading three active murder investigations, as well as a dysfunctional love life. If he didn't get some kind of breakthrough soon, his brain might resemble the mangled wreckage of Gerald Thompson's BMW.

The DCI re-entered the room just as Harris was fiddling about with the projector cable, trying to locate a socket in the wall and coming up about three feet short.

'Be with you in just a second, sir.' His overly conciliatory tone caused another pang of guilt in Gillespie.

The detective didn't say anything; he'd made his feelings clear and could see from the way Harris was frantically yanking at cables and stabbing at buttons that his sergeant was going as fast as he could. After dragging the desk closer to the wall and another couple of minutes scowling at the screen, Harris grabbed the remote control and sat down. He clicked his way through several slides, which showed that regular withdrawals had been made from Andy Cruickshank's bank account.

'The bank has confirmed that every withdrawal was made by cheque, and that these were paid into the account owned by Steve and Tricia Durham.'

Gillespie dusted his hands together above the table, a showy gesture to indicate his patience was wearing thin. 'This is all very interesting, Simon, but I think we've already established most of this. What we're missing is proof that this wasn't just a case of Andy being generous. We need to show that the Durhams were writing their own cheques from his account. Do we have any of the cheques?'

'Yes, sir, we've got all of them. They're in the lab, being checked for prints.'

'Good. But we need to complete the picture. We need CCTV from the bank and hopefully we'll be able to catch them in the act. I want to see Tricia or that man mountain of a husband of hers handing the cheque over to a teller.'

'Way ahead of you, sir. We've got the CCTV and we've logged all the times that the cheques were deposited. Dickson is going through the footage now and pairing everything together.'

'Good work, Simon. We'll make a detective of you yet.'

Harris smiled, relieved. 'Thank you, sir, but don't you ever get tired of using that line?'

'Listen, sunshine, you're having a laugh if you think I'm going to waste all my best new material on you. Now come on, grab your coat.'

'Where are we going?'

'Officially, we're going to haul Davy Henderson over the coals and see what he can tell us about Elena Enescu.'

Harris's eyes narrowed. 'And unofficially?'

'Unofficially, we're going to call in and see Steve and Trish on the way.'

The officers parked across the street. After they crossed the road, Gillespie took a moment to peer into Andy Cruickshank's garden. It looked much as it did when he'd seen it last. The dust was still thick on the windows and the garden still resembled a jungle. If people didn't know better, the neighbourhood hoarder could have been inside right now, watching TV and eating baked beans from the tin.

Only the tracks left by an army of socos hauling their evidence bags through the long grass pointed to anything being amiss. Now, Gillespie noted, even these had started to disappear among the weeds. It was a physical reminder that this case needed a push. From the moment the DCI had set eyes on Andy

Cruickshank's frail, helpless body, he had wanted answers. He felt close to finding them.

The officers rang the doorbell and waited on the step, Harris whispering to Gillespie, 'Remember the last time we were here? Mrs Durham had just come out of the shower. I hope she's decent this time.'

'From what we know, I don't think "decent" is in her vocabulary.'

The opaque glass grew dark as the bulky figure of Steve Durham approached and pulled open the door. He was wearing nothing but small black shorts and a pair of flip-flops. His body glowed an unnatural orange and a pair of goggles were perched on his head. He squinted at the detectives.

'Yes?'

'I hope we're not interrupting,' Gillespie lied—he had absolutely no qualms about dragging Steve Durham away from his sunbed.

'Mr Durham?' said Harris. 'We spoke a week or so back about your neighbour, Andy Cruickshank. I'm Detective Sergeant Simon Harris and this is Detective Chief Inspector Kenny Gillespie.'

'Yeah, I remember.'

'We have some further questions for you and Mrs Durham. Is she at home?'

Durham nodded and beckoned them to come inside.

'Tricia, we've got visitors.'

They waited in the living room. Now that he knew where the cash was coming from, Gillespie couldn't help but look at the enormous television and the fake tans with even more distaste than before. An innocent man was lying dead just so these two could enjoy a pampered lifestyle. Tricia Durham entered the room in her dressing gown and sat down. If circumstances had been different, the detectives might have exchanged knowing smirks, but not even Gillespie was in the mood to joke.

'Mr and Mrs Durham, we're here to interview you about

Andy Cruickshank under caution.'

'*Under caution*?' Tricia spluttered. 'What does that mean?'

Harris knew the drill. 'It means you don't have to say anything, but it may harm your defence if you don't mention, when questioned, something which you later rely on in court. Anything you do say may be given in evidence.'

Tricia looked dumbfounded. Steve sat up straight, his square jaw set firm.

'Now wait just a minute.'

'How long have you been out of work, Mr Durham?'

Gillespie's question took the bodybuilder by surprise. 'Not long. I was at the gym until recently.'

'According to Edinburgh City Council, you were forced to give up the tenancy on Flex Gym nearly two years ago because you could no longer afford the rent. Do you mind telling me how you've been able to pay the mortgage on your home while you've been looking for a job?'

'We get by.'

'And what about the new suite? And the television? How did you pay for them?'

Even through the suntan, Gillespie could see a flush of anger in Steve Durham's cheeks.

'We came into some money. My uncle died just before Christmas, plus we had savings.'

Tricia nodded vigorously, but her agitated voice betrayed a lack of confidence. 'Yes, lots of savings. We've always been very careful with money.'

'And I suppose your financial statements will be able to confirm all of this?'

Instinctively, the Durhams looked at each other and then quickly turned away. Neither ventured an answer to the detective's question.

'I'm going to need to see a detailed account of finances.'

'What the hell for?' Steve's tone was growing more confrontational.

'Mr Durham, I'm conducting a murder investigation. Don't tell me you've forgotten that.'

'And what's that got to do with my bank balance?' He stood up slowly, making a show of extending himself to his full height. Gillespie knew what he was trying to do. Inwardly, he was just daring the big man to have a go. The temperature in the room seemed to be rising quite a few notches.

'I'm the one asking the questions,' said Gillespie, fixing his gaze firmly on his aggressor. 'And if you think you're in a position to challenge me, I can assure you that you'll be proven very wrong.'

Steve raised a finger. 'Look, I don't know what you're trying to get at, but I want you both out of my house right now.'

'We'll be happy to leave, Mr Durham, but I'm afraid we're going to have to ask you to come to the with us to the station.'

'This is outrageous! Are you having a laugh?'

'No, it's no laughing matter. I'm arresting you both on suspicion of conspiracy to defraud and for the murder of Andrew Cruickshank.'

Durham double-blinked and retreated a couple of steps. He put his hands on his hips then raised them up towards the ceiling, seemingly unable to decide what to do with them. He turned away from the officers and then looked back, wiping his mouth with the back of his hand, before sitting down in stunned silence. He shook his head, a look of disbelieving fury on his face. Tricia Durham, seated beside him, looked frozen in time as she stared blankly at the carpet.

'Sergeant, please arrange transportation,' said Gillespie.

The detective turned back to the Durhams. 'You two might want to make yourselves look decent before going over the door.'

Chapter 21

Tricia Durham found her voice when the police van arrived, kicking off like a cornered wildcat. Her howls of protest were still ringing in Gillespie's ears as he and Harris drove away. All in all, though, the visit had gone as well as could be expected. Harris stopped for a red light at the foot of Liberton Brae as Gillespie began fumbling around in his jacket pocket for his mobile.

'I'm just going to let Gemma know we've got a couple of guests checking in.'

It rang for nearly a minute. On another occasion this might have annoyed him, but he took it as a sign she was busy.

'Sergeant Dickson.'

'Gemma, how are you getting on?'

'Almost done, sir. We've got Tricia Durham on camera, handing over cheques to the cashier.'

'And you can definitely tell it's her?'

'Unless she's got an identical twin we don't know about.'

'So she didn't even bother with a wig and sunglasses like they do on that old *Police Squad* show. I don't know. Criminals, they just don't make the effort these days.'

Dickson let out a laugh so loud that Harris could hear it. Gillespie saw the sergeant give him a sideways frown. Probably jealous because Dickson hadn't so much as cracked a smile at any of his jokes. And by the way he tore across the junction and up Mayfield Road, it looked like he was trying to take out his frustration on the accelerator.

'Oi, Simon, take it easy, you're not in Traffic any more. Sorry, Gemma, I'm getting distracted by Lewis Hamilton over here. Anyway, the Durhams are on their way in. Just let them sweat in the cells till we get back. And do me a favour, will you, and grab all the cheques and print out some screen-grabs of Tricia paying them in. I'm going to give them both barrels and then watch them squirm.'

'No problem, sir. When are you planning to be back?'

'Give us a couple of hours. We're on our way to see Davy Henderson, so it depends how helpful he is, and whether Simon can get us there in one piece.'

He shot Harris a grin, but he didn't get one in return.

'There's one more thing before you go, sir,' said Dickson. 'The lab report has come in from Elena Enescu's post-mortem.'

'About time. What does it say?'

'I've only had a minute to scan it, but they've confirmed that she was strangled. They also know for sure the attacker was male, based on the position of the contusions.'

'So far, so vague. Did they find any DNA?'

'None.'

'Okay. Anything else to go on?'

There was a pause and a rustle of paper. 'There was sexual activity, but it looks like it was consensual as there's no sign of sexual assault.'

Gillespie thought for a moment. 'Let's not rule anything out yet. I'll give you another call when we're on our way back.'

'Righto, sir. Bye.'

The detective hung up and put the phone back in his pocket. He reached for his cigarettes and wound down the window. Harris's face was still a picture of concentration as they headed down Causewayside and then on to the Meadows.

'Gemma's a really good fit, don't you think?'

Harris didn't take his eyes off the road. 'Sir?'

'She's a really good fit for the team. I like her.' He paused for effect. 'Don't you?'

Harris was suddenly very interested in the car in front. 'Look at this clown. You've got indicators, *pal*, you should learn how to use them!'

Gillespie smiled and blew a mouthful of smoke out the window. He wasn't going to take the bait. The guy had a crush. So what? What was Gillespie expecting him to do—ask him for relationship advice? He'd be better off asking Mickey Rooney. They sat in silence as they drove through the Meadows.

Gillespie watched what he presumed were students kicking footballs and sitting round disposable barbecues. He couldn't remember whether the council had banned these or not, then he decided he couldn't care less. He had bigger things to worry about—not least of which was the man they were going to see.

'What's the name of Mr Henderson's club again, sir?'

Gillespie gave a start. Harris hadn't spoken for several minutes as he negotiated his way through the various one-way streets of Bruntsfield.

'You know, he's changed the name so many times I don't remember. But you can't miss it. Just look for the bright red sign that says *Girlz, Girlz, Girlz*.'

'You mean like this one?'

Gillespie looked at where Harris was pointing. At first glance, it looked like the club was named *Best Bar None*, but closer inspection revealed a small but strategically placed 'r' and 'a' in the word 'Best'. Gillespie gave an appreciative nod.

'Pretty subtle, by Davy's standards. Makes you wonder what he'd rename Fairview if he ever got his hands on it.'

Harris parked up and thought for a moment. '*Balls Deep?*'

'Detective Sergeant Harris—I'm shocked and appalled.'

There was silence for a moment as the two men looked at each other, stony-faced, then burst out laughing. Gillespie couldn't remember the last time he'd laughed out loud. It felt good, like a valve had been turned and was letting out excess pressure on his brain. They composed themselves and got out.

'Try to keep a straight face, Simon, we're in the Pubic Triangle now.'

'This is pretty embarrassing, but I only recently found out why this area's called that.'

'Yeah, most people think it's because of all the strip clubs, but I think it's because an arsehole is never far away.'

It took a few minutes for the detectives' eyes to adjust from the bright sunshine to the dimly-lit surroundings of Davy Henderson's club. The bouncer, all eighteen-plus stone of him, had given them a curt nod on their way in.

'Do yourself a favour, Simon,' said Gillespie once they were safely out of earshot, 'if smiler back there ever tells you to look but don't touch, do what he says.'

They took a moment to survey the scene. Half a dozen men in suits gathered round the main stage, whooping in appreciation as a topless brunette worked her magic on the pole. They made their way over to the bar, where a scantily-clad blonde was mixing a cocktail. She looked up and smiled, inch-long eyelashes rising in greeting.

'What can I get you, gents?'

'You can get me Davy, if he's around.'

'Who?'

'Your boss. We need to speak to him, right now.'

The girl's smile wavered slightly. 'Can I tell him what it's about?'

'No. Just tell him Detective Chief Inspector Kenny Gillespie wants to see him. I think he'll know why."

She disappeared through a door and emerged five minutes later, beckoning them to follow. They were led down a short corridor and into an office. It had a desk, chair and computer, but the photos of strippers lining the walls suggested it wasn't an everyday place of work. The imposing figure of Davy Henderson, dressed in a dark suit with no tie, appeared from a side-door, the sound of a flushing toilet behind him. His eyes lit up when he saw Gillespie and Harris.

'Gentlemen! Welcome to Breast Bar None. To what do I owe the pleasure?'

'We'd like to speak to you, Davy,' said Gillespie, before turning round to the girl still hovering by the door. 'In private.'

'I think Sonja was just about to offer you a drink, but suit yourself. Sonja, love, you'd better get back to the bar. I won't be long.'

He walked over and gave her backside a slap as she left. He closed the door and sat down behind his desk. He gestured for the detectives to sit opposite.

'Anyone that didn't know you would think you'd come up in the world, Davy,' said Gillespie. 'But I'm not that gullible, and I've got the advantage of having looked up your record.'

Henderson's chair creaked as he leaned back and lit a cigarette. He smiled at Gillespie.

'You mean we're not even going to bother with any small talk first? That suits me. I'm a busy man. Now, what do you want?'

'I want to know why one of your prostitutes was found on a golf course out in East Lothian.'

Henderson shrugged. 'Maybe she was working on her swing.'

'I'm glad you can joke about it, Davy. It must be easy for you to write off Elena Enescu as just another lost asset, but a young girl's lost her life.'

'And it's tragic,' he blew out a white plume of smoke, 'but I genuinely don't have a clue what she was doing there.'

'You're a member of Fairview, aren't you?'

'I am.'

'Did you send her?'

'Now, why would I do that?'

'Maybe to sweeten a deal? Maybe to bribe someone into looking more favourably on your plans to buy the club?'

Henderson flicked ash into a large marble ashtray and nodded thoughtfully. 'Maybe I should have thought of that, but I'm afraid you're wide of the mark there. Elena was a nice lassie and I'm not going to deny she sometimes worked for me, but she was a free agent.'

'We're not talking about the bloody Premier League here, Davy.'

'She ran her own show—she advertised on the internet, for Christ's sake. Anyone could have called her out there.'

'You're right, anyone could've called her—including you. I assume you've got a phone?'

Henderson stubbed out his cigarette in the ashtray and leaned forward. He fixed Gillespie with a cold stare. 'Given the opposition I've run into trying to buy that place, I'd say it's more likely someone was trying to frame me.'

Harris was unable to hide the surprise in his voice. 'Frame you?'

Gillespie gave a derisive laugh. 'Anyone can see you like living in a fantasy world, Davy, but are you seriously suggesting someone would do that, or is doing that?'

Henderson shrugged again. 'Hard as it is to believe, I'm not everyone's cup of tea. I've faced pretty violent opposition from some of these guys. To be honest, I wouldn't put anything past them.'

'Are you referring to the chartered accountants or the actuaries on the board?'

'Don't be fooled by their posh accents and old school ties, there's some hearts of stone beneath those tweed jackets. Some of them developed more than sharp elbows to get where they are.'

Gillespie uncrossed his legs and leaned forward. 'Okay, Davy, let me indulge you. How about you give me a list of names of people who you think might be willing to, not only break the law, but break the law in the most heinous fashion just to show you up.'

'Yeah right.' He let out a spluttering laugh. 'You think I'm about to do your job for you. That will be the day.'

'I'd have a long think about that, if I were you. There might come a point when you'll be cutting off your nose to spite your face.'

'I'll take that chance, for now.'

'Think about what I'm saying. I wouldn't want to be in your position and underestimate my enemies. If you think you're being played, Davy, you're going to have to be smarter than that to avoid going down.'

Chapter 22

Gillespie wondered if the meeting with Davy Henderson threw up more questions than it answered. The man was no angel, but he was no fool, either. The detective had scoffed at the idea of anyone trying to frame Davy Henderson—that would take a person far braver, or stupider, than he had ever met. But there was something about the way Henderson said that he wouldn't put anything past them. There was something in his voice, in his eyes. Not quite fear, but something he didn't expect. Gillespie was about to voice his thoughts to Harris, who was driving them back to the station, when he felt his phone vibrate. It was a text from Louise. The butterflies which had lain dormant in his stomach while he dealt with the murder investigations fluttered into life. He breathed out slowly and clicked on the message:

'I didn't like the way it ended last night.'

Ended? What did that mean? The way the night ended, or was she trying to tell him something more? Had she finally had enough—was it over?

'Is everything okay, sir?' said Harris.

'It's nothing, Simon,' said Gillespie, stuffing his phone back in his pocket.

It was far from nothing, but he couldn't allow himself to get distracted. He had another date with the Durhams. Louise would have to wait. He realised the irony of putting her off, in favour of the job, once again, but what choice did he have? There was only so much space inside his head for dealing with his mounting workload and the pressures of his love life. When it came to the crunch, the job would win every time because it was what defined him, what propelled him, and what kept him putting his shoes on every morning when the world around him was disintegrating. The job gave him perspective; it told him there were people far worse off than he was, some sufficiently worse off to be deceased, and he owed them something.

Dickson was waiting for them at the front desk when they walked in, a white envelope tucked under her arm. Gillespie gave her a weak smile.

'Are we all set, Gemma?'

She handed him the envelope. 'Ready when you are, sir.'

He opened the bulky package and flicked through the photographs inside. Dickson was right. In a series of shots that showed her walking up to the teller and handing over a cheque, there was no mistaking the pointed features of Tricia Durham. Gillespie wondered if it was arrogance or stupidity that could lead to such brazenness. He reasoned it was probably both. He nodded his approval and turned to the desk sergeant.

'Can you arrange for Steve and Tricia Durham to be taken into an interview room? Simon, we'll catch up with you shortly. Come on, Gemma. Let's see how this pair enjoy their Kodak moment.'

As he looked at them sitting next to each other at the metal table, both scowling and arms folded in identical poses of defiance, Gillespie thought the Durhams could have been a pair of comedy bookends. Like sulky teenagers who'd been sent to detention, they appeared ready to defend their actions with all the bleating indignancy they could muster. Gillespie couldn't wait to hear what bullshit story they'd come up with. He pulled out a chair and sat opposite them, 'Are either of the two of you able to explain how such large sums of money from Andy Cruick-shank's bank account ended up in yours?'

Steve Durham peered over the bridge of his nose, his voice firm but calm. 'What money?'

Gillespie looked down at his notes, dangling a pencil by its pink eraser before dropping it like a dart on the page. 'Approximately twenty-seven thousand pounds over the past year.'

'I don't know what you're talking about.'

'Maybe this will jog your memory.'

He slid a piece of paper across the table. Steve cast his eyes down for a moment before looking back up at Gillespie.

'The bank must've made a mistake. Wouldn't be the first time. You saw what happened during the, what did they call it, Trish?'

'The credit crunch,' mumbled Tricia.

'That's right, the credit crunch. The banks are always messing up.'

'So, you're saying you've no idea how this money appeared in your account? Two grand, every month, leaves Andy's account and lands in yours, and you're telling us this is down to a banking error?'

Steve bit, a vein protruding from his temple as he yelped like he'd been scalded. 'I don't know! You can show us as many bank statements as you want—it doesn't prove anything.'

Gillespie fought all his instincts to stand up and belt Durham in the middle of his ridiculous, orange face. 'You're right, Mr Durham. It doesn't prove anything. But I think you'll find this does.'

He turned to Gemma and nodded. Dickson stood up and walked slowly, deliberately round to the Durhams' side of the table. She removed the photographs from the envelope and placed them gently, one after the other, onto the table. Steve snatched the photographs and raised them level with his eyes. His stare was intense. Gillespie sensed the cogs in Steve's brain whirring around as he tried desperately to explain the images of his wife in the bank. Or perhaps he was under the impression that, if he concentrated hard enough, he could make the photos burst into flames, Superman style. Gillespie turned to Tricia. She was staring at the table. She didn't need to see the photos. She knew what they revealed.

'Incidentally, Mrs Durham, we've matched your prints to the cheques you were paying in.' He let that sink in for a few seconds before continuing to pile up the woes. 'We've got all the proof we need. There's no point in denying your involvement at this stage. You're only going to make it worse for yourself if you don't come clean.'

The DCI let his words hang in the air. A few moments of silence followed, before he became conscious of a dripping sound. Tears were starting to fall from Tricia Durham's eyes and on to the cold metal. It wasn't long before the tears were replaced by loud sobs. Her husband threw down the photos and hissed at her.

'Pack it in, Trish!'

She rounded on her husband, 'For Christ's sake, Steve, if you don't bloody tell them then I will!'

Gillespie and Dickson looked at Steve Durham as he mashed his fists, weighing up his options. In the space of a minute, they watched his expression turn from anger, to panic and then, finally, to resignation. He sat back in his chair and stared up at the ceiling. He let out an enormous sigh as he returned his gaze to Gillespie. He spoke slowly, softly, as though he'd just borrowed a voice from a man half his size.

'You've no idea what it's like to lose everything. *Everything*—your whole life's work. Gone, like that.'

He tried to click his fingers, but the sweat on his hands rendered the gesture noiseless. He placed his hand on Tricia's and continued. 'We lost kids, years ago. Miscarriages, you know? Trish could conceive but she couldn't bring them to term. You get over it, well, you grow numb to it. You have to just carry on, don't you? But when the business went down the pan, we lost everything we ever had. Andy didn't need that money. He never spent any. You saw how he lived, for God's sake. What harm was there? It was just all sitting there, untouched.'

Gillespie listened carefully, trying to decide whether what he was hearing was genuine remorse or Steve wallowing in self-pity. He decided to find out.

'How did Andy die?'

Tricia started to sob again. Dickson handed her a tissue.

'Andy was an old fellah—not right upstairs,' said Steve, pointing to his head for emphasis. 'I never thought he would...I mean, why would he? He never touched the money, but he went absolutely spare and started attacking Trish when he found out. I swear, I never meant to. I was just trying to get him away from Trish, like shooing a fly, but he was so light, so frail. There was nothing to the guy—he just fell over. He must've hit his head because he went out like a light and never came round. I never meant to do it. I swear to you, I never.'

'But you meant to cut him afterwards, didn't you? To make it look like a murder? You wanted to deflect attention away from you and make us think someone else had killed him. Is that about the size of it?'

Steve bit his bottom lip so hard that Gillespie thought it would burst open. He nodded slowly and then looked up at the detective. His eyes were moistening, pleading.

'Will they put me away for a long time?'

Gillespie knew he was right to doubt that Steve Durham would show any remorse, at least for Andy. The brute didn't care that a man was dead. All he cared about was how much time he'd have to do.

'That's not up to me, it's down to the courts now.'

He stood up. Dickson collected the photographs and the detectives walked to the door. Gillespie paused on his way out. 'Those kids in Andy's house—you'd've let them go down for this, wouldn't you?'

The Durhams didn't answer.

Gillespie turned and walked out. The only sound he could

hear as he shut the door was the slow tick of the wall clock in the empty corridor.

Chapter 23

Gillespie led the way back to the incident room, a tense shrug and a protracted sigh failing to relieve his tension. He knew some detectives would be pumping fists into the air about now, but not him, that wasn't his way. Despite the Durhams' confession, the DCI didn't feel a particularly strong sense of satisfaction. Even with the lid coming down on the Cruickshank case, it simply crystallised in Gillespie's mind just how many other questions remained unanswered, both in his professional life and at home.

He entered the incident room, closely followed by Dickson, and gathered the team. He felt like he was on one of those stupid reality shows that Pauline gorged herself on, where the presenter would leave a five-minute pause just to announce who'd got the two-hundred-and-fifty-thousand-pound business investment, or which soap star had eaten the most kangaroo testicles. As far as he was concerned, those programmes were a misnomer—they had nothing to do with reality. To him, reality meant long hours for little reward. It meant dead bodies in the morgue, and it meant having to deal with the dregs of humanity daily. There was no glamour in that, and certainly no fame and fortune at the end of it.

Gillespie looked at the rows of expectant eyes and said: 'Steve and Tricia Durham have just confessed to the killing of Andy Cruickshank.'

'Yes,' a few of the team whispered, he was okay with that, but when he saw Harris and Dickson high five each other, he snapped.

'Oi, we're the police, not bloody *Baywatch*. Do I need to remind you that a man has been brutally killed? There's absolutely nothing to celebrate here.'

'Sorry, sir, it won't happen again,' said Harris, his cheeks beginning to glow as he dipped his head towards the floor.

'But you must be glad to get that pair behind bars,' said Dickson.

Gillespie sneered. 'Do they look like master criminals to you?'

Dickson shrugged. 'No, but they did wrong. Surely that's enough, isn't it?'

'Is it really? To me, they just looked like an ordinary husband and wife who got thumped too many times by life. I'm not excusing what happened to Andy, but if you think locking the Durhams up is going to make our jobs any easier then you're mistaken. They had a good business before the economic crash—maybe we should be cuffing a few bankers and traitorous politicians instead?'

Harris was still eyeing the floor, but stole a glance at the DCI. Several other members of the team were staring at him open mouthed.

'Right, I've said my piece, now let's get back to work,' said Gillespie.

Nobody needed to be told twice. Within seconds, the group had dispersed and were setting to their tasks with renewed vigour. Gillespie, still fuming, marched out of the room and into his office, slamming the door. He sat down and inwardly cursed to himself before firing up his computer.

Instinctively, he looked over his shoulder before turning back to the monitor and accessing the criminal records database. He quickly typed in the name of Robert Mitchell and hit the enter key. He leaned forward and scrolled through the record of the man who had suddenly re-entered Louise's life. If he was a gang lord looking to hire another petty thug, he would have added Rob's CV to the 'definite maybe' pile. As he saw one conviction after another filling up the screen—drunk and disorderly conduct, aggravated assault, drink driving, fleeing the scene of an RTA, assaulting a police officer—it made him wonder why Louise would ever want to get involved with someone like that in the first place. But he also knew that lying came easily to the likes of Rob Mitchell.

Gillespie scrolled down to the last entry, dated the previous spring: a double theft of farm quad bikes in Ellon, an act which had earned him nine months in Grampian Prison. By the date of his release, it looked like his trip to Edinburgh was the first thing he'd done since vacating his cell. Gillespie puffed out his cheeks and clicked on the print icon. While he waited for the printer, he reached into a drawer, grabbed an envelope and scribbled Louise's name on the front, then folded the A4 pages and stuffed them inside. He closed down the computer, slipped the envelope into his jacket pocket and stomped into the corridor. Turning the corner, he almost ran into Harris, who he suspected was coming to offer another grovelling apology. He didn't give him the chance.

'Come on, Simon, you're with me.'

Harris followed him, eager as a puppy, to the stairwell. 'Of course. Erm, where are we going, sir?'

'Heriot Row.'

'Heriot Row? To see Gerald Thompson's flat? Isn't that where Robert Louis Stevenson lived too?'

Gillespie grunted. 'I believe so.'

Harris, clearly trying to lighten the mood, didn't take the hint. 'His father built the lighthouse at Turnberry, don't you know?'

'Yes, I do know, Simon. I'm not completely illiterate. Thomas Stevenson built dozens of lighthouses, one at Ailsa Craig, Lindisfarne and Muckle Flugga. Honestly, Simon, I wish you'd stop forcing me to show you up for being so bloody pompous. It's as embarrassing for me as it is for you.'

Harris mumbled an apology as they got in the car. They proceeded to the New Town in silence, but it was little over five minutes before Harris tried tentatively to break it.

'Sir?'

'Hmm.'

'I thought you'd be relieved to be free of the Cruickshank case.'

Gillespie turned to Harris and gave him the faintest of sympathetic smiles as he shifted gear.

'And my grumpiness belies that? Perhaps I've got more on my mind to worry about. Perhaps I've been doing this job too long. Either way, I take the subtle hint, Simon.'

He didn't elaborate, but Harris seemed pleased they appeared to be putting the high-fiving incident behind them. It was, in any case, as close to an apology as he was going to get.

They parked up, about fifty yards from Thompson's flat. Harris gazed appreciatively at the New Town architecture, the precise geometry of the streetscapes and the old world charm of the cobbles, but Gillespie was more interested in one of the lampposts.

'Look at that. There's a CCTV camera pointing right on to this stretch of pavement. See if you can get images from the night before the crash.'

Harris made a note as they walked up to the imposing front door with its authentic Georgian ironmongery.

'What's the story with this place?' said Gillespie, shaking his head.

'It's what I suppose you'd call his theatre abode, sir. Mr Thompson only used it occasionally, if he needed to stay over in the city.'

'Well, if you've got it, flaunt it. Did anything else come up?'

Harris nodded and referred to his notebook. 'He made several noise complaints about one of the neighbours, Nathan Chalmers. One was on the night of the crash, one was two weeks ago and one was made on the ninth of March.' He looked up from the notebook. 'Funny, I thought that date sounded familiar. He must've been in town for *The Oresteia* at the King's. I might have brushed shoulders with him.'

He gave an awkward laugh, obviously conscious that this remark would probably fall squarely in the pompous category. He looked relieved as Gillespie seemed prepared to overlook the comment. The DCI pulled out a key and stuck it in the lock.

'Let's take a look. I doubt it'll tell us much.' The door clicked open and Gillespie turned to Harris, winking. 'Then again, that might just be my Cassandra complex kicking in, eh Simon?'

Chapter 24

The stone stairwell stayed cold despite the heat outside. The walls were tiled in a gaudy Victorian filigree to about three-quarters of their height, where an expanse of yellow plaster took over. It looked nothing like the majority of Edinburgh stairs that the job brought them to. There were no rusting bikes or damaged railings, no graffiti or children's daubings, and pointedly, there was no lingering smell of urine or the caustic disinfectant used to mask it. The black and white chequered floor, more tiles, reminded Gillespie of a Masonic lodge he'd once had cause to visit, but he kept that observation to himself.

The detectives walked up to the first floor, where they found the flat that—up until recently—had belonged to Gerald Thompson. It was obvious the late owner wasn't short of money. In the wide hallway, a grandfather clock stood next to a walnut writing bureau that Gillespie felt sure to be Queen Anne—a knowledge gleaned from his wife's addiction to reruns of *The Antiques Roadshow*. He swept a finger over the leatherbound surface. There was no trace of dust. Gillespie knew the décor met with Harris's approval, before he even opened his mouth.

'It's very spick and span, sir. I wish my flat was this tidy.'

'The upper classes like everything to be in its place, especially plebs like you and me.'

Harris gave his boss a polite smile and let Gillespie lead the way into the living room, where modernity gate-crashed in the form of a fifty-inch television.

'Looks like our friend wasn't all about the roar of the greasepaint, Simon. I hope you brought some popcorn.'

'I suppose it's in keeping with the address that Mr Thompson should be a bit of a *Jekyll and Hyde* character. His wife wouldn't hear a bad word against him—but there were plenty of bad words coming from his daughter. What did you think of that, sir?'

'You mean the "he was a bastard" comment? It could've been shock, but it was more likely to have been a desire to shock.'

'What do you mean?' Harris tilted his head towards his shoulder, a perplexed gaze settling in his eyes.

Gillespie laughed. 'Have you never seen a *St Trinian's* movie, Simon?'

He should have known the answer would be no. The blank look in Harris's eyes indicated a deepening confusion.

'We had a girls' school back home and, by Christ, they could get wild at the weekends. I think it's something to do with the restraint—the shackles of formality and all that walking around with books on their heads. After a while it gets to them and they rebel against the established order. It's a natural part of growing up but, for whatever reason, this particular segment feels the need to go to town.'

'I suppose the boarders will feel an element of rejection too. Some of them need to seek parental attention.'

Gillespie nodded. 'Daddy issues.'

'Indeed. Notice me, senpai!' Harris chuckled to himself as he began to flick through a pile of DVDs. 'I bet you're glad you don't have that problem, sir.'

Gillespie snapped. 'Don't presume to know what I think, son.'

Harris spun round, the sudden change in tone telling him he'd stumbled into an unmarked minefield. 'I'm sorry, sir,' he stammered. 'I was just trying to...'

'Do yourself a favour, Simon, and don't.'

They continued to search the living room from opposite

ends, in silence. Gillespie looked over at Harris, who was keeping his head down in case another salvo was fired in his direction. The DCI felt a twinge of remorse. Had he overreacted? Probably. He was growing to like Harris, in spite of himself, and didn't want to drag him down. He also knew that Harris needed to grow a thicker skin if he wanted to succeed in this game. Was it a fatherly instinct asserting itself? Like the way his old man had been so fond of easing him into the setbacks life was inevitably going to throw at him. 'Stop sugar-coating it for the lad,' Dad was fond of chiding his mother. They seemed like confused moments in his childhood, but Gillespie understood now. Life was far from sweet. He went through to the bedroom. Harris followed in his wake, but at a safe distance.

'Well, wouldn't you know it?' Gillespie looked at the bookshelf and tried to break the ice. 'The complete works of Robert Louis Stevenson. Just for show by the look of them. Either that or Thompson paid someone to turn the pages.'

Gillespie didn't give Harris a chance to laugh. He'd spotted something on the bedside table—a three-digit number scrawled on a notepad. Gillespie held it up.

'Do you recognise this, Simon?'

'Of course, sir. It's the noisy neighbour line.'

'Correct. Looks like Mr Chalmers was causing him quite a few sleepless nights, because here's the number for the local police station too. When we get back to the station, I want you to check the log-books and see how many times he called each one. Come on, let's see if any of the neighbours are home.'

As Gillespie turned for the door, a new purpose in his stride, Harris grinned. Could his mood be thawing?

The newfound optimism drained away as silence met every door knock and ring of a bell. The detectives were heading back for the main door to the street when it creaked open. They took a step back to make way for a young man pushing a racing bike across the threshold.

'Afternoon.'

The man, probably no more than twenty-two and a mass of blond curls poking out beneath his cycling helmet, looked up and put his hand to his chest.

'Christ, are you trying to give me a bloody heart attack?'

'Sorry about that, son. We were just leaving.'

Gillespie gave the bike an admiring glance. 'A Flying Scot? You must take your cycling seriously?'

The young man looked at him quizzically. 'It's just a runa-round, really. I've got another bike back home.'

'And where's home?'

'Perth, if you must know, but I don't see what it's got to do with you.'

'Sorry, I'm forgetting my manners. I'm Detective Chief Inspector Kenny Gillespie. This is Detective Sergeant Simon Harris. And you are?'

His expression soured. 'Nathan. Nathan Chalmers.'

'Pleased to meet you, Nathan Chalmers. Sorry to give you a fright, but we're investigating the death of one of your neighbours—Gerald Thompson. Do you mind if we come into your flat to ask you a few questions?'

'*What?*'

'Oh, you don't mind. Didn't think you would. Lead the way, then.' Gillespie patted the saddle of the stationary bike, 'Lovely piece of kit, that.'

Like Thompson, Nathan Chalmers didn't seem to be too worried about counting the pennies. Gillespie cast his eyes round the young man's living room, which was roughly the same size as Thompson's, and counted the gadgets. They included a wall-mounted television, two turntables, at least four games consoles and speakers in every corner. Connected, presumably, by the spaghetti of wires running all over the highly polished parquet flooring.

'When is Captain Kirk due back on the bridge?'

Chalmers was in the middle of taking off his helmet and parking his bike at the door. 'I'm sorry, I don't follow.'

'Evidently not. What is it you do for a living, Mr Chalmers?'

Chalmers took off his rucksack and balanced it on the seat of his bike. 'I'm a student. Well, sort of. I've just finished my master's and I'm waiting to hear back on a couple of job interviews. Should I offer the two of you a drink? You can have anything, as long as it's water.' Chalmers smiled but Gillespie overlooked the insincerity.

'No thank you, but by all means get one for yourself. Must be hard work tackling the cobbles on those skinny tyres.'

Chalmers disappeared into the kitchen and Gillespie took a closer look at the speakers, which would have been more at home in a city nightclub.

'Have you seen the size of these things, Simon? It must sound like a bloody 747 taking off in here when he watches *Countdown*.'

'*Countdown*? Isn't that a bit of a cliché, sir?'

'He's a student, Simon and, as such, I'm going to stick my neck out and say he watches *Countdown*. If you can stand there and honestly tell me that when you were a student you never watched *Countdown* or paid for a bag of chips with a cheque, then I'll stand corrected.'

Before Harris could answer, Chalmers came back in, slugging water from a Hard Rock pint glass. Gillespie motioned to the speakers.

'We were just saying you must get a decent sound out of these.'

Chalmers flopped on the couch and rested his feet on the coffee table. 'Yeah, they do the job. It's all hooked up—TV, Blu-ray, PlayStation. Everything comes out of those bad boys.'

'And music?'

'Of course.'

'We understand that your former neighbour, Mr Thompson, may have complained to you a few times about noise.'

Chalmers turned indignantly, 'No, he only complained to me once. He came round here and asked me to turn the music down. It was pretty late so I said, "Fair enough, mate" and did what he asked. That was pretty much the only time I ever spoke to the guy.'

Harris began taking notes.

'How long ago was this?'

'Don't know. Three or four weeks ago.'

'So, you're saying this was the only time he complained to you about noise?'

'To me, yes. The next time I knew he had a problem was when a couple of heavies in high-vis jackets hammered on my door demanding I turn it down again. Honestly, the guy must've had ears like an elephant to hear my music from his flat, cos I could hardly hear it from in here. You'd think he'd have the decency to come and speak to me himself, rather than send round a couple of minions.'

'How far apart where these two occasions?'

'Not long, a week maybe. Like I said, I hardly ever saw the guy and only ever spoke to him once.'

Gillespie nodded. 'Well, thank you, Mr Chalmers. I don't think we'll take up any more of your time.' The officers glanced at each other and turned back to the hall. They got as far as the front door before the student's bike blocked their path.

'Let me move that for you,' said Chalmers, relief or eagerness to be rid of the officers flooding his voice. He began to wheel the bike away from the door. A loud noise, like a clanging of metal, came as something fell from the rucksack and on to the wooden floor.

Gillespie looked down, frowning. A long silence played out in the crowded hallway. Slowly, the DCI withdrew his hands from the pockets of his trousers and crouched down. He retrieved the fallen item and felt the weight of the metal in his hand. It was a large monkey wrench.

'What's this, Nathan?'

'It's just…for maintenance.'

'Maintenance of what? A bloody Panzer?'

'It's for the bike, actually.'

'It's a bit of a blunt instrument for a two-grand bike.'

Chalmers took his turn to glower at the floor now. For the first time since the detectives arrived, he didn't have anything to say. Gillespie held the wrench in two fingers, inspecting it closely for a few moments, before handing it to Harris.

'I think we should let the lab take a look at this, Simon.'

'We certainly should, sir,' said Harris. He made a show of removing an evidence bag from his pocket, placing the wrench inside and sealing it up.

Chalmers watched on solemnly.

'If you've nothing else on, young man,' said Gillespie, 'perhaps we should continue this chat down at the station. What do you say?'

'*Station*?'

'Yes, the police station. It's a place where we take a very dim view of criminals…' He turned to the other detective. 'And what's that other group we don't like, son?'

'Liars, sir,' said Harris, regaining his confidence.

Chapter 25

In the cold enclosure of the interview room, Gillespie found some suspects easier to read than others. There were the ones who would be angry, in-your-face and aggressive as they spat out their denials, and there'd be others who'd be terrified into near silence. There were those who'd sit there impassively and greet every question with a 'no comment' and, there were those who'd crack and give him a full confession. The detective wasn't yet sure which of these interviewees Nathan Chalmers would turn out to be, but he did know the boy was hiding something, and not doing a very good job of that. Gillespie let Harris ask him the easy questions, but the student couldn't resist lacing every response with sarcasm. It was a defensive posture, that much was obvious, but it was also irritating and grating on the officers' nerves.

'Would you like to have a lawyer present?'

'I don't need a lawyer,' Chalmers grinned. 'I've done nothing wrong.'

'Would you like to make a phone call?'

'I refer you to my previous answer, *Sergeant*. I've done nothing wrong, so why would I want a lawyer or a phone call? Can we just get on with this?'

Gillespie wanted to resist the urge to talk to Chalmers in what he called his 'gaffer' tones, but then figured that the condescension should go both ways. 'We appreciate your advice, Mr Chalmers, but we'll proceed with this interview as we see fit, do you understand?'

Chalmers leaned back and folded his arms. An impatient gleam entered his eye. He couldn't have affected annoyance more plainly if he had started tapping the face of his watch and exhaling loud breaths.

'Go ahead, but I'm telling you I've done nothing wrong.'

'What kind of car did Gerald Thompson drive?'

The question came out of nowhere. Chalmers's mouth widened before his words started dropping, clanging on the table like a bag of marbles.

'A-a BMW, I think. Yeah. A top-of-the-range Beamer. Black. From what I can remember, yes, black.'

Gillespie followed up with another question, certain that he already knew the answer. It was interviewing 101—know their response and guide them towards the pit you've dug.

'Do you own your flat in Heriot Row?'

'Yes, well, sort of. My parents own it and I stay there during term time, but I don't see how that's relevant.'

'Anything and everything could be relevant, as far as I'm concerned. It always helps if we know the background to a story. For example, sometimes it's the little details that explain how two worlds—for want of a better word—collide. Now, cast your mind back a few weeks, to the night Mr Thompson came round to your flat to complain about the noise. What do you remember about that night?'

Chalmers sighed, as though answering had become a chore. 'What do you want to know?'

'As much as you can tell us.'

'It was a weeknight, me and my friends had just finished our exams. We were celebrating at the pub. We were drinking there for a while and then I suggested we all go back to mine.'

'What time was this, approximately?' asked Harris.

'Surely you can't expect me to remember that?'

Chalmers looked at each of the detectives. Their expressions told him they wanted an answer.

'About half twelve, I suppose, but I can't remember precisely.'

'That's understandable but, when you say "a few friends", can you put a precise number on that?'

'Yes, there were six of us, I think. It wasn't many, anyway. It was a pretty modest gathering.'

'And would you say that this "modest gathering" got out of hand at any point?' asked Gillespie.

'Hardly, it was all very tame. It certainly wasn't some wild college party if that's what you're implying. My friends aren't hooligans, they're Edinburgh University students. They're future engineers and lawyers. One of them's a doctor in waiting. Do you know what I mean?'

'I understand, Mr Chalmers but, if that's the case, how do you explain this...*Sergeant Harris*?'

Harris opened a folder and handed Chalmers a piece of paper. The student accepted it and began scanning the document as Harris detailed its contents.

'In the space of just over three weeks, Gerald Thompson made a total of fifteen calls to the noise abatement service.'

Chalmers screwed up his face. 'Fifteen calls? What, fifteen calls about me?'

Harris nodded. 'All fifteen, including one made in the early hours of the day that he was involved in a road traffic collision.'

The student began to get agitated. 'Look, we'd finished our exams—we were excited. We were celebrating round at my flat and, all right, maybe we were a little more *effusive* than usual, but so what? We weren't doing anyone any harm.'

Gillespie picked up a copy of the report.

'That depends on your definitions of "anyone" and "harm". According to our records, the last call from Mr Thompson was logged at 3:20 a.m. We've got colleagues who are setting their alarms not long after that. If partying until that time is what you'd call a "modest gathering", then I'd hate to see you and your pals letting your hair down.'

Chalmers shook his head angrily.

'Look, Gerald Thompson would complain if someone farted too loudly. The guy was totally deranged.'

'I must confess I'm a bit confused, Mr Chalmers. Earlier, you told us that you'd only spoken to your neighbour once. Are you now saying there were ongoing problems between the two of you?'

Chalmers's cheeks were growing redder, his eyes darkening. 'No. I mean, he was difficult, but I didn't bloody *murder* him.'

The detectives exchanged a long look before Gillespie turned back to Chalmers.

'Nobody accused you of murder, Nathan. Is there something you'd like to tell us?'

Gillespie could see the first signs of tears begin to form in the student's eyes. 'No, I just. God, what have I said?'

He ran his hands through his hair and lowered his head towards the table. After a minute, when it was obvious he wasn't going to look up any time soon, Gillespie broke the silence.

'Let me make this easy for you. We've seen the consoles round at your flat. We know you and your friends like to play games, so let's play a game of "what if". What if some New Town students liked to party and what if their stuffy, upper-crust neighbour liked to object. Let's say this neighbour called the police a few times too many and after quite a lot of drinks and in high spirits—maybe they were celebrating—some of these *effusive* students decided to teach their stuffy, complaining neighbour a lesson. After a visit from the noise abatement team, these students hatch an idea to take a couple of wheel nuts off his top-of-the-range BMW. Of course, the students wouldn't expect the worst. They might expect the driver to be a little inconvenienced—maybe a buckled rim or the wheel rolling off at the first set of traffic lights. They certainly wouldn't expect the car to make it all the way out to the bypass and up to seventy miles an hour because, if that happened, the consequences would be considerably more serious. And we're not just talking about the consequences for the now-deceased neighbour. We're talking about potentially pre-meditated murder.'

Chalmers looked up. He'd been hiding tears that were now flowing freely down his crimson cheeks. 'No, no, no. I didn't do that.'

'Well then, who did?' snapped Gillespie.

'I don't know, but it wasn't me.'

'Well somebody bloody did and, if it's not you, you'd better have a long think about who that somebody might be. That giant wrench of yours, which you say you use on your little racing bike, is on the way to the lab as we speak. If our boffins match your wrench to the bolts on Gerald Thompson's car then I'm going to make sure you're put away. Do you know what *I* mean?'

The arrogant persona had crumbled. All Gillespie could see now was a young boy alone and afraid.

'I think we're done here for now, Sergeant.'

The detectives stood up. The sound of chair legs scraping on the floor made Chalmers wince. His gaze followed Gillespie and Harris all the way to the door. There seemed to be words, and perhaps more tears, welling inside him, but the detectives didn't wait to see if they materialised. Gillespie closed the door, turning the lock noisily before walking away.

Chapter 26

The lights were off when Gillespie arrived home. Only a faint glow from the flickering TV screen beyond the curtains hinted that anyone was inside. The detective stepped out of the car and wondered what Pauline might be watching. Whatever it was, the chances were he would hate it. They'd never shared the same taste in films or TV shows. Pauline had always been taken in by soaps and dramas that bore, as far as he could see, no relation to the real world he knew. At some point everything his wife watched became a sort of joke to him. It were as if the programmers had an agenda to push political correctness to the point of utopia—it was obvious to Gillespie that life simply wasn't like that, and would never be capable of being so. The more hardened he became by experience, the more he sought merely distraction or escapism from entertainment. There'd been a moment, he recalled it now, when he'd settled down on the sofa to retreat into *The Magnificent Seven*, only for Pauline to storm into the living room and demand he turn off the 'macho crap'.

'I thought you left feminism behind when you gave up lecturing,' he'd replied.

'You bastard. What are you trying to say?'

Her reaction to his throwaway remark shocked Gillespie.

'Nothing more than let me watch my movie.'

'No, you're trying to say I lost my job because I'm a woman.'

'I never said that, you did.'

'You think I'd have been happier barefoot and pregnant all these years, instead of building a career for myself.'

'Are you happier?'

She called him a bastard for the second time in the space of a minute and left the room in a rage. The memory, and a million like it, all seemed so familiar, so tired. He didn't want to go back over them but it was like they played on a loop inside his mind. What had happened to them? He felt like a statistic that Harris might point to on a ridiculously long list, perhaps beneath the rubric 'Marriage Failures'.

Gillespie heard Pauline before he saw her, slumped on the couch, snoring above the canned laughter coming from a late-night chat show. On the floor, sitting among a bunch of well-thumbed and now-greasy magazines, was a family-size bucket of KFC. He picked it up. It was empty, save for a couple of sorry-looking crumbs rattling about in the bottom. He looked at his wife and for the first time noticed the large Pepsi that was still in her hand. She stirred slightly as he extracted the half-full container.

'*Jesus*, look at the state of her.'

He switched off the television, laid a throw rug over his wife and took the KFC carcass through to the kitchen. As he dropped the containers into the bin, fighting the urge to retch, he knew the kitchen would soon reek of fried chicken. He tied up the bag and dumped it in the outside bin, closing the door behind him, and lit a cigarette. He walked into the middle of the back garden and looked up at the night sky. The amber glow of the Edinburgh streetlights meant the stars were never as bright here as the ones that used to fascinate him as a kid growing up in the countryside. If he looked hard enough, though, he could still make out the three points of Orion's Belt.

He remembered the night his dad first pointed out the Three Sisters. Meg, one of the farm sheepdogs, had given birth a few months earlier. The first three collies had been snapped up by local shepherds—all except for the runt of the litter, who had a pronounced limp. Now Ben, too, had found a home, this time with a family from Berwick. Young Kenny had grown attached to Ben, who greeted him with enthusiastic licks to the face every time he came home from school. Kenny didn't want to say goodbye, so his dad suggested they take the pup for a last walk together down the bridle path before he began his new life. It was a crisp autumn night, the moon bathing the track in a cool light. He watched Ben sniffing around in the hedgerow and started to get upset. That's when his dad took his mind off the agony by turning his attention to the heavens. He pointed skywards and traced his finger over what he now knew was called Orion's Belt. Instantly spellbound, young Kenny truly believed that if he concentrated hard enough, he could see the great huntsman in the sky. That night, his dad helped dull the pain of losing Ben but, more than that, he had opened his eyes to the wonders of the universe and the infinite possibilities of life.

In his tiny back garden in Edinburgh, Gillespie looked down at the dying embers of his cigarette by his feet and wondered what had become of that excited, wide-eyed kid on the bridle path. Those carefree days of childhood really were the best days of his life. The debt slavery he could just about live with, the dirge existence was something he could handle. But, up until now, he hadn't wanted to admit to the biggest problem of all. It was the fact there was no child by his side—no wide-eyed kid to whom he could show the three points of Orion's Belt. This was the end of the line. When his time here was up, what would he have to show for it?

Once he had gone, it would be like he never even existed. The thought made Gillespie miserable. There was only one glimmer of light in his life right now. He pulled out his phone to see if Louise had sent him a message. She hadn't. He shivered. It was getting cold. He took a last look at Orion's Belt and went back inside.

* * *

The detective made himself a coffee and sat down at the kitchen table. He couldn't stand it any longer. He took a deep breath and called Louise. It seemed to ring forever before a croaky, sleep-deprived voice answered.

'Kenny? What is it? I was asleep.'

He felt ashamed, and desperate not to wake Pauline. 'Sorry, I just wanted to hear your voice.'

'*What?*'

'I said I just wanted to hear your voice.'

'Oh, okay. Well, now you've heard it. Can I go back to sleep?'

'I can't tell if you're joking.'

She sighed. 'Yes, of course I'm joking, Kenny. Where've you been?'

'Working. I solved a case.'

She yawned. 'I'm pleased for you.'

'It doesn't mean anything, though. I've been thinking about you and...'

'Kenny, stop. I don't want to hear this any more.'

'But I mean it, Louise. I can't help it.'

'Kenny, I've been thinking too.' She sounded wide awake now—wide awake and definitely not joking.

'About what?'

She was growing more irritated. 'Just things. I've been thinking about things.'

'I know I'm a detective, but you need to help me out here. What things?'

'I just can't do this.'

'Louise, you're not making sense. What can't you do?'

'This, Kenny,' she snapped. 'I can't do this—*us*. I can't do it any more.'

There was a long pause as Gillespie's mind raced. Why was she doing this? A number of possibilities raced for prominence, but there was only one explanation that made any sense.

'Has he been back? Has Rob been back? Has he been bothering you again? If he has, I'll have him arrested. I mean it.'

'Kenny, just shut up, will you?'

Her voice cracked and she began to sob. The pain and the guilt were eating into Gillespie now. He wanted to be with her, to comfort her and say he knew how to make things right. He'd been wrong, he'd messed her about and hesitated but that was over now.

'Louise, Louise, I'm sorry. I'm really sorry. *Louise?*'

The line was dead. He tried to call her back, but it went straight to voicemail. For a moment, he wondered if her battery had died, but he knew very well she'd hung up, and he couldn't blame her.

'Who was that?'

Startled, Gillespie turned to see Pauline standing in the doorway, arms folded across her chest. Her mass of hair was pointing in a hundred different directions and her belly looked to be evacuating the waistband of her jogging bottoms. Gillespie's neck started to burn.

'I said, who was that?'

He didn't say anything, but stood up and reached across the table to grab his jacket. In the rush, he grabbed it by the wrong end, dropping the envelope in the pocket at Pauline's bare feet. She picked it up and read the name he'd scrawled on the front.

'Who's Louise?'

'Give me that,' said Gillespie. He snatched the envelope from her hand and stomped past Pauline and out the door. His wife screamed at him as he went.

'Kenny, you bastard! How could you do this to me? How could you do this to me?'

The words were ringing in his ears as he got in the car and tore out of the driveway. The dark road passed in a blur of streetlights and oncoming traffic. He didn't think about the turns in the street or which way he was going, he was driving instinctively as his mind welled with grim imaginings. It wasn't long before he found himself parked opposite Louise's place. The house was in darkness. He sat there, cold and angry, trying to find calm and watching for any sign of movement. He wanted to knock on the door, but didn't want to wake Eilidh or have the girl see him confront the owner of the black pick-up—a battered Toyota Hilux—parked outside the house. He knew he shouldn't have come, and now he needed somewhere to sleep.

The voice on the other end of the speaker sounded cautious rather than sleepy.

'Who is it?'

'Simon, it's me.'

'Who's me?'

'Kenny.'

'Sorry, sir, I didn't recognise your voice. Erm, could you give me a few minutes to get dressed before I come down? I'm in my PJs.'

'Don't bother coming down, Simon, just open the door and look out a sleeping bag.'

Chapter 27

Gillespie took the bottle from Harris and eyed it suspiciously.

'Are you sure this is all you've got?'

'I'm afraid so, sir. Like I said, I'm not a big drinker.' He flopped on to the sofa and knuckled his tired eyes. 'My sister brought it back from Greece. It's been in the back of the cupboard for a couple of years but I'm sure it'll be fine, probably good for another century or two.'

Gillespie poured himself a glass. 'Ouzo? Well, I'll give it a go. Where are the olives?'

Harris, yawning excessively, started to stand up. 'Well, actually, I...'

'Jesus, sit down, Simon. I was joking. Seriously, though, I really appreciate this. Cheers.' He raised the glass and downed the liquor in one. He winced, grimaced, then poured himself another.

'Are you sure you won't join me?'

'I'm fine with tea, thanks, sir.'

'This is your place, Simon. You can call me Kenny. At least it's better than what my wife calls me.'

The detective laughed bitterly and took another swig. Harris squirmed in his seat, not sure whether this was an invitation to ask a question.

'What does your wife call you, Kenny?'

Gillespie leaned back on the sofa and sighed. 'Nothing I don't deserve, I suppose. I've left her, Simon. I've bloody left her.'

Harris was now fidgeting with a toy Dalek he'd picked up from his desk. He was about to speak, but Gillespie wasn't finished.

'I should have done it months ago, to be honest. I realised I just couldn't face her any more. She used to have her good points, though. She's a bright woman, Simon, far brighter than me. She's even brighter than you.'

Harris smiled awkwardly. 'How did you meet?'

'She was a professor in chemistry at Edinburgh Uni. She was called in as a specialist witness in a poisoning case. God, she was gorgeous, I mean really gorgeous, and smart and funny. I thought all my Christmases had come at once when she agreed to go out with me, let alone marry me.'

'So what happened, if you don't mind me asking?'

Gillespie took another drink and shook his head. 'I don't know. Life, work...kids.'

Harris looked surprised. 'I'm sorry, sir...I mean, Kenny. I didn't know you had kids.'

'I don't. I think—I _know_—that's the biggest problem. For some reason, we decided early on that we didn't want any.'

'Was there any reason in particular?'

'Not really. We both had really busy jobs, we were both far too ambitious for our own good and we agreed that being parents just wasn't for us.'

'And now?'

'Now? Well, let me think. If we'd had kids, then my wife might not feel guilty about denying every biological imperative in her body, she might not have spiralled into a state of such depression that she spends all day, every day, eating junk food and ordering assorted crap from the shopping channel. If we'd had kids, then I might feel my life was actually worth something, instead of working myself into an early grave to pay her shopping channel bills and spending all my free time down the pub. If I had been spending all my free time with my kids instead of down the pub, then I might not have fallen in love with the woman behind the bar. And if we'd had kids, I might not have started an affair with a woman I've also now managed to alienate, and I might not find myself kipping on your sofa. Cheers!'

There was a long silence. Harris firmed his features. He glanced at the bottle. It was already half empty.

'Sir...'

'*Kenny.*'

'Kenny, are you sure you want to be telling me about this?'

'You mean my sordid little affair? You might as well hear it from me than through the station jungle drums, or from Derek on the front desk. You have to watch that one, Simon. He probably knows more about your private life than you do.'

'I'll bear that in mind.'

'Anyway, there's more. Louise—the woman I've been seeing—well, she was married to a world-class prick. He was violent, hit her a lot, and now he's back on the scene.'

'Back on the scene?'

'Yes. She'd moved here from Aberdeen, hadn't seen him for well over a year and then, bang, he just shows up on her door one day. "How you doing, love?" As if nothing has happened. He tells her he's got his act together, and she says she believes him, but she doesn't know he's just spent the last nine months in prison.'

'She doesn't know? Then how do you know, Kenny?'

'It doesn't matter how I know. All that matters is that the bastard's back and I'm worried about what he's going to do to Louise and Eilidh.'

Harris inflated his cheeks again and let out a slow, considered breath. 'Eilidh. I assume that's Louise's daughter? You obviously really care about them.'

Gillespie leaned forward and put down the glass. He wanted Harris to know that the next words were his, not the ouzo's. He clasped his hands together—it was enough to complete the almost solemn look that was taking him over.

'Simon, I would die if anything happened to them.'

'What are you going to do?'

'Well, first of all, I'll have to leave Pauline. I mean for good. We're over—done. She can have everything. I don't care. I just need to get away. There's nothing I can do for her. You can't save someone from themselves. She's festering. Who knows? Maybe my leaving will give her the kick up the arse she needs to change herself.'

'Do you really believe that?'

'I don't know. How would I?'

Harris didn't seem to know the answer either. He stood up and walked over to an airing cupboard. He took out a pillow and blanket and laid them on the couch next to Gillespie. There was nothing left to say.

'Thanks, Simon, you're a gentleman.'

'You're welcome, Kenny.' He paused, a new thought clearly forming in his mind, 'Am I allowed to speak candidly?'

Gillespie put the pillow behind his head and sat back.

'We've already established this, Simon. It's your flat. Be as candid as you want.'

'Okay, here goes: I know I've not known you that long, but I know you're not the kind of man who ever gives up on things—or people. It sounds to me like Pauline needs help and all you're doing is...'

'All I'm doing is what?'

'Making excuses. You're making Pauline sound bad because you want to make things easier on yourself—to justify why you're leaving. But what if she doesn't get better? What if she gets worse?'

Gillespie chewed over Harris's words. He wasn't used to this kind of candour from the sergeant. He could tell Harris was sweating over what he'd just said, as he picked up the Dalek again.

'Look, Simon. I'm the first to admit I'm not perfect. I've

dragged you out of bed and drunk half your booze and I've not even stayed with you for one night. Imagine living with me for fifteen years. But do you really think I didn't try to help Pauline? Even when she was throwing insults—and sometimes worse—at me? Let me tell you something, I tried. I tried every damn day. But, when those days turn into months and those months turn into years, it gets to you. It grinds you down—it wears you out. I'm worn out, Simon. I've got nothing left to give. Believe me, the former Mrs Gillespie is already dead inside—she couldn't get any worse.'

'I hope you're right.'

'What do you mean by that?'

'I just mean I wouldn't want to see you unintentionally increase your burden.'

Gillespie eyed Harris searchingly. It was the kind of look he usually employed in the interview room. He found nothing at fault in Harris's demeanour; he was clearly speaking the truth, or what he believed to be such. It didn't help Gillespie to hear Harris's concern, and knowing it to be genuine only made it worse. The DCI didn't know how to respond and was now cruelly aware that fatigue, and drink, were rapidly taking their toll on him. He grabbed the blanket and lay down, with his back to Harris.

'Goodnight, Simon.'

Harris walked to the door and switched off the light.

'Goodnight…sir, I mean, Kenny.'

Chapter 28

Gillespie put his hands on the side of the sink and stared into the cracked mirror of the station's gents. His hair was a mess, there were large, dark patches beneath his eyes, and a layer of greying stubble had appeared on his chin. His suit was crumpled but, worst of all, he felt as though someone was boring into his brain with a pneumatic drill. He'd chastised Harris for filling his bathroom cabinet with a selection of moisturisers that would put Boots the Chemist to shame, while neglecting to buy any paracetamol. Gillespie had gone out to his car and searched the glove compartment but found only a couple of Tic Tacs, which had at least helped to disguise the whiff of sickly aniseed from the ouzo. He'd already had a couple of comments at the station about his appearance, including—naturally—from Derek on the front desk.

'Christ, Kenny, what happened?' the sergeant had said, before following up with another of his well-worn jokes. 'Did you spend the night in a hedgerow?' The DCI could manage only a faint smile and a quick flick of the Vs before disappearing into the gents, where his dishevelled reflection now gazed back at him. He gave his face a quick wash and did his best to flatten out his hair before heading for his office.

'How are you feeling now, sir?'

Harris was sitting at his PC, watching Gillespie wash down a couple of emergency painkillers the detective had found in his desk drawer.

'I'm feeling a lot worse than I look, Simon, hard as that might be to believe. I don't think the Greek who invented that stuff of yours will be remembered in the same breath as Plato or Socrates. I'm beginning to wish you'd left it in the cupboard.'

'Perhaps Aeschylus might be a more appropriate Greek, given that he supposedly died when an eagle dropped a turtle on his head.'

Gillespie winced. 'Another fun fact from the annals of classical antiquity…Thanks for that, Simon.'

Harris turned back to his monitor.

'You'd better go through and see how the troops are doing. I'll be there in a few minutes. Thanks again for letting me stay last night.'

'Any time, sir.'

They both knew this was a barefaced lie, but decided to play along for the sake of throwing a crumpled veil over the night before.

Harris's eyes met Dickson's as he entered the incident room. She motioned him over with what he thought to be a conspiratorial tip of the head, and comely smile. If he sensed danger, he was either too flattered to care, or put it right out of his mind in favour of a gaudier fantasy.

'How's the boss? A couple of people are saying he's hung over.'

'You could say that. He drank an entire bottle of ouzo by himself.'

'Bloody hell. I can't believe he's admitted that to you.'

'He didn't have to. I watched him do it. He stayed at my place last night.'

Dickson's eyes widened. She spared her speech to a slow trickle of words, 'Oh my God!'

Harris tried to milk the comedic value of mock offence. 'Hey, sleeping in my flat isn't that terrifying a prospect, is it?'

Dickson laughed and patted him on the shoulder, with a bit more condescension than he'd have liked. 'Er, no, not so much terrifying as utterly implausible, Simon.'

He sensed his market value dive. 'Well it was obviously preferable to his house. He told me he and his wife are...' He tailed off at the look on Dickson's face, which told him Gillespie had just walked in.

'This looks like an interesting conversation. Don't stop on my account, Sergeant. What were you saying?'

Conscious of Harris's look nearing a fatal cardiac arrest, Dickson stepped in. 'Simon, DS Harris, was just asking how Nathan Chalmers was getting on in the cells.'

Gillespie took a sip of coffee and nodded. 'Was he, indeed? And how *is* Mr Chalmers getting on in the cells?'

'He's still very quiet and he still doesn't want to call his parents, or anyone else for that matter. I think he's embarrassed, to be honest.'

'Well, we can't keep him in the cells forever. What are the boffins saying about that wrench of his?'

'No word yet. Do you want to me to check with them again?' She indicated the door, edging a step towards a speedy exit.

'No, forget it. You'll only get fobbed off. I want to speak to the organ grinder, not the monkey. Get your coat, we're going to the lab.'

Dickson's pallor faded as she nodded and walked to the door. Gillespie turned to Harris. 'Simon, stay here and try to get hold of the CCTV footage from Heriot Row. Start scanning it for the day Gerald Thompson had his crash. I also want an update from the squad detectives and uniform on the Fairview interviews. If there's anything at all to report then I want to know about it. I can practically feel Bassett breathing down my neck.'

Harris's shoulders had slumped ever so slightly but, even with a hangover, Gillespie was able to pick up on it. If he had thought his boss being four sheets to the wind a few hours ago was going to herald an easy day, or that letting the DCI stay over would win him any extra brownie points, he was in for a surprise.

'Something wrong?'

'No, sir, of course not. It's just, is there any reason you don't want me to come with you to the lab?'

'Because I want you here, Simon. It's all about squad rotation. You should read Alex Ferguson's autobiography—he was the master at it. Anyway, after last night, I thought you'd be sick of the sight of me.'

Gillespie wound down the passenger-side window of his Golf and let the warm summer breeze touch his unshaven face. With Dickson behind the wheel, he fought hard against the urge to go to sleep. He did, after all, want to retain a modicum of professionalism in front of the young detective, who he suspected was on the lookout for gossipy tidbits to trade around the station.

'This isn't a regular thing, you know.'

'What's that, sir?'

'Me—coming into work with a hangover. I just don't want you to think it's the start of me going on the tear. I just fancied a drink last night. There were…extenuating circumstances.'

They'd stopped at a junction and Dickson waited until she'd moved into traffic again before answering. 'You don't need to explain yourself to me, sir.'

'I know I don't. But I know how people talk and thought you'd be just the one to set them straight.'

Gillespie grinned as widely as he could; it was sufficient to deter any response from Dickson, who engaged the clutch and shifted gear, eyes front.

The DCI looked at the time on the dusty clock on the dashboard. Quarter past nine. For the first time since he woke up, he thought of Pauline and of what she might be doing. Waking up in an empty bed was nothing new to her. He was often out the door before she woke up. But would it feel different today?

Would it feel permanent?

He looked out the window as they drove down Minto Street. As far as he could tell, every other house was a B&B. Quite a few of them had vacancies. That was useful to know, under the circumstances. He looked at his phone. Pauline hadn't tried to contact him, and he felt a pang of hurt. He then internally scolded himself for being so selfish. Would he really have felt this hurt if Louise's lights had been on and he'd been able to fall straight into bed with her? Probably not. He didn't want to have his cake and eat it. If he got to have his cake, that would be enough. The best thing he could do now was throw himself into his work, which wouldn't be difficult. That was at least one good thing about the job—it gave him little time to brood.

'Do you want to tell me about the extenuating circumstances?'

'Huh?'

Gillespie had been miles away. They'd stopped at traffic lights and Dickson was now looking at him expectantly.

'You said there were extenuating circumstances for getting drunk last night. It'd be good to know what they are, just for future reference.'

Gillespie smiled again. 'Maybe later. Just drive for now.'

The lights turned green and Dickson pulled away.

'You're the boss. Do you go to the lab often?'

'More often than I should have to. Dr Quincy's great at getting people to fob you off on the phone or with an email, but it's a lot harder to ignore someone if you hammer on their door. Besides, it's nice to get some fresh air on a day like this.'

'That's true. Erm, who's Dr Quincy?'

Stevie Sloane looked up from his computer monitor and grunted. He jabbed a Biro pen into his top pocket as he spoke, 'I'd appreciate a bit of warning next time you decide to pay us a visit, Kenny. We're very busy at the minute.'

'Detective Sergeant Gemma Dickson, meet Dr Quincy.'

'Pleased to meet you, but you're showing your age, Kenny. That show was canned way before she was even thought of…I'm Stevie Sloane, Chief Forensics Officer. Sorry you have to work with this bloody comedian.'

He turned to Gillespie. 'Are you still calling poor Clements Dr Freud?'

'He likes it. Anyway, speaking of Freud, we're here to find out about what you've made of that big tool we sent over the other day.'

Sloane rolled his eyes, but Gillespie felt he secretly liked a visit from CID. The lab was sterile and soulless, no family pictures on desks or friendly pot-plants cluttering the window ledge. Just stark white walls, worsened by intense and oppressive lighting. It felt unnatural, like a movie set or a giant experiment with everyone in a lab coat playing the role of a white mouse. Any interaction with actual human beings was surely to be a welcomed.

'If you mean the wrench, then I've got nothing to report.'

'What, nothing at all?'

'Not without the bolts from the wheel. If you can't dig up the bolts, then we can't attempt to match the scores on the wrench to them.'

'Can't you even hazard a guess?'

'No. But, for what it's worth, I do think it'd be bloody difficult to remove wheel nuts without a proper tyre iron. You'd need arms like bloody Popeye.'

He smiled and gave Gillespie a shrug before turning back to his computer.

'So, that's it?'

'That's what?'

'The sum total of your scientific analysis.'

Sloan looked wounded. 'Now you're asking for me to do the detective work as well, are you?'

'Hold on, I've got that covered eight days a week, and all the scars to prove it. What I'm asking is if the wrench had any marks on it that could indicate it had been used to remove bolts from a BMW?'

'No.'

'You sound very confident.'

'I am. Were there marks on the wrench? Yes, the thing's about two weeks older than dirt itself. Are those marks consistent with removing bolts from the wheel of a luxury vehicle? Possibly, but I don't know.'

'So now it's *possibly*?' Gillespie fought an urge to roll his eyes; there was no point in antagonising any more than he already had by his mere presence.

'If there were some indication of an unusual alloy present, there would be something to test, to match up. But there isn't.'

'It could have been removed.'

'It could. I suppose a firm wire brush would do the job. But that doesn't prove or disprove anything. I'm sorry, Kenny, I have nothing for you.'

'Nothing at all?'

'Like I said, the wrench is scored and coated in decades of hardened grease. If you had the bolts and they slotted in to the impressions then maybe we could find some unique matches. I don't know, factory impressions, wear and tear scorings, something like that.'

Gillespie put out his hands and leaned on the desk, his shoulders collapsed beneath his jacket as he shook his head. 'You're telling me that our best hope is constructing a jigsaw puzzle.'

'That sounds about right, yes.'

'I can't take that into the court.'

'Well, you can...you just might not get very far with it.'

'This is a bloody nightmare. There's nothing you can do.'

'Oh, hang on, where's my pointy wizard's hat?' He started to look in a drawer, then turned over a grey folder. 'Tch, must have misplaced it again. That and my magic wand...'

Gillespie eased himself off the desk and started to walk away. He mumbled his thanks as they headed out the door.

'Find the bolts!' shouted Sloan. 'We can talk again when you do.'

In the cold car park Gillespie lit a cigarette. Dickson avoided the puddles as they took a slow walk back to the car but the DCI proceeded straight through them.

'So, what do we do now, boss?'

Gillespie took a draw and sighed heavily. 'We'll have to let Nathan Chalmers go.'

'But he's all we've got.'

'And we've got nothing on him. As much as I'd like to, we can't hold him on possession of cocky manner.'

'Well, it should be against the law.'

The DCI glanced back at the lab. 'Might make the job a bit more lively, if that were possible.'

Chapter 29

The DCI's pounding headache had settled into a dull throb, but the visit to the lab had done nothing to improve his mood. This had been exacerbated on the drive back to the station, when he and Dickson were caught up in heavy traffic. The way he was feeling, he just wanted this day to be over. Tomorrow might be no better, but it couldn't be much worse. It was in this frame of mind that he opened the door of the incident room to see DS Harris practically bounding towards them.

'Have I got news for you!'

Gillespie grunted. 'Good news, I hope.'

'Well, sir, this is the murder squad. I'm not the Easter Bunny, so I can't promise too much, but I think you'll be pleased.'

Gillespie smiled in spite of himself as Harris assembled the team around the whiteboard. Harris opened up his laptop, pressed a few keys and an image of a car, shot from a high angle, appeared on the big screen.

Gillespie peered at the grainy picture.

'Gerald Thompson's BMW, I presume?'

'Got it in one, sir. This was taken in the early hours on the day of his crash.'

'Well, David Coleman, are you going to play the bloody film or are you going to ask me what happens next?'

Harris smiled and pressed another key. The DCI turned his

attention back to the screen. A few moments passed before a short, stocky figure could be seen walking into view and crouching by the car's front wheel. The figure fiddled around for a couple of minutes before it stood up, looked down the street and dropped something into a nearby storm drain. This wasn't like the CCTV footage in the bank that helped Gillespie and his team snare Andy Cruickshank's killers. Tricia Durham might as well have been wearing a sandwich board with her name on it. What he was watching still gave Gillespie no clear idea of who had given Thompson's BMW its unscheduled service, but the detective was now certain of one thing—the bulky figure on the screen wasn't the young man down in the cells. He was just about to say something when Harris pre-empted him.

'There's more, sir. Keep watching.'

Gillespie was now looking at a different scene, this time a pathway he recognised instantly as being along the Water of Leith, not far from the victim's flat. There was the same stocky figure, quite clearly hurling an object—presumably whatever he had used to remove the wheel bolts—into the dense undergrowth and then marching off. Harris paused the film and folded his arms, a look of immense satisfaction spreading across his youthful features. As far as Gillespie was concerned, five minutes of CCTV footage had done more than any amount of painkillers, marriage counselling or therapy could do in five years. In that instant, his hangover, his doomed marriage and his anger towards Dr Quincy and his lab team evaporated. His felt a wave of energy surge through his body, like a toy bunny that had just been given a decent set of batteries. After the frustration of driving down a Nathan Chalmers cul-de-sac, the chase to find Gerald Thompson's killer was very much back on. He sprang into action.

'Right, everyone, I want that drain lifted and I want a fingerprint search done along the riverbank. There are two wheel bolts and a tyre iron out there and I want them found, bagged and tagged, and on my desk. Now get moving.'

The team dispersed rapidly amid a flurry of conversation.

Within seconds, only Gillespie, Harris and Dickson were in the incident room. The DCI nodded towards Harris.

'I don't think you could've found much clearer shots if you'd had Stanley Kubrick behind the camera.'

'I couldn't believe what I was seeing when I came across it at first. I guess sometimes we get a break.'

'Well I was bloody due one.'

'The only problem, sir, is that it doesn't look like Nathan Chalmers is our man.'

'No, not unless he's managed to shed four stone in the space of a week. But it's a relief anyway because we have to let him go. Gemma, can you take care of that? Well done, Simon.'

Harris smiled. 'I know, I know, you'll make a detective of me yet.'

'Don't get carried away, son.'

'That's not all, anyway. I've had a look at the uniform's statements from Fairview and I think I've found something useful.'

'I hope you're right. Go on.'

'One of the sauna workers said she'd heard of some girls getting what she called "overtime" out at Fairview.'

'Overtime? What are you on about? You're telling me prossies are picking up caddying shifts now?'

'Er, not quite, sir. She said there were some after-hours get-togethers for the club members, with quite a few girls—no pun intended—jumping on the opportunity.'

'The randy old buggers. Now I can see why they don't want to admit women to their wee boys club—it would spoil their fun. This is gold, Simon. I take it this helpful young lady has supplied participants' names?'

Harris winced, conscious the well of good news he'd been drawing on for his boss had now run dry. He flashed a quick look at Dickson, hoping for some inspiration. None came.

'I'm afraid not, sir, quite the opposite in fact. She's gone to ground.'

'What?' snapped Gillespie.

'She's disappeared off the face of the earth. Obviously she spoke out of turn and she's been suitably reminded of her station, hushed up.'

Gillespie sighed. 'What's her name?'

Harris's cheeks turned red. 'Erm, Kylie. That's all we know.'

'Kylie? Jesus, I should be so bloody lucky. Get out there and find Kylie, then drag her in and throw the bloody book at her. I want names, I want dates, I want places and I want it all on a plate that I can serve up to Davy Henderson. I'll do that bastard. I swear I'll put him away for that girl's bloody murder sooner than he can say, "Orgy, anyone?"'

Chapter 30

On the few occasions he and Pauline had ever gone to dinner parties, Gillespie would invariably get into some kind of argument with another guest. He never felt comfortable in that kind of environment, especially if he was required to make merry with his wife's university colleagues. Everything about them seemed fake, down to the smiles they pasted to their faces when he told them he was a cop. If they really had to socialise with these people, why couldn't they do it over a few pints down the pub instead of a manufactured social crucible? Everyone round the table seemed to be living in a world of make-believe, regurgitating the same *Question Time* talking points. It amazed him how these apparent intellectuals all read from the same script. Not one used their eyes or reasoning to deduce why we were in the state we were in.

The only things he cared about were the dangers thrown up by real life. While he sometimes relied on instinct to help him catch a criminal, the only way he could truly get results was with hard evidence. That's why he'd ended up scoffing at one of Pauline's friends over the After Eights. Gillespie would never forget his name because he'd yet to come across another so pretentious. He was called Christopher but went by the name of 'Tofe'. What was wrong with 'Chris', for god's sake? He managed to bite his tongue for a couple of courses, as Tofe aired his forthright opinions on the state of the nation, but everything changed when he launched into an impassioned rant about the proliferation of CCTV on the streets of Edinburgh.

'It's a complete invasion of privacy,' he'd said, to nods of agreement around the table. 'Sometimes I feel like we're living in some kind of Orwellian nightmare.'

Gillespie slammed down his glass. 'I feel like I'm in an Orwellian nightmare having to listen to you all night. Let me tell you something, *Tofe*, I can give you a list of murderers, rapists and various other bastards I've put behind bars thanks to CCTV. Do you want me to put you in touch with some of the grieving relatives to ask how they feel about it? You can go on until you're blue in the face about how it infringes on your civil liberties, but I can assure you we've got better things to do than watch you flouncing down the pavement. If you don't like CCTV, then you can take a long walk off Wigan bloody Pier.'

He raised his glass and downed the rest of his brandy, feeling particularly pleased with himself. The other guests were shocked, Pauline mumbled some excuse about stress and tiredness, but they were never invited back. The DCI didn't care. He had to put up with enough crap in his line of work without having to take even more from someone like Tofe. He hadn't thought about the incident for years but, as he and Dickson made their way to Heriot Row, he wondered what the opinionated amateur thesp would have to say now. Not that Gillespie cared for the views of a repeater, someone who had their opinions spoon-fed by mainstream media, but it was fun to watch their egos deflate so publicly, and there was always the chance that some of the less far gone might learn something about themselves.

The socos were already in the midst of searching the storm drain while he and the sergeant parked up. They went into the building to see if any of the neighbours were home but, again, Gillespie's knocks were greeted with silence.

'I'm beginning to wonder if anyone actually lives in this place. Maybe Nathan Chalmers drove everyone away with his ghetto blaster.'

Dickson sniggered. 'Ghetto blaster, sir? Yes, I'm sure Run-DMC wouldn't go down well around here.'

'If I knew what you were talking about, I'd put you on report. Come on, let's see if they've found anything.'

Gillespie didn't have to wait too long for his eureka moment. After another half hour of various foul-smelling detritus being pulled from the drain, a soco triumphantly handed the DCI what they'd been searching for. Two metal bolts, deep grooves around the edges where they'd been forcibly removed from Gerald Thompson's car. Gillespie slipped the bolts into an evidence bag and handed it to Dickson.

'That should keep Dr Quincy away from *The Times* crossword this afternoon.'

Dickson gave a distracted nod. Her attention was taken down the street to an agitated resident furiously wafting a hand in front of his nose as he neared the open drain. 'Sir, I think we have an incoming complaint.'

Gillespie turned round to see the man covering his nose with a handkerchief and stomping towards them.

'What's all this fuss about?' His voice was muffled under the hanky, but the disgruntled tone was still detectable.

'A man's died, sir,' said Dickson.

'A man's *what*?'

Gillespie answered. 'A man has died, he lived here. Do you live nearby, sir?'

'Yes.' He put down an overloaded Aldi bag, but kept the hanky in place. 'Right over there.'

'Then you'll likely know him as your neighbour, Gerald Thompson?'

The man lowered his face, covering to reveal a look of surprise; Gillespie clocked it and calculated his age at around mid-forties.

'He's dead? How?'

'A fatal road accident. We're treating it as suspicious. Are you available to answer a few questions? We won't take up too much of your time.'

The man revealed to the officers that his name was Craig Stott. Jabbering constantly, he led them inside and upstairs into a tiny, sparsely furnished studio apartment. The place wasn't as tastefully appointed as some of his neighbours' properties: a single-bed at one end and a Baby Belling cooker perched on a set of chipboard shelves at the other. Gillespie guessed the studio had once been attic space that was opportunistically made into a flat; he wondered how much the rent was on such cramped quarters, and if he might be looking for something similar very soon.

Stott lifted the Aldi bag on to a small folding table and started to empty the contents—which appeared to be entirely composed of cans of budget lager.

'I hope you didn't have to carry them far,' said Gillespie.

Stott smiled as he opened a fridge about the size of a shoebox and crammed in the cans. 'Not too far, but I don't mind anyway. It's good exercise.'

'You must have arms like Popeye.' Out of the corner of his eye, he could tell Dickson had shot him a look. He didn't return it.

Gillespie scanned the rest of the flat as Stott unpacked his shopping. The place was sparse, but spotless. In the 'kitchen' end, on a shelf beneath the two-ring cooker, was an enamel cereal bowl, with a knife, fork and spoon lined up next to it. Like his groceries, and like the long, grey coat he was now hanging on a nail in the wall, there was something stoic about Craig Stott.

The bed linen was so crease-free that Gillespie wondered if Stott slept standing up. There was no television, only a small analogue radio on the windowsill, and nothing in the way of pictures, only an expanse of yellowing bare walls.

'What is it you do for a living?' said Gillespie.

Stott went and stood by the window, hands deep in his pockets. 'I'm between jobs.'

'What did you do?'

'I was in the Forces. Twenty years man and boy.'

The DCI had met plenty of ex-Forces personnel over the years, some of whom he'd arrested and others he'd worked alongside. In almost every case, however, they would always tell him how proud they'd been to serve with the such and such fusiliers in Afghanistan or on HMS what have you in the Gulf. Stott didn't elaborate, so Gillespie asked him another question.

'What did you do after you left the Forces?'

'A bit of security.'

Again, nothing.

'How long have you lived here?'

'A month.'

'Have you had any encounters with Mr Thompson during that time?'

Stott momentarily looked skyward, as though illustrating that he was trying to remember. He shook his head. 'No, I don't think so.'

'You don't *think* so?'

'Well, I may have said "hello" once or twice. Nothing of any note.'

Gillespie took a step closer and met Stott's gaze, the ex-soldier never flinched.

'Can I show you something, Mr Stott?'

He didn't wait for an answer. He reached into his jacket pocket and pulled out the evidence bag containing the bolts from the storm drain. He held it up about six inches from Stott's nose.

'What do you make of those?'

He peered at the objects inside the polythene. He gave a shrug. 'What are they? Bolts?'

Gillespie slipped the bag back into his pocket. 'Someone removed them from the front wheel of Mr Thompson's car prior to the crash.'

'I don't know anything about it.'

'Are you sure?'

'I'm absolutely certain.'

Gillespie nodded and then signalled to Dickson. 'Do you mind if Sergeant Dickson and I have a thorough look around your flat?'

'Am I under suspicion?'

'I don't know yet.'

Stott opened his arms, inviting the detectives to carry on. Gillespie looked under the bed and hauled out a battered, brown suitcase. He unzipped and sifted through the clothes inside. Gillespie was no fashion expert, but he knew none of the items could be termed designer. He also noted there was no chest of drawers. Stott really was living out of a suitcase.

He searched the minuscule bathroom, into which builders had somehow squeezed a toilet, sink and shower-mounted bath. On top of the cistern, a couple of roll-on deodorants, a tub of hair gel and a bottle of Old Spice stood in a perfect row. Even the man's toiletries were regimented. He re-entered the living room, shaking his head. Nothing.

Gillespie turned to Stott, who clearly felt vindicated. 'Where were you on Tuesday night—the night before Mr Thompson's crash?'

'Here, at home.'

'Can anyone confirm that?'

'I was alone. Look, I've not done anything. I don't even know this banker.'

Gillespie looked confused. 'Who says he was a banker?'

'Didn't you say it, when you came in?'

'No, I did not.'

For a moment, Stott's demeanour altered. It was almost imperceptible, like a thought occurring behind his eyes—if anyone had blinked, they would have missed it entirely—but Gillespie never blinked.

'Why don't you put your coat back on, Mr Stott? I've got some footage down at the station I'd like you to see.'

'Is it really necessary?'

'You'd be assisting with the investigation, perhaps even helping us find out how one of your neighbours died.'

'But I've already told you, I don't know anything.'

'Don't you want to help us discover how Mr Thompson died?'

Stott's mouth remained shut, his lips a taut wire.

Chapter 31

Gillespie let out an elongated sigh as the hourglass symbol appeared on his computer screen. He rubbed his forehead as the symbol began its achingly slow rotation, like a tiny space capsule aligning its orbit with a non-existent mother ship. He'd recently read a biography of one of the Apollo astronauts. He found it fascinating that it took television pictures from the Moon little over a second to travel a quarter of a million miles to Mission Control in Texas. How could that be? How, fifty years ago, could they broadcast live pictures across the vacuum of space when his PC couldn't communicate with a printer sitting two inches away?

He was on the verge of ripping the machine from the desk and launching it into the stratosphere when the printer clicked into life. Two minutes later, he was leafing through the service and employment records of Craig Stott. After casting his eye over his long, but not particularly distinguished, military career, he passed them to Dickson. She read aloud as she scanned the documents.

'Joined the Army straight from school. Served in Iraq twice and then Afghanistan. Twenty years in the Army but didn't make it beyond Lance-Corporal.'

'Not everyone's cut out for leadership, Sergeant.' He immediately realised his remark carried an unintentional edge to it;

he noticed Dickson recoil.

'I suppose not,' she said. 'But his service record is spotless.'

'Most of the ones we see are. It's when they come out that they start to blot their copybook.'

'It must be tough on Civvy Street after all those years of not having to think for yourself.'

'Harsh, Gemma, and such little respect for the men willing to make the ultimate sacrifice so you can sit at home watching *Strictly* in peace and quiet, your only care being that you might be running low on designer gin.'

'I didn't mean...' She sounded defensive, like she'd been backed into a corner she had never actually intended for herself.

Gillespie felt the sharp point of his conscience prodding him. 'I know, don't mind me, you know I'm like a bear with a sore head on a good day...I'm just trying to remind you—in my own clumsy fashion—that it's a bit more complicated than most people credit it, with the ex-service men. For some of them, it's like being separated from their families—the only one they've ever known. Anyone would find it hard to adjust.'

'Some seem to find it easier to adjust than others, sir.'

'They do, but they're generally the ones with the support network at their back. Think of it like this: you're a young lad, you've been passed from pillar to post your whole life—foster care, maybe adoption, care homes, young offenders. Then you're told, right you're a man now and you're on your own. You don't know how to cope and the Army seems like the best of a bad bunch of options. Yeah, you might get yourself killed, but you won't need to worry about dealing with the real world. It's an escape route for them, it becomes a source of comfort, a sad, almost perverse comfort you might say, but for many of them it's the only kind they've ever known.'

Gemma looked contemplative, a crestfallen expression that Gillespie had rarely seen on her. He wondered what new neural pathways were being formed behind her eyes. They shared a few moments of silence before Harris appeared in the doorway, coughing dramatically into his fist.

'Yes, Simon, what is it now?'

Harris patted the laptop tucked under his arm.

'Oh, I see you've found the solution to global warming...'

'Erm, sir?' Sometimes Gillespie's humour was too abstruse for even Harris.

'Never mind. I take it our custody's ready.'

'Yes, sir.'

The two men headed downstairs and entered the interview room where Stott, dressed in a white shirt and dark trousers, was waiting for them. Gillespie honed in on a regimental tattoo beneath one of Stott's rolled-up sleeves—a permanent reminder to the tribal family he'd left behind. The muscular forearms rested on the table, thick fingers drumming a jagged rhythm; did time pass more slowly outside of the regiment? It looked like it to Gillespie. He circled the small table and paused before the two empty chairs on his side—all the while Stott's gaze followed him; his head didn't move, though, and his posture stayed ramrod straight.

'Sorry to keep you waiting, Mr Stott. Or do you mind if I call you Craig?' said Gillespie. He placed a manila folder on the table. It sat accusingly between them as the detective took his chair.

A noncommittal shrug. 'Either suits me.'

'Very well, Craig. We've taken a bit of a look at your military service record. Twenty years, three wars. In any other field you'd be flying high now, sitting pretty.'

'I'm no glory hunter.'

'That's not why men like you join up, then?'

'No. It isn't. It's for the pride of defending Queen and country.'

'That sounds admirable. Did they write that down somewhere for you?'

'Are you trying to be funny?'

Gillespie grinned, confident he'd dented some of Stott's

armour. 'We're not that different you and me. I started in uniform. I don't do this job for a flashy motor and a lavish expense account. I'd be bloody disappointed if I did.'

Stott shook his head. 'It's not the same.'

'Isn't it?'

'No. You wouldn't understand…'

Gillespie kept his gaze on the man in front of him for a moment, wondering if he'd actually made any inroads at all with him. The detective opened up the file and started to speak again, 'Today we're actually more interested in what you did after you left the Forces.'

'Oh, yeah.'

'Specifically, I'd like to hear about your stint at McCluskie's Bank.'

'There's nothing to tell. They let me go.'

'Why?'

'You'd better ask them.'

'Will they tell me that it had anything to do with Mr Thompson?'

'No, why would they?'

'You both worked there. You get fired and then you went and rented a flat next door to him. Do you expect me just to treat that as some sort of coincidence?'

Stott shifted in his seat. His shoulders lost some of their angular tension. 'I had to leave my old place,' he said. 'I couldn't afford the rent.'

'And you blame Thompson for that?' Gillespie tried to make the remark sound as pointed as he could.

'No!' Stott bridled. 'What is this?'

'Show him the footage, Simon.'

Harris opened up the laptop and tapped at the keys. The screen began to fill with a video-player. The now familiar scene of Heriot Row appeared, the stocky figure crouching down by the wheel of the BMW and disposing of the bolts. Stott stared at the moving image. He wasn't giving away much, but Gillespie noticed a slight flicker of the eyes as the reality of what he was watching dawned on him. Maybe he was wishing he'd found a more secluded spot to perform the operation, or that he'd got to work on the CCTV camera before he started on his neighbour's car. He seemed almost disappointed in himself, critical.

'It's fairly definitive isn't it, Craig?'

Stott tried to play it cool, but he started to shuffle in his seat, a reddening tinge creeping up the front of his neck.

'That could be anyone,' he blurted.

'You recognised those bolts earlier.'

'No, I didn't.'

'I bet you thought you'd seen the last of them, didn't you?' said Gillespie. 'I must say, you looked pretty shocked when I told you Gerald Thompson died.'

'Why would I want to kill him?'

'I never said you *wanted* to kill him. I think you just wanted to give him a scare, get your own back for getting you sacked. It must be hard for you, trying to settle back in to civilian life, and then your job's taken away'

'You're making this up as you go along.'

'I hear he wasn't a very nice man.'

'I wouldn't know.'

'What was it his own daughter called him, Simon?'

Harris spoke slowly, deliberately. 'A bastard.'

'That's right, his daughter called him a bastard. Was he a bastard, Craig? Did he look down his nose at you when you were working on the door? He couldn't talk to you like that, could he? You were someone—Her Majesty's Armed Forces.'

Stott's top lip had begun to glisten. He took out a chewing-gum-coloured hankie and wiped his brow. The loud, confident voice was growing soft. 'I'm not saying another word.'

Gillespie spoke again, 'Play the second piece of footage please, Simon.'

Stott rubbed his chin nervously as he stared at the screen. The eyes flickered again, his brain desperately trying to think of a way out.

'We've got a team out there right now looking for the wrench you threw away,' said Gillespie. 'It's only a matter of time before they find it and, when they do, you'll have to own up.'

'I want a lawyer.'

'It'll have your prints on it. Won't it, Craig?'

'I'm not saying another word. Not another word.'

'Well, you'll have plenty of time to think about that, because you're not going anywhere. You know the right thing to do: you're outmanoeuvred and outgunned. Think very carefully about your next move, Craig.'

The detectives stood in the corridor as they watched Stott being led away to the cells, his shoulders slumped.

'He's not very good at hiding it, is he, sir?"

'No, he's too bloody honest. He'll cough eventually—it's eating him from the inside.'

'What do you think happened?'

'Who knows? Perhaps Thompson gave him a funny look.'

'Seems like a brutal response.'

'Someone trained to suppress all emotion acting brutally? You do surprise me.'

'Maybe he snapped.'

'Maybe, Simon, maybe.'

They walked round the corner and were almost sent flying by Dickson as she bolted down the stairs.

'Woah there, Gemma. Where's the fire?' said Gillespie.

He tailed off. He could see the panic in her eyes.

'What's wrong, Gemma?'

'Sir, there's been a call from casualty. It's your wife.'

Chapter 32

Gillespie found himself receiving a strange sort of reassurance by listening to the repetitive beeps of Pauline's ECG monitor. He stood in a languorous stupor, disbelieving that the image before him was that of his wife. As he peered through the hospital ward window, the tableau seemed to have been arranged for shock value, as if to jolt him back to some semblance of the man he once was. Surely this wasn't real, because if it were, then he had lost all hold on reality.

It was the first time he'd seen his wife since she screamed him out of the house. That angry exchange, the dudgeon burning in her eyes, came back now. Was she really so full of hate? Did he have that effect on her? Just being there, just inhabiting the same breathing space seemed enough to put his wife into apoplexy. None of it made sense to him. There had been times when they had been blissful in each other's company, but those times seemed long ago now, buried under mounds of the past. They had gone and he knew they could never be recovered. He felt a pang of shame—not for the past times—for the fact there really were no feelings lurking in him at all.

Pauline was either asleep or heavily sedated. She looked anything but peaceful, however, she did look familiar. She looked like she'd just gorged herself on a mound of junk food that had rendered her inert in the rampaging floods of glucose. It was such a well-worn image in his mind that the chunks of matted hair, clinging to her pale forehead, had no impact on him. Only a large needle attached to a plastic tube buried in the back of her hand seemed to disrupt the scene. It made her slovenly appearance seem different, somehow. She looked so helpless, so alone.

'Her blood pressure is very high,' said the doctor. 'You can go in, but no longer than five minutes, please.'

Gillespie wanted to argue, to say that he'd stay in there as long as wanted, but he instead nodded meekly and slipped into the room. How did you deal with a situation like this? How did others deal with it—did they blame him? He'd watched something on YouTube once, a few minutes from a longer documentary, about a morbidly obese woman who filmed herself and posted the images on the internet. She was an American, and that threw him at the time—he didn't make the connection to his own situation—but he recalled now she had a partner who kept her supplied with milkshakes and burgers and bucket-sized tubs of ice cream. Was that who he was? Was he Pauline's enabler? Was all this his fault, as much as it was anyone's?

He crouched by the bedside and took his wife's hand; it felt different from how he remembered. It had been many years since he'd last touched her hand with any affection. Pauline's hands were no longer the dainty things they once were. Like so many other things about her, they'd changed beyond recognition. What had happened to the girl he married? He caught sight of his reflection in the window, a gaunt, stooping figure he hardly recognised any more. What had the years done to them?

Gillespie dropped Pauline's hand and glanced at his watch. The first of his five minutes had already passed. He wanted her to wake up, to know he was by her side. He gave her a gentle nudge; it seemed a pathetic movement and he regretted it immediately. Her eyelids flickered, like she was smarting in bright sunlight, and then slowly her eyes opened. She turned her head in his direction, it looked uncomfortable, forcing the heavy folds of flesh beneath her chin to constrict. She took him in, but her gaze was distant.

'I didn't think I was going to do it.' The voice was soft, seemed far away. All the usual sharpness was blunted by exhaustion. 'I lined up all the little pills on the kitchen table and I just sat there staring at them for almost an hour. After a while, they didn't look like pills at all. I don't know what I thought they looked like, but it seemed the easiest thing in the world to just put them in my mouth, one by one, and that was that.'

Gillespie was confused, lost in his own pride and in pity with Pauline. 'How? I mean, who found you?' he said.

A shadow of a smile crossed his wife's lips. 'A Yodel driver. I think he was there with my new bird bath for the garden. I had the door handle in my hand. I must have collapsed on him. Oh god, I'm so embarrassed.'

She began to sob gently, like beginning the dawn of a kind of realisation. Gillespie tried to picture the scene: the unsuspecting delivery driver, lying flat out, his wife—in her dirty pink dressing gown—lying unconscious on top of him. For a split second, he felt embarrassed for himself, and was then furious with his mind for taking him there.

'We'll get you sorted out, don't worry. We'll get through this.'

Pauline shook her head. 'You don't need to pretend for me, Kenny.'

'What do you mean? I'm here for you, Pauline.'

'When I thought about it, I'd known for weeks, months even. I've been living in denial, pretending she's not real.' She paused and stared at him. Her pale blue eyes were now fully focussed on her husband, but her voice was still a whisper. 'Is she pretty?'

'Pauline, stop it,' Gillespie bit. 'You're my priority now.'

'No, I'm not. I've not been that for a long time. It's okay, Kenny. I can't say I blame you. Look at me, for Christ's sake— I'm like the back end of a bus.'

Gillespie shook his head, maybe a bit too vigorously. No, he wasn't attracted to her in the way he once was, but he wanted to tell her that her appearance wasn't the issue—it was just a physical manifestation of the lazy, spiteful, self-pitying person she'd become. Somehow, he didn't think saying this would help matters, so he instead tried distraction: 'Don't be stupid.'

Pauline ignored him and carried on. 'They had one of those agony aunts on *Richard and Judy* the other day. She was a psychologist or a psychiatrist, I don't know which. Anyway, she said, "How can you expect anyone to love you more than you love yourself?" And I thought, "How can you?" I hate myself, Kenny. I hate what I've become, and I know you do, too.'

Gillespie continued to shake his head. He didn't want to hear this. It had been a thought pushed so far from his mind for so long that it was like an unwelcome intruder in his thoughts now.

'Pauline, how can you say that?'

'It's true. That's why I don't even blame you. That's the real tragedy, when I think about all the things you've done with her, I can't even hate you back—no matter how hard I try.'

The DCI attempted to process her words, but it was too much. The guilt, the remorse, had robbed him of the power to function properly, let alone find the right thing to say. The word 'sorry' was the least Pauline deserved right now, but even this was beyond him.

The door opened and the doctor stepped into the small room. His presence was like a release of all the tension that had built up in there. Gillespie's time was up.

'Your wife needs rest,' said the doctor.

The detective wondered if he should kiss Pauline on the forehead, but it didn't seem right. He made a bumbling gesture, a lunge for her elbow with his fingers that edged dangerously close to a slap.

'I'll come back soon, okay?' he said. 'They'll take care of you.'

Pauline didn't reply. Her eyes filled with tears. She pulled her hand towards her mouth and turned to face the window.

Gillespie felt drained, emotionally as well as physically, as he left his wife. He waited outside the room for the doctor, as if there were essential words to be exchanged, but the doctor stayed inside the small room with his wife. The detective felt exposed in the warm, over-lit hallway. There was no one to turn to; like so much of adult life, the reaction to disaster had to be made up in the moment of crisis itself. He was so utterly bereft and alone that even instinct deserted him, until he quickly gathered his emotions, and realised the solution was to carry on. Just keep going, putting one foot in front of the other, like he always had done.

He was walking through the hospital foyer, listening to the prominent clacks of his footfalls, and trying to extract his parking pass from his wallet, when he heard a familiar voice.

'Hello, sir.'

Gillespie looked up and smarted. 'What are you doing here, Simon?'

The DS held out one of his surprisingly soft-looking hands. 'I never gave you a key. I got a new one cut today.'

The detective looked away, and continued to walk out the door towards the car park. 'Thanks, Simon, but I won't need it. I'm going home.'

There was a moment of what Gillespie read as slightly hurt silence before Harris spoke again. 'How's Mrs Gillespie?'

'Your guess is as good as mine,' said the DCI as he punched his pin number into the parking machine.

'So, er, what about Louise?'

Gillespie stopped and turned to him, his jaw set firm. 'What about her?'

'I just thought...'

'Simon, my wife nearly died on account of me.'

Harris bowed his head. 'I understand.'

'Do you?...Jesus Christ, I wish I bloody-well did.'

Chapter 33

The familiar odour hit Gillespie as soon as he opened the front door. The smell of sick was one he could never get used to, not even after those early years working the beat on Friday and Saturday nights, arresting people too drunk to remember their own name. More than once he went home with his uniform covered in the stuff. He felt his mouth go dry. He stood there with the door open, letting some much-needed fresh air into the house.

The bright yellow stain on the carpet was unavoidable. This was where Pauline had thrown up after collapsing on the delivery driver. The old images flooded back, their potency diminishing none with the short passage of time. He couldn't face cleaning up right now. It could wait until tomorrow. He closed the door and stepped into the hall. He heard a noise. Voices? At first he thought it was coming from outside, but he then realised it was coming from the living room. The television was still on. Yet another stupid game show—this one with what looked like conjoined twins as hosts—was in full flow. He switched on the light and hunted about for the remote control. After several frustrating minutes of throwing aside magazines and cushions, he found it wedged down the side of the couch.

Gillespie hit the off switch and hurled the remote against the wall, the plastic shattering with a loud crack followed by the batteries dropping on to the floor. They could stay there; the room felt alien to him now, it was Pauline's lair. Nowhere in the house seemed like home to him any more. It hadn't for a long time.

He surveyed the shambolic surrounds and collected up what discarded litter and debris he could find. In the kitchen, he flicked on the light switch with his elbow before negotiating the handle of the back door and dumped the trash in the bin. He didn't take the time to check which coloured bin he was lobbing them into. He just wanted them out of the house. If the city council wanted to send him a bill for daring to use the wrong one, he'd tell them where they could stick their receptacles.

With the smell of sick finally gone from his nostrils, Gillespie realised he hadn't eaten, and probably should if he wanted to continue functioning. Finding nothing in the fridge, he began to open cupboards. They weren't bare, but they might as well have been. Each one was stuffed with junk food. He was half tempted by a Pot Noodle, until he saw it was a bootleg version with the ingredients written in a language he didn't recognise. The real thing was haute cuisine by comparison.

On the counter was a large, unopened box from Amazon. He ripped apart the cardboard to find a set of brand-new saucepans. He shook his head. The only chance of them being used was if Jamie Oliver dropped in. There was a deafening clang as he upended the box on the counter. He then began to stuff the box full of noodles, crisps and chocolate bars from the cupboard. After several trips outside, the bin was beginning to overflow so he took to hurling Kit-Kats and Twixes on to the lawn. He threw out the empty box, for what seemed like good measure, and slammed the door.

Gillespie momentarily wondered what the neighbours might have thought had they seen him decorating his back garden with confectionary, but then concluded that he didn't give a damn what his neighbours thought. There may yet be a call at some undisclosed point in the future from one of the sticky-beaks that passed for the *bien pensant* round his way, probably complaining about attracting vermin. He vowed to be prepared for such an eventuality, and have a suitable rejoinder at the ready.

He lit a cigarette and started to feel its calming influence. Though his heart-rate had dropped a few beats, he knew he wouldn't be back in the safe zone until he took some action. A wash of wild thoughts flooded through his mind. He was Pauline's enabler, just like the weedy dude who supplied the YouTube blimp with milkshakes. He was a philanderer, a cheat. He'd been a husband but now he wasn't even worthy of that title. He'd driven his wife to despair, to suicide, for God's sake. He thought about that, let the message mingle with his imagination and wondered how he might feel at Pauline's funeral. He didn't care what people would say, or think of him, but he did care how he rated himself. It was the fact he could still get up every morning and look himself in the mirror that allowed him to keep doing his job. If he lost that, then absolutely everything was lost. It was the job, the sense of righteousness that it lent to him, that kept everything on the level. He needed to act.

'No time like the present,' was it his old man's voice? He couldn't tell. He quite often wondered where all these traditional gems of wisdom he carried came from. Some were surely his father's but there was another voice too.

He would phone Louise and tell her it was over. Yes, it would hurt, but the pain would pass. It was temporary, like everything else. Right now, his biggest concern had to be Pauline. He had married her, those vows meant something. What kind of a man ignored his responsibilities? What kind of a man deserted those in their most desperate hour of need?

He looked up Louise's number—she was listed as 'Brian' in his contacts, something he thought would be a foolproof way of keeping his dirty little secret—and pressed the green button. He let it ring a couple of times before hanging up.

A cramp lodged itself in his chest, spread up his neck into his throat.

He couldn't do it. He couldn't locate the words, even if he'd wanted to.

He put the phone on the table and buried his head in his hands. Was he going to be a failure at this too? What a mess. What a bloody mess he'd created for everyone.

Seconds later, his phone began to buzz. He snatched it and held it to his ear.

'Louise?'

'Er, no, sir. It's Simon.'

Gillespie wished he'd checked the number first. The ache in his chest vanished. 'What is it, Simon?' he snapped.

'It's Kylie, sir.'

'*What?*' he snapped.

'You asked me to tell you as soon as we'd found her.'

The DCI's thought process was about as malleable as lead. He had a wife in hospital and a mistress he'd left hanging. The last thing he needed was a colleague talking in riddles.

'What are you going on about, son?'

'The street worker, sir.'

Gillespie greeted the politically correct term with his usual disdainful silence.

'The prostitute, sir. The one who told us about the late-night get-togethers at Fairview.'

'Right, yes, I remember now. Great. Is she at the station?'

'No, sir. She's at home, in Leith.'

'Christ, the Links, I imagine. It'll be a nice, easy commute.'

'No, sir. She lives in Dalmeny Street—it's just off the Walk.'

'I know where it is. Be there in twenty minutes, Simon.'

He ended the call, rose briskly and shoved the phone in his pocket.

Gillespie's loud curses were drowning out the sound of the heavy-beating rain. He'd never got round to buying new wiper blades for the Golf and now every shuddering scrape across the windscreen made him wince. It was coming down in stair-rods.

There were some days that the detective could see Edinburgh through the rose-tinted glasses of its tourists. It was beautiful, historic and deservedly spectacular in some places. But today wasn't one of those days. Today, as he drove through the capital's streets beneath the grey skies and black clouds, all his eyes could focus on were the things VisitScotland left off its website.

He saw drunks weaving their way into the road, he saw litter strewn across the pavements and, when he stopped at a set of lights, he watched a young couple having a blazing row outside a pub. Why did he ever move into the city? It certainly didn't seem the kind of place he'd ever want to start a family. His own childhood had been filled with fresh air and wide-open spaces, and he'd spent virtually his entire adult life longing to go back there. He thought of little Eilidh and how much she'd love to live out in the country. He'd been planning to take her and her mum on the new Borders Railway, to have a day out, maybe even a picnic, and show them where he grew up. But it was too late now, or was it? Could he really bear to let them go? They were, after all, the only thin rays of a vanishing sunshine in his grim existence.

If Gillespie thought his own house was a tip, it had nothing on Kylie's. There was a school of thought among some estate agents that an empty property gave potential buyers the illusion of greater space. This girl's furniture amounted to a single mattress on the floor—several condom wrappers lying next to it—but the flat still looked tiny, not to mention filthy. The windowsill was home to an ashtray overflowing with cigarette butts, while, in the middle of the floor, lay a crushed Red Bull can.

Kylie herself looked exactly as Gillespie imagined the person who lived here to look. She was small, skinny, and in her late teens but with a haggard expression that added a good ten years to her face. Her cheeks were so sunken, he reckoned a good artist could limn her skull in perfect detail, with little effort. Her lank brown hair was scraped back in a ponytail so tight that he was convinced it was holding up her eyebrows. He looked her up and down. He reckoned she probably had five years of sexual market value left—if she lived another five years.

'Okay, love, talk.'

'I'm saying nothing.'

'Look, I don't think that playing the silly wee lassie has been a successful strategy for you so far. Maybe it's time to think again.'

Kylie scowled, at least Gillespie thought it was a scowl. It was hard to tell given the unusual contours of her face and the absence of muscle tone.

'I want a fag,' she demanded.

Harris reached into his coat pocket and produced a packet of Rothmans—a sweetener he kept for occasions like this—but struggled to remove the cellophane. Gillespie snatched the packet and impatiently threw it to her.

'Here, have the pack, Kylie.'

She ripped into the packet, pulled out a cigarette and lit up. She pointed at Harris. 'He said you'd keep my name out of it.'

'Simon makes a lot of promises.'

'I'll lose my job if Hendy finds out.'

The DCI laughed. 'And I bet the retirement package from Davy Henderson is a belter as well.'

'*What?*'

'Look, love, I'll do what I can, but I want names and dates, and I can't guarantee I won't have to put you on the witness stand.'

She took a long, thoughtful draw on her cigarette. Gillespie watched as a lengthy cylinder of ash appeared where there had once been a tightly-rolled tube of tobacco.

'It was all the high-flyers from the golf club, like.'

'Go on.'

'Hendy was playing up to them, really laying it on, so he was. I'd never seen him playing up to anyone, so he must've wanted something from them. It was all this "happy to be of service" nonsense, and all this "ask and you'll receive". We were told to give them whatever they wanted, no question. They were all decrepit old men as well—mind you, none of them had any bother getting it up, though.'

'Viagra is indeed a miracle, so I'm told,' said Gillespie. 'And where did this happen?'

'At the golf club, in the actual clubhouse, with the wood panels on the walls and the plush tartan carpets. We all got swapped about like pieces of meat. It was shocking in a way but you get used to that sort of thing. I just thought it was funny, with all the old giffers sloshing the malt whisky about and just grabbing you. It was kind of all a big joke, I don't think the old boys could believe their luck, really. They were all legless. But Hendy paid us, paid us well.'

'And Elena, was she there?'

Kylie nodded. The humorous recollection left her face.

'On the night she died?'

She nodded again.

'I can't hear you, Kylie.'

The girl snapped. 'Yes, she was there. There was a scuffle.'

'What do you mean?'

'Hendy showed up and told us to get out. He was spewing about something. The place just changed in a matter of seconds. There was no laughing and carry on now. All the old bastards were really pissed and some went apeshit and started slapping us about. The girls weren't having it, though. It got nasty. Really nasty. There was biting and scratching...and then we all got thrown out.'

'Out where?'

'Out of the club. Some of the girls walked up to the main road and flagged down taxis or passing cars and that.'

'And what about Elena?'

'She wasn't dressed. She couldn't find her dress, one of the old gits had hidden it. I stayed behind for a bit, and she found her dress, but I wanted to go up to the road with the others and she wanted to set off across the golf course.'

Gillespie could feel himself getting angry. He'd been lied to, and the thought rankled.

'So Elena went off on her own?'

Kylie paused, then her voice cracked, 'We left her there.'

Chapter 34

Gillespie was glad to step out of the oppressive confines of Kylie's cramped flat. He felt like he had been breathing the musty air for too long. What was it about junkies and prossies that they seemed able to exist on stale air? Did it just never occur to them to open a window? On the way down the dark stairwell, he looked back at Kylie's door. The paint was peeling off the panels in long strips, hanging there in leprous flakes like some strange symbol for what went on beyond. He wondered about the girl, about her state of mind. It had been a long time since he stopped caring about Kylie and her sort; he knew you couldn't allow yourself to care on the job. There were too many of them, waifs and strays, the dregs of humanity.

'Everything all right, sir?' said Harris, turning his head back towards the flat to follow the line of Gillespie's gaze.

'Did you see that?'

'See what?' Harris turned back to face the DCI. 'The girl…Kylie?'

'Aye, the way that despite everything she'd done to herself, the million and one ways she'd destroyed any semblance of humanity in herself, she still cared.'

'About Elena?'

'Exactly. She didn't care a damn for herself any more but she cared about that girl. Why?'

Harris shrugged. 'It might just be an instinct, a residual impulse.'

'Like a corpse twitching, you mean? Maybe you're right.' The detective continued down the stairs, his mind awash with strange thoughts. He was finding it difficult to process this case and he wondered if he was up to the job. Was there too much on his plate? Had the incident with Pauline affected his judgement? He hoped it hadn't, because there was only one way to work this job and that was with your eyes open and your attention undivided. He couldn't afford to lose focus.

Outside the night air was cool. A hint of haar was settling over the skyline, blocking out the familiar shape of the Walk. The city looked even more uninviting without its signposts, its conspicuous markers. Gillespie could live without seeing Edinburgh Castle ever again; it was for tourists and weekenders, city-breakers. It meant nothing to him, none of the history or the lore; these medieval streets were where blood ran between the cobbles as far as he was concerned. The famous churchyards and tourist traps were crime scenes, sights of murders and rapes. They had no other meaning left to the detective.

Gillespie lit a cigarette and then checked his watch under the glow of a streetlight.

'Right, get them in,' he said bluntly.

Harris raised an eyebrow. 'Now, sir?'

Gillespie took another draw on his cigarette and nodded. 'Right now. I want them in a divvy van. I don't care if they're fast asleep and I don't care if they're watching *Heartbeat* with a mug of Horlicks. Bring them in their bloody jammies if you have to. I want them all to know we're serious and ready to make them aware of it. So do not, under any circumstances, spare the rod.'

Harris reeled slightly, grabbing the iron railings of the street for support. 'And what about Henderson?'

'Get Hendy, too. We'll start on him when I get to the station.'

'You're not coming?' Harris sounded confused, wary.

'Not yet. I've got somewhere I need to be.'

'It's a disgrace, I'm telling you, it's an absolute disgrace.'

Gillespie had switched on his car radio to be greeted with the sound of Ally Murdo—Edinburgh's Jock Shock Jock—ranting merrily over the airwaves. The DCI wondered if it was still the female golfers who were getting his goat. That wouldn't do his case any favours, but Ally seemed to have moved on.

'We're supposed to call these people refugees, but let's call them what they are—scroungers.'

Gillespie was relieved not to be even loosely associated with the topic of discussion, this time.

'We hear all these sob stories about how their own countries are dangerous. That they're only trying to flee war zones. Then why are they all fighting-age men? Aren't they the ones that are supposed to stay behind and protect the women and children? Looks to me like it's survival of the fittest they're playing, not women and children into the lifeboats first! You see folks, they're economic migrants—not refugees—and that's the long and short of it. They want in here for the handouts, and big business like the banks want them here to get them loaded up with credit cards and debt. The idiots that represent us love it, because they get more votes for more lunacy and they can bang on about rising GDP. Of course GDP's rising, if you add a million folk to the population every year that's a lot of hot dinners and shoe leather that needs to be bought.'

The detective found himself hypnotised by the sound of the DJ's voice, the cadence of the word-flow. The burning anger, tempered by the steel of injustice, real or imagined, it didn't matter. By comparison, all other media pundits were so anodyne, so meat and potatoes. He wondered if he was being taken in, and then he laughed out loud.

'It's a Ponzi scheme,' yelled Ally from the car's speakers, 'I'm telling you. It's short-termism writ large. There's more to life than the sacred cow of the economy—Western civilisation's at stake here, make no mistake! And do you think these childless leaders like Angela Merkel or that puppet Macron care what they're doing to your children's futures? Dream on. They care only about getting their snout in the trough now. Hard times are on the horizon, folks, and you can take that to the bank!'

Gillespie had heard enough. He switched off the car radio. Who was this ranting mad man? It scared the detective to think such people were given a public platform. Ally Murdo couldn't have been more wrong: the hard times had already arrived.

He pulled up outside Louise's house and turned off the engine. It seemed unusually quiet inside the car now, cooler too; he felt almost exposed. Gillespie pulled up his collar and sank further into the seat. He didn't know what he was doing there, or to be more accurate, he didn't want to admit to himself what he was doing there.

He scanned the street, up and down, and was relieved to find no trace of the Toyota Hilux he'd seen parked outside earlier. Could that particular problem have sorted itself out? Had the *bad penny* rolled off in another direction? The living-room light was still on in Louise's home, but the curtains were drawn. He focussed on the lit-up window and watched intently, after a moment a shadow passed. She was home.

Gillespie raised himself up in his seat and tried to calm his eddying emotions. He was there for a reason, there was no point pretending otherwise. He took out his phone and texted her.

'Hi. Are you busy? X'

He drummed his fingers impatiently, nervously on the steering wheel as he waited for a reply. He didn't have to wait long. The phone buzzed.

'Not really. What do you want?'

'I'd like to come in for a cup of tea. X'

A few seconds later, he saw the curtains of the living-room window slide open and Louise's face appeared. She shook her head and then disappeared from view, reappearing at the door a few seconds later.

Gillespie got out of the car and walked towards the door.

'Keep it down, will you? Eilidh's asleep.'

The detective stepped into the living room and assumed his usual position, standing by the fireplace. He used to feel comfortable standing there, but now he felt only tension. Louise came into the room and closed the door. She was wearing a T-shirt and a small pair of red shorts. Her hair, scraped back in a scrunchy, was beginning to escape in long strands over her face. She looked tired and ill at ease. Gillespie wanted to say how good it was to see her, but he was cut off.

'Did you phone me, earlier?' she said.

'Not that I know of,' he lied. 'Sorry, I must've pocket-dialled you.'

'So you didn't want to speak to me?'

'Of course I did.' It sounded like a trick question. 'I've just been busy, that's all.'

Louise slumped on to the couch and folded her arms. 'There's a surprise—said no-one, ever.'

'Has Eilidh been playing up? Or, is the sassiness all my own doing?'

'Why are you here, Kenny?'

Gillespie shifted uncomfortably on his feet. 'Well, it's not exactly been good lately, has it?'

'Are you just here to state the obvious?'

There it was again. The attitude. He decided to ignore it. It was clear the conversation was going to play out like a game of *Pong*. Each of them trying to score points off the other.

'I've found out something I think you should know,' he said.

'If it's the fact you're a workaholic who only shows up at my house when your job permits it, then I already know.'

'It's about Rob.'

Louise sighed and grabbed a bunch of her hair. 'Kenny, not this again.'

'Did you know he's just done nine months in prison?'

Louise sat up straight, untucking her legs that had been beneath her. The dark circles of her eyes widened as she stared at him. 'And just how would you know that?'

'It's called using my initiative, Louise.'

'It's called playing dirty, Kenny—really dirty.'

'For Christ's sake, Louise, I can't believe you. You've been swallowing the guy's sob story.'

'So, so what? He made a mistake…'

'Another one.'

'Okay, he's made a few mistakes, but he's acknowledged them and he wants to make up for it. He wants to make a fresh start with his family.' She shook her head. 'You wouldn't understand.'

'Who's playing dirty now?'

'Bloody hell, Kenny, I only mean you wouldn't understand because you don't have children.'

'But I've got you and I've got Eilidh, or at least I thought I did. I can't tell you how much you've both meant to me these past few months. I felt I was in this shitty little bubble and you came along and burst it for me. I've felt like I've actually been living for something, like there's a reason to everything for the first time in my life.'

He stopped himself. He'd put her up on a pedestal but he meant every word. He turned away, hoping in vain that Louise might stand up and put her hand on his shoulder and tell him that everything would be all right.

She spoke softly, 'Kenny, the only thing that matters to you is that job of yours. You care more about solving crimes involving complete strangers than you do about anything—or anybody—else. Go back to your wife—she needs you.'

His pulse quickened. 'You heard what happened?'

'Nothing stays a secret for long round here. Go back to her.'

He felt he was missing a piece of the puzzle. Like the conversation should have gone another way. There were too many factors to consider here and now, and pride got the better of him. Gillespie turned away from Louise and headed through the door.

Outside in the cold he felt numb, his dreams falling all around him, slipping away like snow off a dyke. He walked to his car and looked back at the little house. He waited, staring at the window for a few moments, hoping to see Louise at the window. Hoping to see her come running through the front door. But nothing happened. The curtains stayed shut and the door remained closed. He reached down for the car's door handle, and spotted something moving out of the corner of his eye. It was the tiny figure of Eilidh, at the upstairs window, standing there in her Peppa Pig pyjamas. She held up a soft toy—a little white cat. She made it wave to Gillespie with its paw. He smiled and waved back; why wouldn't he? She couldn't know it would be for the last time.

Chapter 35

Desk Sergeant Derek McCall's round face was growing a darker, angrier shade of purple. The top button of his shirt appeared to be threatening to ping across the reception area as he struggled to make himself heard above the raucous din.

'Can we get some order please, gents?' he roared.

A crowd of fifteen or so middle-aged rich men, a number of them with pyjama bottoms poking out from beneath their overcoats, were demanding to see lawyers. Gillespie strolled in unnoticed and quietly surveyed the chaotic scene engulfing St Leonard's Station. Standing in the corner he watched Henry Montrose, the Fairview president, demanding to see his lawyer. The PC on the receiving end of Montrose's strafe seemed to be doing a good job of keeping his cool, despite the provocation of a finger poking in his chest every few seconds. Gillespie smiled when he noticed Montrose was wearing a pair of backless leather slippers, with an embroidered crest on the front. He didn't think he'd ever known full satisfaction until that moment—watching a pompous old bastard trying to maintain his dignity while standing there, ankles freezing, in his baffies.

Montrose wasn't in his golf club now. He and his big-time buddies were on Gillespie's turf, and the DCI had no intention of giving them the rub of the green.

'Welcome to the last-chance saloon, gentlemen!' yelled

Gillespie, both arms raised aloft for full effect.

A hush descended on the room and the detective felt the burn of many a concentrated gaze on him. He conceded to himself that the feeling the attention gave him was quite messianic. He went with it; after all, somebody had to be the star of the show. The detective knew he was the man every Fairview member understood was responsible for their late-night predicament, and he wanted to milk it for all it was worth.

'I'm afraid St Leonard's isn't quite as glamorous as your lovely golf club gentlemen,' began Gillespie, 'and it certainly doesn't come with anything like the perquisites but, if you play fair by me, I think I can guarantee some of you will see your comfy beds and warm wives soon. As for the rest of you, I think it's probably too late for that.'

Murmurs of discontent swept around the reception area. Gillespie spotted the desk sergeant lowering his head on to the polished wood of the counter. Montrose immediately began a quick march towards him, but the PC held out his arm.

'Halt!' he blasted, 'I'll deal with you when I'm good and ready. And not before.'

Gillespie had already spotted the man he wanted to speak to first. The man at the top of his 'to-do' list.

'Right, you first, Henderson. How about you and me have a little chat?'

Harris rushed over to the imposing figure of Davy Henderson and latched hands on his arms, awkwardly ushering him into the nearest available interview room. As they went through the door, Gillespie turned back and called to the others for hush.

'Up until now, I've been Mr Nice Guy, but I'm long past tolerating any more of your secrets. I'm not going to ask you again—either you tell us what we need to know or there'll be arrests tonight and names given to the press in the morning.'

The response was a rumbling murmur. Not quite protest, the sound was closer to fearful disbelief. Gillespie had achieved exactly his intention. He'd give the assembled Crombie coats and striped pyjama trousers some time to chew it over, while he gleefully roasted Henderson over an open spit.

'Okay, Davy, there's no dancing girls in here to distract you—spill your guts.'

The big man shook his head, a look of resignation on his pockmarked face. 'I've told you all I know.'

'That's not going to wash any more.' Gillespie began to grin. 'You see, I've found a wee songbird by the name of Kylie and she's singing a very pretty tune to my ears.'

Henderson gave a quick sideways glance in the direction of the door. His pallor darkened a little, highlighting the dark shadow of his unshaven chin. 'I want my lawyer.'

'I'll take a mental note of that.'

'You've nothing on me, Gillespie.' Henderson locked his fingers together; it looked uncomfortable and he separated them again, brushing the surface of the desk with the heel of his right hand.

'Not quite nothing.'

'Not enough, anyway.'

'We'll let the courts decide that.'

'You're not serious, Gillespie.' Henderson's face was a portrait of open-mouthed stupefaction. He was in disbelief.

'I'm deadly serious. A young girl died—she was murdered. Now, Elena worked for you. She was working for you on the night she died at Fairview, and I think you know more about it that you're letting on.'

'You can't prove that.'

'I can't prove the moon's made of cheese, Davy, but I don't need Professor Brian bloody Cox here to help me. The balance of probability's on my side and you're treading a very dangerous path, pal.'

The amount of venom with which he laced this final word surprised even Gillespie. Anyone who'd ever met him knew that Davy Henderson wasn't a man that was easily shaken, but he was definitely getting close now.

'Okay, look, Elena was there but I don't know a damn thing about her murder. Jesus Christ, it was as much a shock to me. Do you really think with everything that's been going on lately that I would want any more police attention?'

'Well perhaps you can tell me why your girls were out at Fairview entertaining the cast of *Cocoon* that night.'

Henderson weighed his open palms. 'It was a sweetener, that's all.'

'A sweetener for what? So you could buy the club?'

Henderson gave a slow nod.

'Bollocks,' snapped Gillespie, thumping the table. 'Do you really think I'm going to believe that? A wily businessman like yourself would have more cards up his sleeve.'

'Like what?'

'Don't play dumb, Davy. You were blackmailing them. What was it? Were you filming the action? Did you have the security cameras turned on them?'

Henderson paused and nibbled his lower lip. His complexion turned towards the greyer end of the scale. A few pustules of sweat erupted on his brow. 'What did Kylie tell you?'

'Never mind what Kylie told me. Where's the footage you were going to blackmail the board members with?'

Henderson shook his head.

'There isn't any footage.'

'Do you think I button up the back, pal?'

Henderson paused. His words came in a slow, strangled drawl, like he was trying to stop himself but couldn't. 'I've only got photographs. A snapper from out of town took them. You don't need his name, do you? No, you wouldn't. There's no need for that, surely?'

'I need his name and I need those photos. And if you give me them both quickly and you speak nicely to me, I might let you have a cup of tea in the morning.'

'*What?* Are you serious? You're keeping me in?'

Gillespie stood up. He let the legs of the chair scratch eerily along the hard floor surface. The noise came like nails on a blackboard. For a moment the DCI paused, ran his gaze over Davy Henderson's face. He knew he had him now, by the short and curlies, as they said. It must have been a long time since Henderson had spent a night in a cold cell, but he'd possess some long-ago memories of the hard bunk and maybe even the odd visit from a burly uniform using his cuffs to protect the flesh of his knuckles.

'Oh, I certainly am keeping you in, Davy. I hope those fancy porcelain veneers can manage a night away from your toothbrush.'

Henderson slumped back in his chair. His plump hands reached up and grabbed tufts of his hair.

'How long?' yelled Henderson.

'That depends on you, Davy. How long have you got?'

Gillespie and Harris stepped coolly outside the interview room, ordering the uniformed officers to take Henderson down to the cells. They watched as Henderson departed in handcuffs, the crowd of grey-haired men in camel coats parting like the Red Sea in an old Charlton Heston movie. The officers were surveying the room when Henderson had gone, discussing who they should bring through next, when they heard the unmistakable clack of Dickson's heels on the floor. She was clearly in a hurry.

'Sir, I think you should look at this.'

'What is it?' said Gillespie.

She held out a notepad and pointed to a series of bullet points running down the margin. 'It's a description of someone,' she said. 'Someone uniform missed.'

Gillespie grabbed the pad.

'Yes, I bloody-well should look at that.'

Chapter 36

It took a few moments for Harris's words to penetrate the fog of Gillespie's thoughts. He was so overloaded with work, balancing so many cases, and under so much stress that he had to think hard about who the DS meant when he said that Stott had 'coughed'.

'He did?' said Gillespie, the grainy image of the man throwing the tyre iron into the undergrowth suddenly popped into his head. He knew Stott would admit it eventually. He wasn't a criminal, not a serious one anyway.

Harris continued: 'Yes. Doesn't sound like it was a rush of blood to the head, more like an unintended consequence of not thinking things through. He said he had just wanted to "rattle Thompson's cage" a bit, but it went too far.'

'Well, he can tell that to the judge,' Gillespie snapped. He slumped against the wall and rested his chin on his chest. 'I've got more to worry about right now.'

Harris led Gillespie towards the whiteboard, where yet more concentrated cerebral activity was clearly expected of him. The detective lifted his gaze and surveyed the dozens of photographs that had been stuck to the board. Little flickerings, like amber shards catching glints of light, began to appear before his dim eyes.

'This is a mess,' said Gillespie.

'It's not very pretty, I'll give you that.'

'If we'd had these organised earlier then we wouldn't be facing this shambles now.'

Harris said nothing.

Gillespie continued to study the images, any one of which he could imagine accompanying a lurid headline on the front page of a tabloid newspaper. The vision of his own name, taken out of all context, amid the column inches added further vinegar to the open wound. He girded his jaws and gazed upon the debauched setting, trying hard to separate himself from the depraved depths of humanity on display.

The photographs were taken through various windows at Fairview. The images showed members of the golf club roaring drunk and slugging back whiskies, the scantily clad girls in their arms, and in their laps, feigning uproarious laughter. It was a far cry from the sophisticated front these same old men were more adept at projecting in daylight hours. It seemed the perfect symbol, to Gillespie anyway, of the schizophrenic heart that beat within Edinburgh. It was all Morningside tea parties by day, and rollicking in the knocking shops by night. Even Stevenson, that doyen of Scottish letters, had earned himself the title 'Velvet Jacket' for the scarlet garb he wore when he was out whoring in the Old Town. *Jekyll and Hyde* had never made so much sense to the detective until now.

Gillespie and Harris were distracted by a loud thump on the table behind them. They turned to see Dickson putting her weight behind a large plastic box to manoeuvre it closer to the middle of the desk.

'Right, some more pics from the lab,' said Dickson, panting heavily now. 'Johnny Wiseman's the snapper—he says that's the lot, sir.'

The lid was peeled and the three of them began to remove handfuls of the latest collection of photographs. They were all more of the same: more drunkenness, more groping, more seen that would never be unseen again.

The group drew up chairs and started to assemble the photographs by known faces, in piles on top of the desk. The photographer had clearly been given strict instructions on who to target, as some of the offenders had multiple angles captured. The moves were base, but hardly gymnastic given the ages of the men involved. Gillespie could imagine marriages being tested, broken. There would be children, grandchildren probably hanging their heads in deep shame. This was potent stuff, he thought, conceding almost a sneaking admiration for the cunning displayed by Henderson.

'Oh, God...' said Dickson, 'is that what I think it is?'

'Now that depends,' said Harris, 'if you think it's a wrinkly, old male testicle in a young girl's mouth, then the answer's yes.'

Dickson threw down the photograph and started to gag. 'I can't do this.'

Gillespie watched her put her hand to her mouth.

'I'm sorry, sir. It's just too gross,' she said.

Harris white knighted for her: 'Maybe we can manage without her, sir?'

'Hang about, Simon,' said Gillespie. 'Have you seen the size of this? And no, I'm not talking about some wrinkly chopper. We could be here all day with the three of us, and believe me if young Gemma is so delicate as to be offended by this, then she certainly won't want to think about accompanying us on an indecent child rape.'

'Sorry, sir, I wasn't thinking,' said Harris.

'No, you were, but not with your head. Maybe it's you I should be asking to step aside.'

'Sir!' Dickson's chair legs scraped across the floor. She leaned forward excitedly. 'I think you should take a look at this.'

The DCI took the photograph as it was presented to him. 'What in the name of hell?'

This picture was different. It was a view of the outside of the golf club, obviously taken before Wiseman had moved in for a closer look at the goings-on inside. A gaggle of Henderson's girls were arriving in taxis and being ushered inside but there was another figure. There was a young man in the background, to the side of the building, slumped halfway over the line of the building's shadow, but seemingly observing everything. Gillespie held up the photograph to Harris and pointed to the figure. The DS peered at it.

'He looks familiar.'

'It's Grozan. I thought of him when Gemma brought up the description uniform missed.'

'Elena's boyfriend? It can't be. He didn't arrive here until after Elena died.'

Gillespie stared at Harris and Dickson. His voice came low and firm, 'Tell me we checked his passport.'

Both men turned to Dickson. Her face was turning red and her eyes widening. 'Yes, yes, I checked, I checked, okay?'

Gillespie felt a cold shiver pass over his heart. He ran to his desk and grabbed the case file. He began frantically flicking though the documents until he found what he was looking for.

'The file says Grozan's passport was checked, but it wasn't stamped. Did someone run it by Border Force? I can't see anything about that in the file.'

He looked at Dickson and Harris, who both shrugged before looking at each other.

'Bloody hell!' yelled Gillespie.

The rest of the room fell instantly into silence. All eyes were on Gillespie; the DCI was breathing heavily, his shoulders rising and falling. 'Right, you pair, do it now. I want to know where Grozan is. I want him traced and I want him picked up by bloody yesterday. This isn't happening. Tell me, dear god, this isn't happening.'

Harris and Dickson were jolted out of their shock and into automatic action, diving towards their desks, trying desperately to find a way of rescuing the situation, of reversing the shame, of saving their jobs.

Gillespie, in the midst of the flurry, took what he felt was the only appropriate course of action under the circumstances: he located the nearest chair and kicked it as hard as he could. It skidded across the floor, hit a wastepaper bin and teetered for a moment on its castors before toppling over. Harris and Dickson pretended not to notice.

Still deep in rage, Gillespie stormed out of the incident room, marching towards the toilet where he pushed the door so hard it continued to swing on its hinges for several seconds. He slammed his fists either side of the mirror above the sink and tried to discern just what blind rage looked like.

He was as furious with himself. He was furious with his two sergeants. But the buck stopped with him. No one would ever say any different. His anger was justified, though, and that was the worst kind, the most potent. Indignant rage was dubious, could be caustic but more often than not, its results were merely messy. Righteous anger, the kind that fuelled revolutionaries, that's what was running in him now.

He'd been paying more attention to the shit show that was his love life. It had distracted him, taken him off guard, weakened his focus. If he'd been on the ball, then all the proper checks would've been done and he'd never have let the Romanian out of his sight.

The thought rankled because it intensified his self-loathing. He knew he was a failure as a family man and now he was also a failure as a cop. If he'd got the first one right, the second one would have followed. Why couldn't he? *Why?*

He remembered Pauline trying to calm him, in the early days of their marriage. She'd say things like, 'It was nobody's fault.' Or, 'You just need to treat it like a regular job.' She never understood. She never knew how much the job meant to him. If he'd chosen better, more wisely, if he'd had Louise and Eilidh at home, things would have been different. Wouldn't they?

His heart was pounding, his face and neck a riot of red blood vessels. He turned on the cold tap and splashed himself with icy water. It caught his breath but it re-focussed his mind.

He was a fool. He was letting voices inside his head lead him astray. There was no parallel world where the grass was always greener; there was no way of changing the past. Life was life.

He turned away from the mirror and dried his hands. He was resting on the sink, letting his heart-rate return to normal, when he had an urge to check his phone to see if Louise had sent him a message.

There was nothing since yesterday. It was actually a relief. She really was part of his past now. So he could file that away. Let it go. There was only the here and now to consider, and that meant finding Grozan.

He headed back to the incident room, his footsteps reassuringly firm and loud on the tiled floor. From a few feet away he could hear Harris's voice, it was raised, he was shouting. The sound jarred.

Gillespie opened the door.

'You should've checked it, Gemma!' yelled Harris.

'I did!' she yelled back.

'But the passport wasn't stamped.'

'I didn't know that meant anything.'

'Well we bloody well do now, don't we?'

The detectives stopped when they realised Gillespie was standing behind them. He took his hands out of his pockets and displayed one open palm towards the rowing couple. 'What's all this? Is love's young dream turning sour?'

Harris looked at his shoes.

'I'm not a dentist, Simon. I can't pull teeth.'

Harris looked at Dickson and mumbled, as though he were a schoolboy explaining why he hadn't done his homework. He seemed much more awkward, ill at ease, than ever he did.

'It's Grozan, sir. He arrived in Edinburgh two days before Elena died.'

Up until that moment, Gillespie had clung to the faint hope that there had been a mistake. A genuine error. A foul-up. That somehow they'd got it wrong. These things happened; the administration of a large police station was a complex business. Files get lost, pictures get removed, slipped back in the wrong place. People made mistakes. They were known for it.

But, it was now clear that forlorn hope had vanished.

Gillespie eased himself on to the edge of the desk and started to massage his forehead with his finger and thumb. It was a rare show of weakness he felt helpless to hide.

'Oh god,' he said.

'I'm afraid it's worse than that, sir.'

'How could it possibly be worse, Gemma?'

'The passport he was travelling on was stolen. It's only just been flagged on the national computer by the Romanian police.'

Gillespie eased himself up. 'Right, run that through the airport. See if he has a return flight booked.'

For a split second, nobody moved.

'Now!' screamed Gillespie.

Harris and Dickson didn't need to be told a third time. They bumped into each other as they leapt for their phones. The tension in the air was almost combustible. One stray piece of static electricity from an acrylic shirt could prove explosive. Gillespie watched the action nervously, switching his gaze between the clock and the frantic officers. After a few minutes, Dickson stood up and shouted out.

'Sir, I've got a hit!'

The team ran to her desk.

'Go on,' said Gillespie.

'He's on the three forty-five KLM flight from Edinburgh to Amsterdam, connecting to Bucharest.'

Gillespie turned back to the clock. 'It's quarter past three now.'

Within seconds, he was racing out of the room and taking the stairs two at a time, with Harris and Dickson in pursuit. He grabbed the keys to a squad car on his way past the front desk. The desk sergeant yelled obscenities then apologised to an old woman, sitting with a shopping basket in her lap.

The squad were soon screeching out of the station, siren

wailing, on their way to Edinburgh Airport. Harris, mobile clamped to his ear, was desperately trying to stop the flight and cursing the fact he'd been put on hold. Dickson was in the back, clinging on for dear life as Gillespie weaved in and out of traffic, throwing the car around corners and speeding across junctions.

'Don't kill us, please,' said Dickson.

Gillespie grinned. 'That comes later.'

The DCI's knuckles were white as he gripped the steering wheel. He shifted through the gears, recalling the ball-breaking police instructor who had managed to get him through the advanced driving module without getting a smack in the teeth, and then he thought even further back, to a happier time when he was hurling his dad's old beige Escort round the dirt tracks of the farm and sending hens diving for cover.

The vision of his dad's smiling face shattered with the screaming of Dickson and the blast of a horn as a huge artic lorry cut across their path at the Gyle. Gillespie slammed on the brakes just in time as the lorry whistled past the front bumper. He looked at Harris, whose eyes were getting watery, then he checked the clock on the dashboard. It was nearly three thirty-five. He put his foot down and tore away again.

Cars and vans moved over as they sped past the Royal Bank of Scotland headquarters and then, seconds later, the airport control tower came into view. Somewhere beneath that building, Nicolae Grozan was probably kicking back and listening to the pre-flight safety instructions. He imagined him leafing through the duty-free magazine, selecting his preferred in-flight movie. He couldn't let the bastard leave. He couldn't let him get away with it.

Gillespie took the turn-off and sped through the network of mini-roundabouts that led to the terminal.

'There they are!' yelled Harris, arms flailing wildly to his left. 'They're heading for the main runway, but you can't go through this way, sir...'

It was too late. Gillespie had already stepped on the gas and smashed through the perimeter fence. Harris and Dickson screamed in strangely similar tones, but their boss was a man possessed now. There was no way he was giving up the chase. He slammed the car into fourth and then fifth as he tore across the tarmac, like a cheetah sprinting across the plain—eyes only for its prey.

The car bounced unevenly as he cut across a short section of grass, trying to head off the aircraft as it turned its giant metal body for the last time before joining the main runway—and delivering Grozan to freedom.

Playing chicken with an aeroplane was not something he had on his bucket list but today, there it was. Gillespie had taken the big gambles his entire life, he knew it. But, even to him, this felt like it could be a last throw of the dice. He turned on to the runway, yanked up the handbrake and brought the car to a screeching halt in a cloud of smoke.

Now it was the pilot's turn to lock up. The enormous tyres squealed, the engine howled and the wings shuddered. The plane's nose tipped forward before rocking back and finally coming to a halt. Gillespie got out and slammed the door, immediately gesturing for a set of portable steps to be brought across the runway. There were shouts of confusion and anger as airport officials ran towards the plane.

When the steps arrived, along with uniformed backup, the three detectives boarded the plane and began the aisle-by-aisle hunt for Grozan. The passengers were in uproar, firing moans and groans and threats of complaints in every direction. Some of the younger ones had the foresight to film the unfolding drama on their mobile phones. But there was one passenger who seemed very interested in what was written on the back of his vomit bag as he tried desperately to hide his face.

'I hope you realise you're going to be a YouTube sensation after this, sir,' said Harris.

'Who cares? Get the cuffs on him, Simon.'

Gillespie didn't say another word as they led Nicolae Grozan in handcuffs down the steps and towards the waiting car.

Chapter 37

Gillespie sat in the interview room and stared deep into the eyes of Nicolae Grozan, a man he now knew was called George Podescu. There seemed to be nothing there, a blankness, a hollowed-out soul. Maybe there had been a marker there once but the DCI couldn't find it. It never failed to amaze him how those he knew had committed the most heinous of crimes could carry on their day-to-day existences as if nothing had changed. What did that make them? Animals, seemed like the closest answer Gillespie could supply. Animals didn't carry around the baggage of remorse. Did a cat feel guilty about toying with a mouse in the seconds before its death? He was sitting in front of an animal. An animal who had killed and was now going about its everyday business, blissfully unaware that it had even transgressed another's laws.

Gillespie drew the paperwork closer to him. One of those winding, red-string clasps held the file closed. He unfurled the string slowly, exhausting every drop of tension he could extract. This was his turn now. The hunter had become the hunted. Podescu was his prey. Gillespie longed for the killer to have the intelligence to be aware of the turnaround, the reversal of fates. He wanted Podescu to be aware enough to feel the weight of consequence now pressing on him.

The detective pored over the papers in the file. Podescu's

record was extensive, the old American cop shows would have used the cliché 'a rap sheet as long as my arm'. It was fair to assume that stealing a passport was among the least serious offences the thirty-five-year-old had committed over the years. There was an act of grievous bodily harm, drug dealing, multiple vehicle thefts, assault and battery (numerous counts)—murder was about the only thing missing from the list and that, too, could be about to change.

As he went over the list of previous convictions, it occurred to Gillespie that he now seemed to be spending more time in the interview room than in his own home, exchanging more words with killers and crooks than with his wife. It wasn't how he saw his life panning out when he thought about it. But there it was, a bizarre intrusion, a strange observation made at the most inappropriate time.

The DCI drew his focus back and spoke, 'So, George Podescu.' Podescu's eyes twitched. Perhaps he wasn't used to hearing his own name spoken these days.

'Our colleagues in Romania have been good enough to share a list of your previous convictions. It's quite a rogue's hand-book, but let's take a look at some of the highlights.'

'I know what it says,' spat Podescu. 'All lies, you police are all the same.'

'I'm sorry,' Gillespie made a vault with his fingers above the papers, 'am I keeping you from something else? Oh, that's right, you were heading off on a nice little trip, I must have interrupted your plans. That explains your brusqueness. I'll try to keep that in mind, because I'm pretty sure you're not going anywhere else in a hurry now.'

The detective loosened his fingers and proceeded to leaf through the pages once again. 'You did six months in jail for supplying cocaine in 2005 and, shortly after you came out, you were convicted of punching your ex-girlfriend. This, of course, was before you served two and a half years for fracturing a man's skull with an iron bar. I could go on, but I'm not surprised you had to "borrow" someone else's passport for this little trip over to Edinburgh. You're a very different man to the Nicolae Grozan who sat upstairs and wept in front of me a few days ago, aren't you?'

Podescu stiffened, his breathing audible now.

'It must get confusing, living these different lives. Did Elena know who you really are?'

'She knew me.'

'She certainly did in the end.'

Gillespie swept up a small pile of black and white photographs. He laid them carefully, one by one, on the table. Each picture showed the pale, broken body of Elena Enescu, lying lifeless on the golf course. The stark whiteness of her flesh was given more contrast by the blackness of the contusions that covered her torso and ran down her legs.

'She was a pretty girl, very pretty. Even after your handiwork.'

Podescu snorted and shoved the pictures away, refusing to look at them. Even now, he couldn't hide his disdain for the woman he had previously professed his love for.

Gillespie chose his next words deliberately. 'It's such a shame to see a beautiful young woman cut down in her prime. The loss of innocence has a cruelty all of its own.'

'Shut up!'

'Excuse me?'

'I said, shut up. Just stop talking. Who are you to pass remarks on Elena? You didn't know her.'

'And you did?'

'Yes, I did.'

'Then tell me what I'm missing.'

'I don't need to tell you anything.'

Gillespie picked up one of the photographs. 'How about I tell you what I see when I look at this? I see a pretty young woman, pale and weak. She's been preyed upon by a much stronger hand, she's been used and abused. Why would *you* do such a thing?'

Podescu smirked. 'You know nothing.'

Gillespie pointed to another picture, a close up on the bruising around Elena's neck. 'I know more than you think. Elena's body can tell us everything we need to know. You see these finger marks? Our friends in the lab can work out the exact spacing between each one and even determine how much pressure was applied. It's an exact science; there's books written about it. Experts travel the world making a living explaining just these kinds of marks.'

The detective gave Podescu a hard stare. 'You can't get away with killing her—you must know that. It's an absolute impossibility. Not here and now, not in this world.'

Podescu shifted in his chair, moved his weight around. 'I want a cigarette.'

'Simon.'

'But, sir. He can't smoke in here...'

'Just give him a cigarette, Simon.'

Harris gave a resigned look and reached into his pocket. He passed over a cigarette and held the lighter, watching as Podescu took a long, deep draw before holding the cigarette in his cupped hand.

'Tell me about that night,' said Gillespie.

Podescu's top lip was beginning to glisten. He gave a shrug. 'There's nothing to tell.'

'Weren't the two of you engaged?'

'She was a whore, for god's sake.'

'And that upset you?'

'She deceived me. She told me she was working over here in a hotel, as a service worker, a cleaner. She was nothing of the sort.'

'How did you find out?'

'I followed her.'

'From her flat?'

'Yes, from her flat,' he snapped.

'All the way out to Fairview?'

'I followed her there.'

'Did you intend to kill her?'

The rapid-fire questioning stopped abruptly. Podescu's eyes thinned as he took a drag on the cigarette. 'No, of course I didn't.'

'So, something happened?'

The cigarette ran out. The long, grey funnel of ash separating from the filter tip and falling on the table's clean surface. The relentless questioning was starting to take its toll. Podescu let out an agitated sigh.

'I followed her to the golf course. I saw them coming and going. Old men, rich old men—old enough to be her father, her grandfather, even. That made me sick. I couldn't watch. I just couldn't watch Elena give herself away like that.'

Gillespie lowered his voice to a whisper, 'You felt let down?'

'I was disgusted. It was disgusting,' Podescu began to shout, 'they were all whores. Drunken whores giving themselves away to pathetic old men.'

He clenched his fists and pressed them into the surface of the table, his face was growing redder beneath his white expanse of brow.

'I understand. It must have made you angry.'

'Yes, it made me angry. What do you think?'

The DCI nodded slowly. 'I think you went there to satisfy your suspicions and, when they were confirmed, you followed Elena on to the golf course, where you did what you thought was right.'

'It was an honour killing.' Podescu slammed his fist on the table. His eyes groped around for something to alight upon but all he could find was the taunting black and white photographs of Elena. He swept the photographs from the table and on to the floor.

'Honour?' said Gillespie. 'That's a word murderers forfeit the right to use.'

The detective rose and walked from the interview room. Harris, crawling on his hands and knees to retrieve the photographs, trying desperately to preserve some of Elena's lost dignity, looked up in confusion. He followed the DCI's paces across the floor and hastily got up, running after his boss as the door was closing. Outside in the corridor Harris fumbled to get all the pictures back inside the folder. A few stray images escaped and landed, face up, like a terrible reminder to the way Elena had been murdered.

'Calm yourself, Simon.'

'Sorry, sir…I'm just trying to.'

'It's okay.' Gillespie placed a hand on Harris's shoulder and made eye contact. 'Take a break, son. Go get yourself a cup of tea and a Kit-Kat.'

'We got him, sir,' said Harris. 'We bloody-well got him.'

Gillespie nodded and turned away. As he walked his shoulders slumped into amorphous mounds beneath his coat. His feet dragged below him. A delicate hum, like the sound of a computer running, set up shop inside his head. He felt tired, worn out.

'So, what now?' cried Simon.

'Good question. Very good question.'

'*Sir?*'

'You go home. You have a home to go to, don't you?'

'Yes.'

'Then go home, son. At the end of every day, that's all you can ever do. Go home.'

'Yes, sir.'

Harris seemed to be contemplating the words for a moment and then he bent down to retrieve the last of the evacuated photographs of Elena Enescu from the floor. As he rose, Podescu was being escorted from the interview room by two uniformed police officers.

Gillespie was already out of the door, staring at the mobile phone in his hand, something else already required the detective's attention.

'Goodnight, sir,' said Harris.

Gillespie considered a reply, a wave perhaps, but didn't bother.

TONY BLACK is the author of more than 20 books. He has been nominated for eight CWA Daggers and was runner up in The Guardian's Not the Booker prize for *The Last Tiger*. He has written three crime series, a number of crime novellas and two collections of short stories. His acclaimed author interviews series was collected under the title *Hard Truths*. His novella, *The Ringer*, was adapted for the stage and the Ayr Gaiety performance can be found on YouTube.

TOM MAXWELL is a former journalist who lives in Edinburgh. He is the author of several acclaimed sports books and an award-winning guide to Scottish films. He first met Tony Black while working with him at the Edinburgh Evening News. *Slings & Arrows* is his first novel.

BOOKS

On the following pages are a few
more great titles from the
Down & Out Books publishing family.

For a complete list of books and to
sign up for our newsletter,
go to DownAndOutBooks.com.

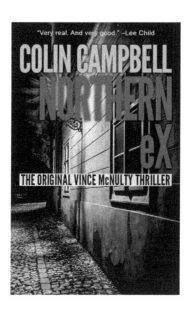

Northern eX
A Vince McNulty Thriller
Colin Campbell

Down & Out Books
August 2021
978-1-64396-214-6

Once a cop always a cop.

Ex vice squad cop Vince McNulty copes with life outside the force by visiting the Northern X massage parlours he used to police. Until a return to his old stomping ground prompts a change of fortunes. Several girls have gone missing. All young masseuses. All from parlours that McNulty has visited.

When one of them turns up dead everything points to a regular customer being involved. And McNulty is top of the list.

Watch for Me
Martin Bodenham

Down & Out Books
August 2021
978-1-64396-215-3

Happily married, Tom Harper cannot understand why a woman not much older than his teenage daughter is suddenly obsessed with him.

This is the story of one man's struggle in the face of overwhelming psychological and physical torment.

"Deliciously creepy with a twist you won't see coming!" — Helen Hardt, #1 *New York Times* bestselling author

Stalker Stalked
Lee Matthew Goldberg

All Due Respect, an imprint of
Down & Out Books
September 2021
978-1-64396-229-0

What happens when the stalker gets stalked?

A fan stalks a reality show personality only to discover that she's being stalked as well, and learns the only way to beat her stalker is to use her own prowess to outsmart them at their own game.

Blood Like Rain
A Big Island Mystery
Albert Tucher

Shotgun Honey, an imprint of
Down & Out Books
August 2021
978-1-64396-192-7

Detective Errol Coutinho of the Hawaii County Police faces the most difficult case of his career, when his wife's best friend is murdered.

Eleanor Swieczak's current boyfriend is a man without a past, but Eleanor's own history turns up other suspects, and someone is trying to put Coutinho among them. And what do a legendary marijuana dealer, a rightwing militia, and the coldest murder case in Hawaii history have to do with the case?

Must blood fall like rain before Coutinho finds out?

Lightning Source UK Ltd.
Milton Keynes UK
UKHW010647161021
392321UK00001B/108

9 781643 962337